WITCH WAY TO....?

By Lucy R. Fisher

A sequel to *Witch Way Now?*

CHAPTER ONE

June 1970

I'm writing this in an exercise book I bought in Chancellor cards in Kentish Town high street, because if I become a student I'll need a lot of stationery. I've got a fountain pen my parents gave me, and I got a pencil case, but I don't think I'll fill it with six-inch rulers and compasses and protractors. Though the compass might come in handy for drawing complicated diagrams to repel witches and demons.

I never did A Levels at school due to being "asked to leave". I didn't do most of those things they accused me of, and they never knew what I'd REALLY done. Anyway, so I've only got a few rather bad O Levels. My friend Murray from school is very into Nature, and so am I, in a way, and he thinks I ought to do Biology.

So I went along to the Working Men's College, which is quite near where we live now in Kentish Town, and got some brochures from an office at the entrance. They said a student would come and show me round so I hung about the foyer which had the usual tiles covered with muddy footprints. It was a bit like the hostel near Hyde Park where I lived when I went to secretarial college.

Then Fiona came and showed me the lecture rooms and the science labs. They were like the ones at school (both schools I've been to), with wooden benches and a nice-nasty smell which is probably the stuff they use to pickle the specimens. There were Bunsen burners and a few grisly things in jars I tried not to look at.

Fiona had thick dark straight hair cut in a chin-length bob without a fringe. She was wearing a baggy burgundy jersey, an olive corduroy skirt to the knee, black tights and lime-green Hush Puppies. I thanked her for the tour and walked off home with my brochures to show to Mike, my husband.

You may think I'm a bit young to have a husband but I'm nearly 20 and I was 18 when we got married. He's a policeman and I work as a temp typist most of the time though I used to work in a boutique which was not as groovy as it sounds. I'm Anna, and our surname is Savage. Mine was Lestrange before we got married.

When Mike came home from work I opened a tin of soup and then made sardines on toast which we ate off a small table beside the window in the kitchen, which is really just the end of the living room. We talked about getting a house in a suburb, but we've never done anything about it. I think we like it here.

"I went by the Working Men's college," I said. "And a girl showed me round the science labs. Murray thinks I ought to do Biology A level."

"Do you think you'll go? You could start in September."

"What do you think?"

"Depends if you like the idea."

"I bought a lot of new stationery, anyway!"

"You can keep it in the cupboard with your old school books." I have kept a lot of exercise books, and index books with interesting useful stuff in. Some of it's even about plants, and whether they are ruled by Venus, or soveraigne against the plague, or the evil eye.

"I dunno, though. I don't want to cut up animals – or plants."

"It might spoil the magic – unweave the rainbow."

"Who said that?"

"Um – Isaac Newton? Einstein?"

"I think I'll just loaf in the local library and read books some more." The library is just up the road from us, too.

"OK, doll! Whatever you like."

"I suppose you did A levels."

"Yes, I got a few, but I can't say it was fun. You seem to do OK without college."

"I might get a corduroy skirt and some green Hush Puppies and just pretend to be a student."

"A bit casual for work?"

"Yeah, perhaps."

Just then the phone rang. Mike picked it up and listened for a bit and passed it to me saying "Here she is." It was a husky, stammering voice.

I said: "Ginevra! How nice to hear from you. How's the baby?"

She said he was fine and was two now. Then she asked us to come to dinner at their flat next week. Mike passed me his notebook and I wrote down the date and the address. We chatted a bit more about the old days in the hostel, which was where we met, and being terrible at tennis, and said we'd see each other next week.

"I didn't know you played tennis," said Mike. "We could play at those courts at Parliament Hill."

"I am truly awful," I said. "Ianthe and Ginevra – that was Ginevra – and me and another girl used to play when we lived in a hostel near Hyde Park."

"We could still give it a go, though."

"Yes, let's!"

"Fun, these light evenings. Tell me about this hostel."

"I was lucky to meet Ianthe and Ginevra. They'd been to the same kind of schools as me, with nuns. Then Ginevra was having a baby and got married – we were her bridesmaids! I wonder if Ianthe will be there? I still write to her sometimes. She's quite intellectual but OK."

The next day after work I made stuffed baked potatoes (you mash the insides with Philadelphia and parsley and put them back into the skins, and then put the whole thing under the grill), and then we walked up College Lane to Parliament Hill to look at the tennis courts. We watched the people playing for a bit.

"Remember those people in Blow Up playing without a ball?" asked Mike. "I never did understand that film."

"It was one of those ones you're not supposed to try to understand!" I remembered being sneered at by the girls at the boutique for wanting to know what films meant. We walked on up the path where there are street lamps and benches.

Mike said: "I'll never forget that Halloween party at the top of the hill here where we rounded up some of your friends!"

"They weren't my friends! Oh OK, some of them were."

"They'll be out of prison in a few years. The girls, anyway. If they're not out already."

"I was just thinking about them. They weren't very matey."

We walked on for a bit. Mike doesn't know it, but I was at that party, watching weird people dancing round the bonfire in antlers and monks' robes. My "friends" turned out to be drug dealers and worse.

"This lot we're meeting next week sound nicer," said Mike.

"They are! They're very normal."

"Isn't that an acquaintance of yours, though, back there on the bench?"

I looked back, but I could only see a shabby man with black hair, hunched into a dark raincoat.

"Who? There's only some bloke."

"That old bird with the wispy hair and old-fashioned clothes I thought was a shoplifter that time."

I looked back again – no Elsie.

"Perhaps we'll bump into her," I said.

Elsie is someone I met in a Lyons teashop when I was feeling a bit lonely. She's been a good friend to me – she just happens to be dead. Most people can't see her. She's the only ghost I know, so far – but when you walk among the crowds in Oxford Street, how many of them are ghosts? Elsie likes haunting John Lewis the department store and criticising the new fashions. Was she trying to get in touch?

"Perhaps she's gone on ahead – I remember she moves fast!" said Mike.

We reached the top of the hill, where there's a bench and where the bonfire was. There's a famous view of London, and we spotted St Paul's and the Shell building and a new skyscraper near Oxford Street.

"Look – the sky's the colour of apricot yoghourt," I said.

"I suppose it is. How delicious!"

"Sister Violet used to tell us to use unusual similes, but if you do people usually look blank!"

We looked at the view for a bit more then ran back down again. The shabby man was still sitting on the bench, and he looked at me in a friendly way as we passed, but no sign of Elsie.

*****

So we went to dinner at Ginevra's at the weekend. She and David and their little boy live in a groundfloor flat in a suburb, and I hadn't seen her since their wedding. The flat had a little front garden with a tiled path and a door with small window panes. She met us and gave me a hug and said how nice it was to meet Mike. He smiled and tried to look less serious than he usually does. He was wearing a blue work suit and a tie and I was wearing a brown velvet midi skirt, a silver cardigan and a brown velvet choker and boots. I'll briefly say what we look like without pretending to be looking in a mirror or anything: I am quite short and slim, four foot eleven, and have very long straight black hair and green eyes and look a bit like an elf. Mike is tall, well perhaps average, and wiry and has short pale brown hair like mouse fur in a widow's peak, and greeny blue eyes.

We went into Ginevra's living room which was knocked through front to back (like ours), and she'd put a table in the back bit near the kitchen with a flowery table cloth. There was a brown three-piece suite and a beige haircord carpet and a brown corduroy pouffe, and lots of turquoise and orange paperbacks on shelves. We said hello to David and sat about with the other guests drinking Mateus Rose. I'd better describe Ginevra and David as well – she's small but curvaceous, with curly dark hair and long eyelashes, and he's medium height with brown curly hair and a short beard. I'd never really met him except at their wedding and the reception.

Then the doorbell rang again and another guest arrived and when she came into the room I jumped up and hugged her – it was Ianthe, my other friend from the hostel. Her red hair was very short now and she was wearing dungarees and the same old glasses. I introduced her to Mike.

Then we all had conversations along the lines of "What do you do?" Mike confessed to being a policeman and some of the men boggled a bit like a horse that's seen a paper bag.

"What are you up to now?" I asked Ginevra. "Did you go back and finish your course?"

"I got a bit sick of interior design," she said. "I only did it because my mother thought I ought to do something. Ianthe persuaded me to go to college so I'm doing history – I've just done my first year."

It seemed the other people were fellow students or lecturers. The men had longish hair and beards and glasses, and wore a lot of tweed and corduroy and elbow patches.

"How about you?" asked Ginevra, politely.

"I worked in a boutique for a bit, but then it shut, and I went back to temp typing and I'm still doing that."

"You could always be a mature student."

"I'm so mature, I don't think! Tell me about your little boy – is he asleep?"

"Richard – he's staying with my mother. I'm afraid he wouldn't have gone to sleep with all these people here. Do come to tea another day and we can take him to the park."

"I'd love to!" She got a picture of him in a silver frame off a table and I said how cute he was, which he was.

"It starts when you sink into his arms, and you end up with your arms in his sink!" said Ianthe. I noticed she had a new way of talking, with a slight accent that wasn't quite Cockney. "Come and visit me in Oxford and we'll go to a consciousness raising meeting at a women's group. At least you haven't tied yourself down with children yet!"

"Haha, I can tell when you're joking. Fortunately. Are you still working at Radio Oxford?"

"I'm in the office of one of the colleges. But I thought I'd go into teaching instead of radio and I'll start the training soon."

"Then you can tell all the girls not to get married and be scientists instead."

"That sort of thing."

"So how did you meet Mike?" asked Ginevra.

"Through work – when I was at the boutique. He came and made inquiries about a missing person. We got talking somehow."

"What kind of boutique?" asked another guest. She had shoulder-length red hair and was wearing a baggy russet corduroy dress over a petrol blue roll-neck. It was nearly midsummer, but still pretty cold.

"It started off very trendy – you know, when everybody was a dolly bird. And then everybody seemed to want to dress up as Queen Guinevere."

"Rather impractical for everyday life!"

"There was a green velvet dress I rather liked, and a huge black cloak – but imagine going upstairs on the bus in that kind of clobber!" It all seemed like a long time ago. For a brief moment we were all going to be medieval and live in woods, and now here we were, typing and filing and studying history and giving dinner parties.

Soon Ginevra called us to the table and we unfolded our cream paper serviettes and she doled out vegetable soup in little cups with handles. Everybody chatted away and seemed a bit disappointed that Mike and I weren't going to help them change the world. Apart from Ianthe, she doesn't mind what I do, really.

"Do you find it interesting, always going somewhere new?" asked one man, who looked disapproving about everything.

9

"It's interesting going to new bits of London and finding new sandwich shops," I said.

"I got banana and bacon the other day," said Ianthe. "It was that or date and cream cheese. Whatever will they think of next?"

"It can be hard to make friends, though," I said, "When you keep moving on."

"What happened to your chums from the boutique?" asked Ianthe.

"They all kind of scattered when it shut," I said, feeling that I couldn't say they'd all gone to prison because the shop was a front for the drugs trade. And I never liked the girls particularly, though Lawrence the boss was OK. There's a lot I have to keep my mouth shut about.

Ginevra brought on some chicken supreme on white rice, with a green salad and everybody said "How delicious!", which it was. Perhaps I could try making it, Mum taught me how to do a white sauce. The others started to gossip about "departments", which seem to be where you study subjects, and the conversation started to go like this:

"Have you still got that copy of Thompson?"

"I lent it to Bernard."

"He's got my Durkheim. Or did I give it to Malcolm?"

"Do you think Sandy is a fair marker? He only gave me a B plus plus query plus for my essay on the invention of childhood."

"Has anyone talked to Christine recently?" asked red-haired Rowena. "One minute she's your best friend and all over you. And then I go up to her in the library and she looks through me as if she didn't know me. She talked to me eventually, but kind of stiffly."

"Perhaps she's a bit schizophrenic," said Ginevra seriously. "Or depressed."

"A lot of our year are depressed," said Rowena, as if it was something to be proud of. "They go to the medical centre and get given valium."

"Is that such a good idea?" asked Mike.

"Can you be just a bit schizophrenic?" said one of the men. "RD Laing says it's all due to the nuclear family driving you mad."

"What's the nuclear family?" I asked. "Are they worried about the Bomb?" I meant the Atom Bomb, which the Russians might drop on us one day.

"The standard two parents and children," said the bloke, who had wild hair and an untrimmed beard so nothing could be seen of him apart from the end of his nose. "In the medieval period, and still in southern Europe, families were extended, and it was far healthier."

"Well my mother is baby-sitting," said Ginevra, "Perhaps it's because she's Italian!"

"But wasn't it more about power relations?" asked Rowena.

"You must have read RD Laing?" the man asked me.

"Actually, no, should I? I mainly read detective stories and books from the library about Greek and Celtic myths."

So he told me all about RD Laing, who didn't approve of mad people taking drugs, or perhaps he thought they should take different ones, and we had coffee ice cream to end the meal, and I helped Ginevra carry stuff out to the kitchen.

"It's terribly old-fashioned," she said, meaning the pale green cupboards and tiles. "I want to get it all redone in stripped pine."

"You're so lucky to have a garden!" I said. "We just look out onto other people's at the back. But we're very near the Heath."

The two of us nipped outside – it was still light – and had a look round. There were a lot of plastic toys among the shrubs. "I haven't really had time to do much to it," said Ginevra. "Look at us! Here's me with a little boy and talking about gardening – shouldn't we be going out to discos and having fun?"

Ianthe came out and joined us. "Remember those light evenings in Hyde Park? How's your tennis coming along?"

"Not going anywhere! More fun than a disco, though?"

"I always hated them," said Ginevra.

"Same here."

"These days I play pool," said Ianthe.

"Did you ever finish that purple Twiggy jumper you were crocheting?" I asked Ginevra.

"I'm afraid I didn't – but I've knitted a beige jersey in reverse stocking stitch. I do like that silver cardigan."

"It's just from a shop," I said. "I'm hopeless at craft."

We went back into the kitchen where David was making coffee and setting out a tray with tiny cups – Ianthe carried it in. We sat around on the sofas and pouffes and David folded up the table and put it away. "It's not usually as tidy as this," he said, smiling.

"I can imagine," I said.

Mike flashed me a look. He'd been valiantly talking to the students and lecturers, and listening while they told him about juvenile delinquents, which he probably knew more about than they did. I'd better try harder and remember some techniques from those ghastly teenage parties when Murray and Elspeth used to rescue me and we'd all go and make tea in the kitchen. Mum always used to say that if a silence fell you should say "I hear they've had snow in Northampton". I do miss her.

I was sitting next to Rowena, the red-haired girl in the corduroy dress, so I asked her what she was studying.

"Sociology," she said. "It's the science of how people live, improving conditions, people in greeps, problems of yeeth, and all that."

I supposed she meant "groups" and "youth" and said it sounded very interesting, and she asked me if I'd read Sheila Rowbotham, who I'd never heard of either, but Ianthe had and soon they were nattering away. I talked to another girl, Beth, who was wearing a pale green smock. She told me that if you didn't wash your hair it would eventually clean itself, and that deodorant gave you cancer and you could sharpen razor blades under a cardboard pyramid.

"What DID happen to the Age of Aquarius?" I asked her. "Did it ever dawn?"

"That was just a fad, wasn't it?" she asked.

"Anna used to be rather a hippy chick, didn't you?" said Ianthe.

"I was just thinking it seems like a long time ago," I said. "When everybody was living in a fantasy and wanting to go back to medieval times."

"But you told fortunes with Tarot cards, I remember," said Ginevra.

"Ginevra's very into astrology, now," said David.

"Have you done my chart yet?" asked Rowena. She'd turned down the coffee and David had made her some peppermint tea.

"Yes, I finished it yesterday! I'll go and get it."

She went and got a folder full of file paper and diagrams which she laid out on the coffee table. The charts were coloured in, and looked rather pretty. I recognised the symbols for the planets – Venus, Mars and so on. She explained it a bit, all about signs rising, and being on the cusp. Beth looked wide-eyed and nodded gravely.

"Rowena, you're a Pisces, that's a sign with negative polarity," she read from her notes. "You're driven by intense feelings and you like to solve problems peacefully. I'll give you the full reading later – we can meet in the common room."

Rowena looked delighted.

"It all looks rather mathematical to me," I said.

13

"All this stuff is making a comeback," said one of the men with beards. He was wearing a tweed jacket the colour and texture of porridge. "It'll be table turning next. Didn't the Victorians levitate dining tables?"

"The spirits never seemed to do anything terrible useful, did they?" I said. "Just played trumpets and chucked violets about."

"Have you ever been to a séance?" asked Rowena.

"Yes, once," I said.

"Did anything, you know, HAPPEN?"

"Well, the medium went into a trance and talked in different voices. It was a bit scary. A friend took me."

Mike caught my eye again.

"But you read the Tarot yourself?"

"Very fashionable now," said the porridge-tweed man. "I blame the rise of the paperback."

"I really started doing it because I'd just gone to a new school and it was a way of getting to talk to people," I explained. And then I started to see a bit too much, but I wasn't going to tell them that.

"You don't really think the stars can have an effect on your life though, surely?" Mike asked Ginevra. "But don't worry, telling the future isn't a crime any more."

"We're 90% water – and the moon controls the tides!" said Ginevra.

"Surely you must admit there must be something in it?" asked Rowena.

"But the stars are flaming balls of gas!" said Mike. "They're millions of miles away!"

"There are more things in heaven and earth, Horatio!" said one of the tweedy men.

"That's just a line in a play," said Mike.

Ianthe said that logic was a male conspiracy, and they went on arguing. I picked up the charts to look at them more closely. "It would be fun to illustrate these with pictures of the constellations," I said. It seemed mean to throw cold water on the whole idea, and I liked the idea of the Greek gods being just out there in the night sky.

While they talked I tried to follow the chart, but I couldn't make head or tail of it. It just looked like geometry. Then the diagrams blurred, and I looked beyond them at the shiny brown surface of the coffee table. I began to see scenes, the same way I see things in my crystal ball, and even in a cup of black coffee once. I could see Rowena in different clothes (though just as frumpy). If I was Madame Sosostris I could ask "Do you have a peach jumper?" and she'd be amazed, even though it could just be a guess. I watched her mill about in a big room that looked like part of their college – perhaps the entrance hall. The other students looked just as conservative, except for one wearing a striped skinny-rib jersey and an A-line button-up miniskirt. She had a smiley face and a dimple in her chin and shoulder length pale brown hair. I was just trying to see what kind of boots she had on when Ginevra spoke to me and the scene faded.

"You're miles away, Anna! I thought you'd be interested. There's a lecture on modern astrology at the college next week. Rowena and I are going. Do you want to come along?"

I said yes I'd love to, and wrote down the time and the address, and directions of how to get there – it's near the BBC. I wondered if I'd like higher education after all. There's something safe and secure about institutions. And uniforms.

"Just because I admit there might be something in astrology," said Mike as we walked off towards the tube, "How does that make it true?"

"You were very restrained."

"More than usual. Poor kid – Rowena, I mean. There I was casting doubt on her present."

"And her future, ha ha."

"How could anybody see the future? I'm not sure I'd want to."

"I don't think anybody can," I said. Just the present and past and the hidden. It hadn't happened to me for a bit, and I keep my Tarot cards and crystal ball wrapped in black velvet in a box in a cupboard.

"You know what the Americans say?"

"No, what do they say?"

"I knew when to get out of college! But they were nice people, especially your hostel friends. But this doesn't mean WE have to give a dinner party, does it?"

"I hope not. Why did they boggle when you said you were a policeman?"

"Guilty conscience. No, probably think we uphold the establishment and all vote Tory."

And we went into the underground station and went home.

CHAPTER TWO

June 1970

I met Ginevra at her seat of learning, Regent Street Polytechnic, and it was just as I'd imagined (and seen in the table-top). It was a cross between the place I'd got the brochures from, the convent, and the hostel. People were hanging about: lots of Indian and Japanese and West Indian boys and girls wearing studenty outfits and carrying folders and briefcases and pads of file paper. I thought students were supposed to be revolting, but perhaps that's all over now too.

There was a smell of dust, and books, and furniture polish, and sandwiches. I'd brought one of my new notebooks. I looked around for Ginevra and Rowena and found them sitting on a bench in the corridor. I was wearing work clothes – a yellow shirt and grey skirt, with my hair up in a big plait twisted round and hairpinned to the back of my head. These days I just want to look dull.

We chatted a bit and then they led me towards the lecture hall. There was brown lino on the floor, and the walls were painted dark green up to my head height. In the lecture hall there were seats in steep tiers. There weren't many people there, so we sat near the front and put our notebooks and pens on the sloping shelf. I wondered if there'd be any other "extra-mural" lectures I could come to. People chatted quietly and shuffled papers and then the lecturer walked out onto the stage. She had a long wooden stick to use as a pointer, and a clicker in one hand to prompt the person in the control box to change slides. She was about 40 and had short dark hair and wore a dark-green blouse and a bright green sari. I recognised her at once.

She was Naheed — someone from that time in my life when I had adventures that were exciting but also scary and could have gone horribly wrong. And just when I'd been feeling so safe. She began to talk about the history of astrology and I took a lot of notes. I liked the stuff about Greek gods, and personality types – she'd always talked a lot about those – but when she got onto how to cast a nativity I drifted off a bit although Ginevra was concentrating hard and writing stuff down.

I'd met Naheed with a lot of other – I don't know if you'd call them a coven, but they studied the occult, and held séances, and the leaders Gilles and Dorinda tried to call up demons to do their bidding and deflect the bad vibes onto innocent bystanders. They also dealt in hard drugs on the side and were safely in prison, for a bit. So I could relax, I thought.

But I'd always liked Naheed and she'd been friendly to me, and perhaps she hadn't been involved in the drug side of things. And I had a friend on either side of me, and we were in a room full of students. The lecture came to an end and Naheed asked for questions. Ginevra put up her hand and stammered out a question (she can't help stammering), and Naheed answered it. There were a few more questions, and then instead of going backstage, Naheed came down the steps from the stage and into the hall.

"I'd like to ask her about the Ancient Babylonians," said Ginevra.

"You were brave to ask a question like that!" said Rowena. "Let's linger, she's talking to some other people."

I looked back, and Naheed was standing in a group, smiling and talking to them and tidying her notes. She caught my eye and smiled. We walked up to the group.

"Hello!" said Naheed to me. "I saw you there with your friend. I appreciate your interest." She nodded to Ginevra.

"I, I would love to know more about Babylonian mythology," said Ginevra. Naheed gave her a book title and I wrote it down as well.

"Would you like a reading list? How about you, Anna?" And she handed us out some typewritten sheets.

"Have you met before?" asked Rowena.

"Oh yes, we were friends a couple of years ago," said Naheed. "That group rather broke up, didn't it? Though I still see some of them." She looked at me a bit narrowly.

We walked slowly towards the exit up the stairs – it was a bit narrow, and Ginevra and Rowena went ahead.

"It is nice to see you," I said to Naheed. "I'm glad you're OK."

"Well, I was never part of the other shenanigans, you know."

"No, nor me!" I said.

"I visit them sometimes."

"Gilles and Dorinda?"

"Dorinda, certainly, and Lawrence. Poor man, I'm sure he'd appreciate a visit from you. I bring him books to read."

"I've never been to a prison. Where is he?"

She told me, a prison in London, and what the visiting days and hours were, and where to go, and I wrote it in my notebook.

"So you are still seeking after the higher truth?" she asked.

"I mainly go and hang out in the library," I said. "I'll look for that book about the Babylonians."

"I feel you are an Old Soul!"

I said I'd visit Lawrence, and we said goodbye and I caught the others up. They were impressed that I knew Naheed and I said I'd met her at a few parties, which was sort of true. And we went home to our husbands or to a flatshare in Rowena's case. I wondered if she was going out with anybody – one of those men with beards at the dinner party, perhaps.

I got home and found Mike reading a book about the lost rivers of London. "Fancy going out at the weekend and looking for them?" he asked. "How was the lecture?"

"It was OK – a bit technical, but I like the stuff about myths and legends and gods. Guess who was giving it – Naheed! She was one of the gang, you remember."

"Did she wear a sari?"

"That's her. She was quite friendly and says she visits Lawrence in prison. You know, my old boss."

"She was in the clear – just involved in the spiritualist side. And we can't do anything to them unless they defraud anybody."

"Would you mind if I visited Lawrence? It must be awful being in prison."

"Yes, it's not much fun. But you go if you want to. He wasn't so bad, if I remember."

"He was always nice to me."

******

I had a half-week coming up, so I went to the prison on visiting day, following Naheed's instructions, and asked to see Lawrence. I sat around in a room lit by fluorescent strips, with lots of little formica-topped tables and metal chairs, and girls with babies. The girls were smoking cigarettes and stubbing them out on tin ashtrays. One of the officers told me to sit at a table, and not to touch the prisoner or pass him anything. I said I'd brought cigarettes and a lighter and he asked to see them. He examined them and put them on the table and told me not to touch them again. I sat there for a bit, and then they brought Lawrence over to my table and he sat down in front of me.

"Anna!" he said. "How nice of you to drop by."

"I bumped into Naheed," I said. "She said she visited you and Dorinda."

His dark hair was cut very short and was now sprinkled with grey, and he was much thinner, and he'd never been very fat. He was wearing a dark navy-blue uniform.

"You win some, you lose some!" he said. "The barnet, darling? It was always dyed. I've got to act my age now."

"How awful, being in here."

"It's hardly the Ritz."

"How long -?"

"I'm trying to get time off for good behaviour. Are these for me? Thanks. I know you don't, unless you've taken it up."

He opened the cigarettes and lit one. His fingers were shaking. A tear rolled down his face and he brushed it away.

"Tell me about you," he said. "What have you been up to since shopping us all to the police?"

"You're being very nice about it."

"I suppose you didn't like the idea of the drugs," he said. "And there was that friend of yours you were worried about. You kept shtum about knowing her but I put two and two together."

"Ursula? She wasn't exactly a friend, but I was worried about what might happen to her."

"She'd have been OK. All that Devil Rides Out stuff was just a lot of play-acting, you know. Dorinda used to fake those trances. It was a giggle! I just went along for the ride. And Naheed's a good egg. She's got her head screwed on despite the 'your fate in the stars' bit. So, enough about me, what about me? I mean, tell me the story of your life."

"I went back to working as a secretary, and I got married."

"Well, fancy that! Who to?"

"A policeman."

"Not the one who came sniffing around the shop?"

"That one."

"Married into the fuzz! Have you heard from the girls – they've been out for a while?"

"No, I haven't."

"You used to hang out together, didn't you?"

"We did – but I don't think we really had much in common."

"Well, you are a dark horse. Still look about 16."

"I wonder if I always will."

"You might manage to grow a bit."

"I try!" We laughed.

"Just the thing for selling teenage fashion, mind you. How about Gilles, seen anything of the Master of the Dark Arts?"

"Wasn't he going to be in prison for a long time? He's not in here, is he?"

"No, he was in the executive suite. But he escaped, don't you read the papers? Naheed says Dorinda is spitting tacks about it in Holloway."

I felt rather cold.

"I didn't know, no. How?"

"Helicopter, ladder made of knitting needles, one of those! Actually it seems he just finagled his way out. In an ambulance? Or did he just ask nicely?"

"Anyway, I'm glad you forgive me."

"I hope you forgive ME – for kidnapping you that time!"

It's true, he spiked my pink champagne when we were celebrating shutting down the boutique, and drove me to Harpsden Manor, the headquarters of the operation. It's a Gothic pile in the country — or suburbs really — owned by the coven's high priest, Gilles Lemaitre. He'd found out I had some wild talents, and wanted to use me to channel some dark powers and gain his heart's desire.

"You were only doing what you were told, I expect," I said.

"I never knew why they wanted you in particular. Unless you look so innocent nobody would think you were passing out the stuff. They told me some mystical rigmarole, but I never really listened."

"Would you like me to come again?"

"Oh, please do. It's lonely in here with all these people. Except some of them aren't too bad."

"What would you like me to bring?"

"Flowers. I miss them. And chocolate and fags are always welcome. And the odd magazine or book. Don't put yourself out."

I wanted to shake his hand, but he said the screws would think we were passing contraband. Two officers moved towards us, and he got up and went away with them and I went home. I'd never told anybody, eg the police, about his part in it, just said I woke up at the Manor and found I was a prisoner. Kidnappers probably get really long sentences.

***

"I've seen Lawrence," I told Mike as we ate a celery and white grape salad I'd got off a recipe card from Sainsbury's.

"How was he?"

"Pretty miserable, I think. I'll go back, and take some flowers and chocolate."

"He's not in hospital!"

"No, but he said he missed flowers."

"Poor bloke. He was just a minnow."

"You mean not one of the big fish?"

"Right. He should be out in a couple of years if he's good."

"He said he was trying to be. But he said Gilles had escaped."

"Lemaitre — Yes, he's gone AWOL again. Probably left the country. I didn't say anything because I didn't want to upset you." He looked worried.

"Don't apologise. But how – surely you can't just walk out of a prison? Did someone throw a ladder over the wall?"

"I shouldn't really tell you."

"Go on, though."

"Nobody really knows how he did it. The simple explanation is that he disguised himself as a visiting psychiatrist and walked out through security that way. But where did he get the civvies? And there was no spare psychiatrist tied up in a cell. And he's pretty noticeable. Like they say, you can't disguise height. So Lawrence wasn't too resentful?"

"No, he seemed quite pleased to see me, despite everything."

"He left some pretty strange books behind in his cell, though. Lemaitre, I mean."

"What happened to them?"

"Bagged up as evidence. They were all written in some kind of code symbols and diagrams. A bit like that astrology chart your friend showed us."

We cleared up the plates (they came with the flat), and looked at Time Out to find a film to go to.

***

I had another day off, so I went up to the Heath – that's Hampstead Heath and it's big and quite wild – and picked some rowan branches and some yarrow, and found a few white feathers. I was wearing a brown and purple summer dress with a scoop neck and little sleeves, and my hair down. I looked out for Elsie, but "her" bench was empty. I pinched the yarrow leaves and sniffed them – they smell sharp and spicy. When I got home I put the plants in a vase with the feathers, and pencilled some small signs on the wallpaper next to the door frame outside the flat's front door. I put a stone with a hole in it I found on a beach next to the flower arrangement.

Then I got out our Scrabble set and picked out the alphabet, and wrote YES and NO on two squares of paper. I put them all in a circle on the table and put an upside-down glass in the middle and rested a finger on it.

23

I whispered, "Elsie, are you there? Elsie?"

The glass began to move round in circles, and then it spelled out: "Hello, dear."

"Were you looking for me?"

"Yes."

"Do you want to meet?"

"Yes."

"Usual Lyons café teatime?"

"Yes."

And then the glass went "dead". I tidied up a bit and put the Scrabble away, then got a bus to Oxford Street and went to the Lyons where I'd first met Elsie. Our table was free, so I sat on the banquette facing the door to the street, and ordered a cup of tea. I took off my cardie (brown crochet) and put it on the seat opposite as if I was saving it for someone, which I was.

I wondered if she'd turn up. More people came in, and I hoped they wouldn't come and sit next to me. I read a paperback for a bit. Someone brushed past the seat and I looked up to try and put them off coming to join me, and when I looked back there was Elsie sitting opposite, with a man on her left. I hadn't seen or heard him sit down, either, or say "Is this one free?" as people usually do. He looked like the fellow who'd been sitting on the bench on the Heath that day.

"Hello, dear!" said Elsie. "Speak low, and don't forget to look down or at the wall," she said.

"OK, I remember." I pulled my hair over my face so that people wouldn't think I was talking to myself, and looked down at the book.

"I'd like you to meet my friend Francis," said Elsie.

"Oh, hi, are you - "

"One of them? A revenant?"

Francis looked at me and smiled. He had untidy black hair – not long like the sociology lecturers, but like a short haircut grown out a bit. He was wearing a dark raincoat and a dark suit. All his clothes were slightly shabby and rubbed at the cuffs, and the ends of his shirt collar were frayed. He had a gaunt face and was quite good-looking.

"I know revenant is French for -"

"We like to return to our old haunts, don't we, Elsie?"

"Francis is an educated man," said Elsie. "He had a college education, didn't you, Frank?"

"I was a disappointment to everybody," he sighed. "In life. And now I just hang about here. Or Soho. There are a lot of us there. People whose lives didn't go according to plan."

"I thought he might be of some help to us," said Elsie. "I've known him for simply ages."

"Will we need help?"

"I'm sure you know by this time, dear," she said. "THEY are among us again."

"Yes, I saw Lawrence in prison."

"it was kind of you to visit."

"He told me Gilles had got out of prison somehow, and nobody knows where he is."

"That's right. And you know, I don't like his friends. And they don't seem to like YOU. Getting the police to interrupt the ceremony, and getting them all, well..."

"Put away," I said.

"It all sounds most intriguing," said Frank. "Elsie has been too discreet. Who are these people, Lawrence and Gilles, and why don't they like you?"

"Oh, Lawrence likes me," I said. "At least, I think he does. He used to be my boss at the boutique, but I suppose Gilles and Dorinda — she's a spiritualist medium, and he's a wizard — I suppose they got him to employ me in the first place so that they could kidnap me and use me in their ceremonies, as well as another girl called Ursula."

"I told you Anna has gifts," said Elsie. "The kind you're born with."

25

"I'm not telling this very well," I said. "You see, Frank, they knew about the gifts because the other coven I was involved with in the country must have told them, and that was why they wanted me. I just happened to do a couple of spells that worked, and word got around. I even made someone fall downstairs and break her leg. I felt awful about that."

"You were looking for the other girl when we met," said Elsie.

"Ursula, yes, I was worried about her. And then when Lawrence kidnapped me I woke up at Harpsden Manor, this Gothic chateau they had in the country, and Ursula was there, but she didn't want to escape, but I did. The grounds were huge, there were woods, and there was a high wall all round. I found a way out along a stream in a thicket that went under the wall. And then I rang Mike – he was my boyfriend then, he's a policeman. We're married now. And then the police were mainly interested in the drugs part. I never told them I'd stolen some money from the hippies to buy a train ticket, either."

"The drugs part?" asked Frank.

"Yes – they were using Harpsden Manor as a drugs factory, it must have been hidden somewhere. And they had a lot of boring hippies as dealers or couriers or distributors. Apart from Alan, he was all right. So anyway, they were going to hold a ceremony on Parliament Hill at Halloween, and use Ursula as a shield so they would get the magic, but she would get the side-effects. But the police turned up dressed in Halloween costumes and Ursula and I flew away and I took her home and she's fine now. I think she's studying interior design."

"How fascinating, do go on," said Frank.

"If you don't believe me, ask Elsie! She helped me a lot." I said. "And Gilles and Dorinda and Lawrence and some of the girls went to prison for the drug-dealing bit. I don't suppose you know how long Gilles has been free, Elsie?"

"I'm afraid not," she said. "I read about it in an old newspaper that was blowing about the gutter, and then I asked a few questions, and bumped into Frank here, and he said he'd heard something on the grapevine."

"Drug baron flies coop," said Frank. "There was a modicum of gossip."

"Mike never told me," I said. "He didn't want to frighten me."

"And of course he's not sure how friendly you were with them all," said Elsie. "But you should protect yourself."

"I'm trying," I said.

"Don't forget you're more powerful than he is," she said.

"Yes," said Francis. "And if you don't call us ghosts, we won't call you a witch!"

"I don't know how that happened," I said. "It just started with trying to read tealeaves."

"What about your parents?" said Elsie.

"How much did I tell you? You don't know where they are, do you? They disappeared when I was about 17," I explained to Frank.

"They know how to hide, I'm afraid," said Elsie. "They've had practice."

"Yes, if you never age, you'd have to keep moving on and changing your name."

"Anyway, we're here if needed," said Francis. "I can see why this lot might be rather irritated with you."

"Call us any time," said Elsie. "But we must go now. Some people want this table."

She nodded towards some shoppers who were looking crossly at me as if I ought to make room for them. I looked back, but Elsie and Francis had gone. I retrieved my cardy and left too. Of course my parents would know how to hide themselves from the spirit world as well as this one.

I wandered down Oxford Street where Mike and I had looked up at the architecture through binoculars, in search of statues – there are lots on buildings once you start noticing them, even some beavers. I saluted the large lady in purple on Selfridge's clock, then turned round and strolled the other way, past C&A. I stood and looked at the skirts and dresses for a bit, and then a smartly dressed woman with short dark hair came up and said "Excuse me". I thought perhaps she was a tourist who wanted to know the way to Piccadilly Circus or somewhere so I smiled back at her.

She said: "Look, I'm sure you've been told not to talk to strangers – is your mum inside the shop?"

I said: "No, I'm on my own."

"Really? Out window shopping?"

I nodded.

"Let me explain," she said. "I work at a model agency – now, I know alarm bells will start ringing all over the shop, but here's my card. I think you've got the look and I'd really love you to come and have some pictures taken. Don't worry! I'm not going to spirit you off somewhere! Get your parents to ring me and we can have a chat and see what they say."

"Actually," I said, "I haven't got any parents. I'm nearly 20, and married."

"Well, blow me down!" said the woman. "Are you really?"

I showed her my wedding ring.

"I'd still love you to come and have some pictures taken. I can't promise anything, of course, but you'd look fab in a teen range. Teenagers are a big market now, and all the department stores have boutiques."

"I used to work in one – a boutique, I mean. And I suppose we all modelled the clothes – we wore them at work, anyway."

"Well, that's useful experience. What do you do now?"

"I work as a temp, I've just got a few days off."

"Well, DO give me a ring, won't you? I'd love to hear from you!" And she clacked off in her sling-backs, and I went to get my bus. I looked at the card, which read "The Stella Orrin Agency" in copperplate writing.

When I got home, Mike kissed me and said: "And how was YOUR day?"

"I had tea with some friends," I said. "You know, Elsie, the woman with the wispy hair? And then guess what, I was talent-spotted by a scout from a model agency."

"Don't models have to be tall?"

"It's an agency for child models." I showed him the card. "It would be more fun than dreary temping."

"Honestly, you're not safe out! Well, I suppose they just might be legit. I haven't heard anything against this lot."

"I could just go and see them."

"And never be seen again? You like to live dangerously."

"Yes, yes, I'm much too trusting, aren't I? And Mum told me never to join a cult."

"OK, but only if I can come with you."

***

I rang the Stella Orrin agency the next day, and the number worked and it all sounded quite above-board, and after asking to speak to my mother, and me explaining, they made an appointment for me. They still asked if I'd be bringing a chaperone. I kept telling them I was nearly 20 and said I'd bring my husband and I could hear them boggling a bit over the phone. Perhaps they just didn't believe me.

You see, I stopped growing or looking any older when I was about 14. I think it was the herb tea Mum kept making me drink. I thought she got it at the health food shop, but there's a "longevity" recipe in the old handwritten book she left behind for me when they both disappeared. Mum and Dad must have taken the potion too, and that's why they never aged either – they left me some photos of them in old-fashioned clothes captioned with different names and I suppose they thought I'd work it out.

I only hope my mind will get older. I wonder when it all started, and when they were born? Mum had a few what she called family heirlooms that she said were 18th century. Or were they older? How long am I going to live? Do you have to keep topping it up if you want to live for ever? Is there an antidote? Most of the time I try not to think about it. And I haven't told Mike, obviously. I haven't told him about any of it.

Of course I don't want to die. But I don't think I want to live for... 200 years? 300 years? And then just crumble? While Mike ages? And all my friends? Elsie and Francis don't seem to mind not being alive in the generally accepted sense of the word. But ghosts don't like being asked about that, I've found.

CHAPTER THREE

June 1970

At the weekend we went out with Mike's book about the lost rivers of London.

"We can do Hampstead Heath another time," he said. "That's where the Fleet rises in a spring – it's now the bathing ponds."

"I think I'll go to the Ladies' Pond when the weather gets nicer."

"And leave me at the Men's Pond – thanks!"

"You can go to the mixed one – the Lido."

"It's miles away down by Gospel Oak station."

"We'll go together."

He smiled to show he wasn't cross really, and we took the 214 to Kings Cross and started following the Fleet River past Old St Pancras Church, which the book says has been "extensively modernised" by the Victorians and has a lot of old gravestones piled up with tree roots growing over them.

"Boys used to swim here," said Mike, "And that was a Workhouse." He pointed to a grim edifice with narrow windows. "This hotel is curved because the river went round here."

We crossed over Euston Road to Gray's Inn Road where there's a statue of Hermes on top of a building that has some winged lions carved on it too.

"We need to go down St Chad's Place," said Mike, consulting the book and turned into a little cobbled alley.

I looked up at Hermes and quickly muttered:

"Hail to thee
Great Mercury
Where e'er I be
Look after me."

I wonder if that spell I cast for a joke in the British Museum, to bring statues to life, is still working? Perhaps it will go on working until I reverse it. I ran after Mike.

"There was a holy well here," he said. "And the river ran down this alley."

There were a lot of gratings and we peered into them all. They smelled a bit dank.

"Look!" said Mike, bending over the smallest, a slit-like grille in the middle of the cobbled alley. "People will think we're bonkers, but look."

I looked through the grille, and many feet below I saw water flowing.

"Wow!" I said.

"It might just be a sewer. But apparently you can see and hear it in Farringdon Road – we could always get a bus. Now I think it goes through that door and along the back of the houses."

We walked out into the road through a tunnel in the houses at the end, and on towards Farringdon. We found a tiny shop that must have been built right on the river bank, and then we decided to go home, and find the Farringdon Road bit and the outfall into the Thames another day. Mike marked our route on his map and we walked back to get the 214.

I wondered if the Fleet still had Naiads, and how they felt having to run through pipes and sewers, or if they just stayed up on the Heath in the ponds. They are good nature spirits, and should be on my side, so all the more reason to visit the ponds.

***

Mike works shifts, so sometimes he gets days off in the week, and he wangled one and so did I, so we could go to the audition at the model agency. I took my birth certificate and he wore a work suit and a face suitable for interrogating villains.

"I've checked them out," he said. "There's nothing known against them, but you never know."

The office was in Soho, in among Italian sandwich shops and striperamas and a veg market with men shouting "Bananas! Bananas! Pound a pound!"

We went upstairs where there was a receptionist behind a typewriter and she asked us to take a chair and wait. I'd read somewhere that model agencies like you to wear very plain gear and a white T shirt so I was wearing one with some cut-off jeans and plimsolls, and my hair down. After a bit the receptionist answered the phone on her desk, talked for a bit, and then called us forward.

"Anna Savage? Come with me, and would you like to come too Mr...?"

"Savage," said Mike.

She led us into another office, where there was an older lady in a bright pink skirt suit who sat us down in front of her desk. She said it was nice to meet us and that she was Stella Orrin herself, and said to Mike: "So, has Anna done any modelling before?"

"No, I haven't," I said, "Though I did work in a boutique and wear the dresses. And in case you're wondering, we're married, and I'm nearly 20." I got out my birth and marriage certificates and handed them to her. She put on some glasses and looked at them with her eyebrows raised.

"I see," she said, handing it back to me. "So you'd rather call yourself Anna. That's understandable. Well, Anna, would you like to do some modelling?"

The name on my birth certificate is "Inanna" – she was a Babylonian goddess.

"It sounds fun." I said. "I'm working as a temp and it's quite dull most of the time."

"I expect it is!" She smiled. "Can I ask how tall you are?"

"Four foot eleven."

"Would you mind standing up and doing a twirl?"

I did that.

"What lovely hair!"

"I promised Mum I'd never cut it." I don't know why she got me to promise her that, but Mum probably knew what she was talking about, so I'd better not.

"This isn't really relevant to you, but we're very protective of our models, and the young ones are chaperoned everywhere."

Mike said he was glad to hear it.

"And what do you do?" she asked politely.

"I'm a policeman."

"Well, you can see we're complying with the law!"

"On children working? I should hope so."

"Now come through, both of you, and Helmut will take a few shots."

We went through into a quite big studio that must have been built out at the back of the old house we were in and there was Helmut wearing black jeans and a black T shirt. He had a pale, quite good-looking face and short fairish hair. There were a lot of cameras and white umbrellas, and sheets of shiny silver stuff, and a white backdrop.

"This is Anna, Helmut. You know what's required." And Stella Orrin went back to her office.

Helmut said hello, and gave Mike somewhere to sit, and got me to stand in front of the backdrop and smile, and not smile, and twirl round, and fling my hair around while grinning.

"So how old are you, Anna?"

"Nearly 20, and this is my husband, Mike."

"Oh, I see! I thought maybe your brother!" He smiled, and put some music on and got me to dance to it. I did the silly dancing we used to do at parties – I never really learned to do groovy dancing properly. I preferred the ballroom classes at the convent, with girls dancing together. Then he got some little boxes and got me to leap off them with my arms in the air while looking ecstatic.

"That will do for now, I think! Very nice! You know, not all our children are children. Just most of them."

"Fun for you!" said Mike.

"It's a living!" said Helmut, and ushered us back to the office again where Stella Orrin was waiting for us.

"We'll see how the shots turn out, but I think they'll be fabulous, and we'll be in touch, I promise! Now we'd better talk money, Mr Savage. You don't mind, Anna?"

"Oh no, please, I'm clueless with money and stuff."

She got out a contract and explained it to Mike, and then she got me to sign it.

"I'm used to dealing with parents and sisters," she explained, gave us her card and told me to ring on Monday mornings. "Janice will take your measurements," she said, ushering back to reception. Janice measured my height on a scale on the wall. "And now I'll just take your vital statistics! And what's your shoe size? I see you don't pluck your eyebrows – you won't, will you?"

I promised not to. It's fashionable at the moment to have thin eyebrows that make you look like an insect but mine are quite thin anyway.

***

"Did I look a complete fool?" I asked Mike as we went down the stairs.

"No, you looked lovely. I wonder if they'll paint on some freckles?"

"Yuck, I hope not."

We wandered around the fruit and veg market a bit and bought some bananas, then got frothy coffee and avocado-bacon sandwiches in the Bar Bruno, then went home.

"I wonder if you'll hear from them," said Mike. "I was worried they'd ask YOU for money. That's how these dodgy model agencies work."

"Don't they ship girls to Istanbul?"

"That sounds like a fairytale, but they do sometimes – offer you a job in Istanbul and take your passport away 'for safe-keeping'. Don't fall for that, will you?"

"No, I'm going to type boring stuff at something or other enterprises and I doubt if they have a secret basement or anything so exciting!"

"What about the bosses – don't they ever make suggestive remarks?"

"I probably wouldn't notice if they did."

"Keep it that way," he said.

***

I rang the model agency on Monday, trying not to sound too eager, and the receptionist, Janice, said the pictures had come out well, there was nothing at the moment but to keep ringing in. My usual secretarial bureau had got me a job right next to the building with Hermes and the winged lions in Gray's Inn Road. It was a big open office and we typed stuff about inspecting college courses. It was quite interesting, though the courses sounded a bit feeble and I didn't fancy going on any of them. I learned a new word – "module".

I went out at lunchtime and bought a bunch of flowers from a stall outside Kings Cross station, and left some outside the Hermes building. I walked down the little alley we'd found, and dropped some flowers into the river through the grille, while murmuring:

Like the Styx, your stream is dark
Naiads of the Fleet, now hark!
Though in Thames your river ends
Don't forget that we are friends.

I took the rest of the bunch into the office and was putting them in a basin in the Ladies when one of the other girls came in.

"Lovely!" she said. "I'm sure we can find me a vase for those."

She took me to a stationery cupboard and there were several vases, so I filled one with water, stuck the flowers in it and put the vase on my desk.

"From a boyfriend?" she asked, going back to her own desk.

"No, I just bought them for myself," I said.

"Oh, yeah!"

I took the bunch home. There were some lavender roses in it – that means "enchantment". Perhaps I could take Lawrence a bouquet that would make him feel happier. I must find the little book on the Language of Flowers that the Haslemere Museum had given me. A coreopsis in a pot – it means "always cheerful", but he might find that difficult. Haslemere was where I lived with my parents and had all that trouble with the coven, and got kicked out of school when the witches spread lies about me. Where can I get some verbena, dill and St John's Wort (Fuga Daemonum)? Lawrence could probably do with all of those too.

"So where have you been today?" asked Mike, while we laid the table and fried some sausages.

"An office near that little alley where we looked for the Fleet. There's an older lady who reads the Bible all the time, and a girl who wears orange every day – she belongs to some sect. Nadine was telling her all about how she got picked up on the tube and taken away for the weekend."

"Nice behaviour, I don't think!"

"I think all the others were rather shocked. She bragged that she didn't have to pay for anything. I don't think they like her, either."

"That's rather sad."

"But she found me a vase for my flowers."

Ginevra rang me, and we arranged to go to the park with her baby at the weekend. Mike was working, or he could have come too, but Ginevra said perhaps he didn't like babies. I said I didn't know.

36

Anyway, I went down south to where they live and we pushed Richard (he's quite big now) to the park and took him out of the push chair and sat on some tree stumps and pretended to have a tea party. It was great fun and then we went back to their house and had some real tea and biscuits, and then I went home. Mike came back in the evening and I told him all about it. We ate some taramasalata and crisps, and then some soup I'd made, and had a glass of Blue Nun. I was just thinking a gingham tablecloth would like nice on the table in the back window where we usually eat, looking out at trees, and wondering if green or blue would be better – or perhaps brown or red or yellow – when Mike said: "How do you feel about having children?"

"It would be nice."

"It would be nice to be a family."

"I suppose it would."

"You just suppose?"

"It was always just me and my parents. And now they've gone missing."

"It was just me and my parents, too, when they were around. But that's a family."

"I think it would be brilliant. Where would we put it – the baby, I mean?"

"We can always find room." He smiled. "People used to have loads of kids in places this small."

"Can't have been easy."

"They probably sent them out to work as soon as they could walk."

"But – you know, we've never taken any precautions. What if I can't have children?"

You probably think we're irresponsible, but we'd never really talked about it. I think we were too shy.

"Perhaps you should go and see the doctor. Do you mind?" he asked anxiously.

"No, they're all pretty nice at the Health Centre."

The next day Mike was working a night shift, and it was Midsummer Eve.

"Shame I've got to leave you, babe. We could have wandered round the park and watched the sun set at about 11pm. Those are nice flowers."

I'd got some more, and put them in a vase on the table. The shop even had some St John's Wort and I asked them to mix it in. It has yellow, whiskery flowers and black berries. Mike went off to work, and I put the bouquet in a plastic shopping bag with some wet tissues at the bottom, and stuffed a candle and a lighter and a book in my handbag. I put on a dark T shirt and some baggy dark trousers and got the bus up to Parliament Hill, carrying the flowers. I put the strap of my handbag over my head and one arm in case of muggers, and walked up the path that goes up the side of the park for quite a long way and eventually gets to the Heath and the ponds.

It was still quite light, and there were people around, flitting through the trees, getting up to naughty things according to Mike, though he wouldn't say quite what, but I thought they would probably leave me alone. I walked on, under the trees. There were a few houses on the right – I could just see their lighted windows through the leaves. What a place to live! Those people must all be rich. Mike would be furious to think I was out here on my own in the semi-dark, though. Not cross with me, but worried.

Eventually I passed the Men's Pond on my left, and soon came to the Ladies Pond. There was a board up saying that it was very deep and children under 15 couldn't come in. The gate was padlocked shut, but I climbed over it and went towards the changing huts. They were locked too, but there was an open kind of deck, with a ladder down into the water. The pond was quite big, more of a lake. In the deepening dusk my flowers looked dim and colourless, and the pool was black. There were high trees and hedges round the pond, to stop men looking in, so nobody would see me.

I knelt on the deck, and one by one threw the flowers into the water. I lit the candle and quietly read from the book:

Listen where thou art sitting
Under the glassy, cool, translucent wave
Listen for dear honour's sake
Goddesses of the silver lake
Listen, and save!
By scaly Triton's winding shell
And old soothsaying Glaucus' spell
By Leucothea's lovely hands
And her son that rules the strands
By Thetis' tinsel-slippered feet
And the songs of sirens sweet
By all the nymphs that nightly dance
Upon thy streams with wily glance.

That's by Milton and it's really about the River Severn, but I think it's beautiful. I wonder who Leucothea was, and her son. I love that bit about the translucent wave. I added a bit.

Listen, Naiads of the Fleet
From your dark and watery seat
Listen to my sacred ode
Spirits of the Farringdon Road
Help me, keep me safe from harm.
Listen, listen to my charm.

I threw in the last of my flowers, then put all my things down and quickly peeled off my clothes. I can almost wear my hair like Lady Godiva, so I was quite decent just in case anybody was peering in. I descended the ladder into the cold, cold water and swam about a bit, then came out and dried myself on my T shirt and climbed back into my clothes. Then I picked up my stuff and packed it away, and put my handbag over my head again and headed back to the gate. It was much darker now.

There was someone standing by the gate, with his back to me. I stood still. Perhaps he was just waiting for somebody. He looked in my direction, then set off down the path and down the hill.

I let him go on a bit and climbed over and went in the same direction. He walked on without looking back. He was wearing a kind of cape, and perhaps nothing under it as I could see his legs. As we came out from the trees he looked back at me, and

I could see he was my friend Hermes – not the one in Gray's Inn Road, but the one from the top of the building in Finsbury Square where I had a temp job once, and where he rescued me from Gilles in the underground car park. I raised a hand, and so did he, and then he ran quickly down the path, faster and faster until when he reached the road he was just a blur, and a streak of light vanishing southwards.

I squeezed some of the water out of my hair and tried to arrange it so that it didn't look too awful, and walked into the glare of the street lights and crossed the road to the bus stop outside the convent at the bottom of Swain's Lane. I got home and had a bath, and read some more of Comus while my hair dried, even though it was awfully late. You were supposed to throw flowers in the water, and the River Severn "can unlock the clasping charm, and thaw the numbing spell, if she be right invoked in warbled song". Perhaps I should have sung the poem, though I'd have had to make up a tune. And the character talking said he'd address the river in some "adjuring verse", so I hoped I'd done the right thing.

CHAPTER FOUR

I carried on phoning the Stella Orrin agency on Monday mornings and they'd say "Nothing this week!", but to keep phoning. I made an appointment at the health centre and rang Ianthe and fixed a day to go and see her.

I got books from the library and read about Greek myths and made notes. "Hermes is god of transitions and boundaries. Quick and cunning, moving freely between the worlds of the mortal and divine. Messenger of the gods, conductor of souls into the afterlife. Protector of thieves, wit, literature and poetry, sport, roads, boundaries and travellers." He's my protector – Naheed told me that. There was some ancient author thought that incantations were just strings of beautiful sounds.

I carried Mum's book of recipes about with me and wrote out bits of it. It's all in ye olde spelling and quotes from "The Lylye of Medycyne". There's the potion for "longevetie", but where is the antidote? They left me some money, too, with some lawyers, and I'll get some more when I'm 21.

I had a week at Magister Enterprises, in a super-modern tower block near Tottenham Court Road. I'd pinned up my hair in a plait again. It takes a lot of old-fashioned long hairpins from an Indian shop – Indian ladies have the same kind of hair as me. And I'm very slightly short-sighted and managed to wangle some specs which are almost plain glass. Very different from the old hippy me in the velvet bell-bottoms.

I arrived and stared up at the building, which is quite famous. It's like a hotel, with rows of zigzag white bits all round. It's set back from the road with a kind of forecourt in front with spotted laurels and a few vans and cars. The entrance was through some revolving glass doors into a big marble foyer with security guards standing around and one behind a big desk. I told him who I was and he rang someone up and he told me which floor to go to and someone would meet me at the lift.

It turned out I was in the typing pool, where there were a lot of Scottish girls. It meant I didn't have to try and talk more London. I used to speak quite nicely, especially when I was at the convent, and Mum was always very keen on me not saying sumpthing or everyb'dy, but the local school rubbed the shine off a bit. It's OK, because it makes people think I'm even stupider than a girl who looks 16 ought to be. Mum and Dad used to talk rather precisely – as if they were trying to fit in, too.

The girls were quite chatty and started reciting nursery rhymes for some reason and I wrote some of them down. There's a canteen where you can get school-type food with soggy boiled cabbage and something called bacon and onion roll which is basically suet pudding. Even I might put on pounds here. I think I'll stick to cheese rolls.

Here are some of the rhymes:

I love you, I love you Almighty Almighty,
I wish your pyjamas were next to my nightie,
Don't be mistaken and don't be misled,
I mean on the clothes line, not in the bed.

Oh where is King George? Oh where is he-o?
He's out in his longboat, all on the salt sea-o.

Up flies the kite, down falls the lark-o.
And Old Mother Birdwood, she had an old ewe,
And she died in her own park-o.

They started doing clapping games to them and the older lady overseeing us shut them up at that point. She's called Olive – she has dyed black hair and wears a leopard-print cashmere jersey. We typed the usual boring stuff about investments and executive homes. But it made a change from insurance, and letters, and tables of figures. I saw the doctor one evening that week.

"How was your day?" asked Mike when I got home.

"OK, the canteen's nice but the food's pretty stodgy. I've just been to the doctor's."

"So what did he say? What did he do?" He put down his book and we sat by the window.

"It was a she – she's very nice and has a pudding basin haircut and very thick eyebrows. She examined me, and that was about as much fun as you can imagine."

"Well, you are brave."

"She said I seemed a bit undeveloped, and asked about periods and stuff and she seemed to think I ought to have them more often. Plus she said anyone under five foot had to have their babies in hospital, and everybody did for the first one. I said we'd been married about a year and she said it usually took about six months, and no need to worry, it could take longer."

"Not so bad, then."

"No, she said wait and see and she couldn't see any reason why not, but wasn't I a bit young and I had my whole life ahead bla bla bla!"

"Perhaps she thought you ought to have an exciting career first! Did you hear any more from that modelling place?"

"They keep saying 'Nothing, ring back.'"

"At least they haven't taken your money for a portfolio and disappeared. What shall we eat?"

"Oh, I don't know."

"Let's go out and get fish and chips. Or a kebab."

So we went out and had a kebab and salad at a little place which is terribly cheap and had a glass each of retsina which is wine that tastes of varnish.

****

One weekend when Mike was working, I got the train to Oxford and met Ianthe. She met me at the station and we walked into town via a big indoor market. We stopped at a clothes stall and Ianthe held up some World War One land girl's breeches: "What do you think?"

"I'm not sure," I said. There were a lot of cool girls in short haircuts and pencil skirts. They looked a bit like Olive. I wondered if it was the fashion and where I could get a skirt like that. Ianthe didn't buy the breeches and we went on towards the centre of town and had a sandwich in a café, and then Ianthe said she'd take me to the Pitt Rivers museum because she knew I'd love it. It's a strange place with glass cases full of things like an ox's heart studded with nails, and witch bottles (I know all about those) and "mammets" – dolls for sticking pins in if you want to curse someone. There were rings set with wolves' teeth and toadstones. There were even some South American shrunken heads.

"They mocked them up from monkeys' heads," said Ianthe, "Like the Fijian mermaid. And the toadstones are really fossil sharks' teeth, not jewels from a toad's head."

We walked out through a hall full of huge animal skeletons. "It was all carved by local workmen," said Ianthe, pointing to the decorations of stone flowers and leaves. She said there was time for a stroll through the Parks, so we went and walked beside the river.

"Sweet Thames flow softly till I end my song," said Ianthe. "It's part of the Thames, you know. It's quiet now because it's the holidays. I can't wait for my term to start at Westminster – oh, I'm not coming to London, Westminster is the teacher training college here. So what's on your horizon?"

I told her about going to the doctor and wanting to have children. I didn't tell her I wasn't sure if I could, or whether I should. What would they turn out like?

"But anyone can have children," she said. "You don't want to be a cow! Or a cabbage! Your brain will atrophy! You should read some Margaret Drabble, have some ambition!"

"I just want to be normal."

"What, dull and beige?"

"No, like everybody else! And I might get some work as a child model."

"That won't be very fulfilling!"

"We want to go and live somewhere like Ruislip."

"You wouldn't like it really! Or perhaps you're joking! Why not join a Women's Group?"

"What do they do?"

"Self-examination and consciousness raising."

"I've heard about that, but what does it mean?"

"If anyone needed their consciousness raising... At least you saw a woman doctor."

"But what do you become conscious OF?"

"Being oppressed, and then you do something about it."

"Like?"

"Start a revolution!"

"Wouldn't it be quicker to just tell people?"

We talked some more and I told her about Ginevra's little boy and how sweet he was and how happy they seemed and she walked me back to the station. She seemed happy too. I waved out of the window as the train creaked off past a graveyard.

***

I rang Stella Orrin's on Monday as usual and they actually said they wanted me and could I come in next week – they gave me a day and said to be there at ten. I rang the temp agency and explained I'd need a day off and they ummed and erred and in the end said that was OK. I was at a different office by that time, older and shabbier and near Hatton Garden. If being small gets me modelling work, perhaps I'd better not reverse the longevity spell for a bit.

I turned up at the Stella Orrin agency at the required time and sat about in reception with some children of about 12 and younger, with their mothers. Janice the receptionist came in and out, calling out names and taking people into the studio. I smiled at a girl who was with a small blonde child in a pink dress. She had a round face and a dimple in her chin, the grown-up one, I mean. Eventually she said, "Are you on your own? You must be older than you look."

"I'm nearly 20," I said. "I'm just naturally tiny."

"Have you done much modelling?"

"No, this is my first 'gig' or whatever you call it."

"This is my sister Paula – she does a lot of shoots."

Paula smiled at me and went on reading a Ladybird book. She looked about seven.

"What about you?" I asked. "Were you ever a model?"

"Yes, when I was little. I think I'm too ordinary looking now. When I was a kid they liked the dimples and the snub nose. I really want to get into acting. In fact I've got a sort of acting job at the moment."

"I usually work as a temp typist, though I did have a job in a boutique once."

"That must have been fun. All my friends do things like work in shops or waitress and try to get parts in fringe plays."

"I'm Anna by the way."

"And I'm Christine."

Before I could ask her more about acting Janice came and called Paula and me and we all trooped into a big room with rails of clothes and some more girls came up to us and led Paula away. I wondered what Christine's job was –

demonstrating ironing board covers in a department store? They always have women in John Lewis doing that – or vegetable slicers.

They showed me a rail and told me to put on yellow tights, denim clogs, blue shorts and a check smock with a red yoke and puffed sleeves. Mine not to reason why. I put the stuff on and by that time we were all dressed in primary colours. They took us into the studio which was now decked out in red, blue and green plastic cubes, bright pink hula hoops and green beach balls with blue spots.

Helmut the photographer was there, and he got us to stand on the cubes and throw the balls around and hula the hoops while grinning crazily. Paula also had dimples and looked cute when she smiled. There was a girl of about 14 with wild red curly hair, and a little West Indian boy with an afro hair cut and a couple of other little ones. I mucked in and played catch and ring-a-roses with the children, and they handed out bubble sets and we blew bubbles all over each other. There was a wind machine to make the bubbles float around and the kids tried to catch them. Of course they were taking photos all this time, and the chaperones sat round the edge on chairs and read magazines and knitted.

We changed our clothes a few times, and went through the same kind of routine. After a bit the little children had their own things put back on and they left, but I was asked to stay. Christine waved goodbye and said "See you again! Hope you get more work!"

I called out "Thanks!" and they gave me and the red-haired girl new outfits to wear. This time I had a brown plaid dress with a lace collar and a black velvet ribbon tie. With it went knitted brown openwork stockings and a suspender belt, and buckled shoes. The girl with red hair had the same kind of costume, also with knitted stockings, and they took us out into the alley to take some pictures of us running down it and leaping about and cavorting with glee, with the wind machine blowing our hair about.

"It's for Golden Fingers," explained one of the staff. "They're printing the pattern for the stockings and we'll all be knitting them for ourselves. I don't think."

"They're pretty uncomfortable," I said.

"They're probably recycling patterns from the war."

Eventually they said "That's a wrap!" and we went back inside and got back into our own clothes and I went off and wandered round Soho a bit looking at the outsides of "Non-Stop Striperama" and shops selling red plastic leotards, and eventually had egg and chips in a Chinese café. I was quite hungry. I wondered if our pictures would encourage anybody to knit the stockings, and how I'd fill in the rest of the week.

CHAPTER FIVE

July 1970

I rang the secretarial bureau and got three days work for the end of the week. I filled in the time reading in Kentish Town Library, browsing in Oxfam (I bought a rather nice dress), and sitting in the café next to the railway station that has a jukebox like the one next to the cinema in Haslemere, where we'd met some unsuitable boys. I wasted rather a lot of money getting it to play songs I liked. The dress has pale blue and buff stripes, and the woman at the till said it was "quality". I dropped back into Ginevra's college in Regent Street too and got some brochures about evening classes and read them.

I went to a rather scruffy office in the City for three days wearing the Oxfam dress over a cream polo-neck jersey, cream tights and strap shoes. It was full of men in three-piece gangster suits saying the word "premium" in squeaky voices. They were OK. One of them was called Mr Novak. I was in the care of a large woman called Gladys. She said they needed someone to do "audio" and if I didn't know how she'd soon show me. I said I was game for anything so she got out some rather scary beige plastic devices and plonked them around my desk. I had to wear big headphones and have a foot pedal on the floor, but I soon got the hang of it. It was easier when I took my shoes off. I typed a lot of stuff about insurance. I wondered what Lawrence would like me to bring him so I typed him a quick letter, too. I went out to post it in case anyone noticed I was writing to someone in Brixton.

47

Next week I was back at Magister Enterprises which seemed even more shiny and modern by contrast. I told Olive I'd been "trained in audio" and she said "Okey dokey!" and gave me a desk with the equipment and some tapes to do. They were labelled: "Focus Group One – Focalor Project". Olive was wearing a turquoise blue cashmere top with a tie collar today, and a pencil skirt like the girls in Oxford.

"What's a focus group?" I asked her.

"They get members of the public together and put ideas to them. You get tea and biscuits, and sometimes travel expenses."

"That sounds like quite a good wheeze," I said. "Where can I put my name down?"

"You're not exactly the target market," she said. "They're mostly more middle-aged and established."

Anyway the tape was quite fun, with people talking in a chatty way and someone in charge asking them how various pictures of houses made them feel. They occasionally said things like "return on investment" which we'd learned how to write quickly in shorthand at secretarial college. You have to write it "retur-vestent". More fun than insurance. Sometimes I never find out what the firm I'm working for does, or makes.

I carried on doing that all week, all groups of people talking, with someone asking questions. I'd do half of one session while someone else did the other half, so it was all a bit disconnected. And one evening I went home via Regent's College and signed up to do an evening class in Classical Civilization.

I went to the Magister canteen at lunchtime, but got ham and cheese rolls and yoghourts instead of lasagne and mashed swede. One day it was really crowded and I sat at a table where there were some men in suits talking about various "projects".

I was eating my lovely chewy white rolls washed down with a cup of milky coffee and reading a Margaret Drabble like Ianthe had told me to – A Summer Birdcage, all about these two sisters, and one of them goes to Oxford then works at the BBC, no wonder Ianthe liked it. It was a good read but I didn't like the girl much – she had a boyfriend in America who she might or might not marry and another one who hung around hopefully that she was a bit mean to.

A woman with a tray came and hovered by the empty place opposite me and said "Can I sit here?" So I said "Yes, of course." She put her tray down and began forking in sausage and mash and boiled cabbage. She had rather pink cheeks and dark wavy hair.

"I don't want to disturb you," said the woman, which is what people say when they want to talk to you, and you're reading.

"Oh, it's just a romantic novel," I said, shutting it.

"Something like Barbara Cartland?" she asked gently.

"That sort of thing." Margaret Drabble would cringe. I'm sure Miss Cartland never went to Oxford.

"I expect you're new, too," she said.

"Oh, are you new?"

"No, I've been here ever so long. About 15 years in September." She had a slight Scottish accent, like the girls in the typing pool.

"I'm just a temp."

"What department have they put you in?"

"I've been in the typing pool for a bit. There are a lot of Scottish girls."

"Yes, it was a scheme started by the original Mr McRobbie. They all live in a hostel he built for them."

"I must ask them about it. I used to live in a hostel."

"This used to be McRobbie's, you know. Of course we were in a different building then, not this monstrosity. But Mr Magister is in charge now."

"Really? I thought it was just the firm's name."

"Of course, we hardly ever see him. Just occasionally you'll spot him getting into his private lift. It goes straight to the top floor. Mr McRobbie used to eat in the canteen. It was a really friendly place then, I knew a lot of people. Now I see new faces every week, and I wonder what happened to so-and-so, and find they've gone months ago. And somebody threw out the rubber bands I'd been saving for years. Such a waste! McRobbie's used to build houses and offices, but now, well, I don't know..." Her voice tailed away.

"What does he look like, Mr Magister?"

"Oh, distinguished, you know — very tall, thin, dark suit, white hair. I gather it's very plushy up on the top floor, lots of these modern indoor plants, and grey carpets."

"It sounds like a hotel."

"Perhaps you'll get the chance to go up there. They move you around if they like you and they're pleased with your work. I'm Marian, by the way."

"I'm Anna."

I got up to put my tray back on the rack and she said "It was nice talking to you."

I said: "Perhaps we'll meet again on my progress round the building!"

"Perhaps," she said, a bit doubtfully. The other people on our table got up and left, clearing up plates and trays and chatting loudly, but she stayed sitting down.

"Just a moment!" she said, leaning forward. She went on. "It's not just the way people just get replaced by new faces. The work we're doing. It doesn't seem to make sense any more. I can talk to you. Everybody else seems to think it's all fine."

"Really? I just type what I'm given."

"If I'm right..." Her voice turned into a sigh. "Are you here next week?"

"I expect so."

"Would you meet me for a coffee on Monday, after work?"

"Of course – I'll meet you in the foyer at half past five."

"Oh, not in the foyer – on the corner of the street. Turn right as you go out."

“All right.” I picked up my tray again and she smiled at me rather sadly as I walked away.

When I saw Mike in the evening I said “I told someone today I was JUST a temp!”

“Is that how you feel?” he asked a bit anxiously.

“No, it’s just what you’re supposed to say. ‘I’m JUST a secretary, JUST a housewife.’”

“Have you been brainwashed by that red-haired friend of yours?” He smiled. “The one in dungarees?”

“Ianthe? No, though I did read the book she told me to. But it was a novel, not politics. Anyway, I’m PROUD to be a housewife! And I’m a model too. Nobody says ‘I’m just a model’.”

“Why not be the first? What was the book like?”

“Oh, OK, about these two sisters who leave college and don’t know what to do next.”

“None of that ‘It starts when you sink into his arms...’?”

“Not that I could see. Perhaps I’m just thick.”

While we ate some dinner – avocado salad – I said: “I signed up to do a course at Ginevra’s college.”

“When did you change your mind?”

“I didn’t – but they do classes in the evening, all kinds of interesting stuff, like astrology and psychic development.”

“Did you go for botany or biology?”

“No – Greek and Babylonian mythology. It’s one evening a week.”

“That’ll come in useful for... naming our children? Or our house? Or even our boat!”

“Oh, do let’s have a boat!”

“Our dog, er... Why not the Egyptians?”

“I think they come into it. It’s all the ancient world and people I’ve never heard of.”

"Perhaps they come in the Bible."

"I wouldn't know – I'm a Catholic, we don't read the Bible!"

I washed up, and he dried. I don't see what's wrong with washing up – I rather like it.

***

The next day I finished the Margaret Drabble over lunch (soup). The heroine decides to marry her boyfriend in the end, as if she was doing the world a big favour. I wasn't quite sure I got the point about the older sister being rich and marrying for money. Why was the younger one so shocked?

There was a cart stacked with leaflets and prospectuses dumped outside the lift, so I nicked a couple so as to have something to read on the bus going home. There was one with pictures of an olde-worlde village in the country somewhere, built new, like reproduction furniture. So the firm still built houses after all – what was Marian on about?

I got home and found Mike sitting at the table reading a book about some people who got given a miracle drug. There were a few letters for me so I put my shopping bag down on the table and picked up the letters and sat in the other kitchen chair. The Magister brochure fell out of my bag and Mike picked it up and flicked through it.

"Is this where you're working? Do you fancy living in a place like this one day?" he asked.

"It looks like a fake version of the village I really grew up in," I said. "I preferred it when we lived in Haslemere, there were more shops."

"Shall we go and look at a suburb at the weekend and pick our dream home?"

"Yeah, why not. Oh look, I've got a letter from Lawrence."

It was written in biro on the kind of paper they make rough books and scratch pads out of. He said he'd appreciate another visit and more fags, and some fashion magazines.

"I don't mind you visiting him again, but watch out, won't you?" said Mike. "Those on the inside just want to use those on the outside and will tell them anything."

I said I'd be careful though I didn't see what harm Lawrence could do to me now.

"If you see any more of your old friends – you'll tell us, won't you?" he said, and I said I would. I wondered what Lawrence wanted the magazines for but supposed he was desperate for something to read.

***

On Saturday we got the tube all the way to Ruislip and got out and wandered about hand in hand and looked in some estate agents' windows. It was a grey day. We walked down a few avenues and found little patches of green with noticeboards on them, and pink roses in front gardens, and bungalows and greenhouses and British Legion huts. The houses had bay windows and Mike said they looked pre-war. We went down a cul-de-sac called Midcroft which ended at a hedge and a ditch full of rubbish, with fields and trees beyond. We went back, and took a different route to the station, past a brick Catholic church with a shrine to Our Lady of Lourdes outside, with the figures painted white.

"What's that all about?" asked Mike, stopping to look at it.

"That's St Bernadette – she saw a vision of the Virgin Mary when she was a teenager, and there was a miraculous spring that healed people."

"Do you mind not going to church any more?"

"I don't miss it. So, what do you think?"

"It's a bit soppy."

"I didn't mean the statues – Ruislip."

He shook his head. "It's too much like where I grew up. Let's stick with London for the moment."

"Yes – what do people get up to round here? It's so quiet."

"Join clubs and have wine and cheese parties."

"Don't they swap wives?"

"They probably do that as well."

"Anyway, London can't really get on without us." I think Elsie told me that once.

We had spaghetti and meatballs at a trattoria near the station, which we agreed must be Ruislip's one attempt at night-life, and went back to Kentish Town. I wondered what Marian wanted to tell me.

CHAPTER SIX

On the Monday I went to meet Marian on the corner of the street and find out what she was being so mysterious about. Perhaps she wanted to know who had stolen her rubber bands — but she never turned up, and after waiting for about half an hour I went home. I looked out for her in the canteen the next few days, but I didn't spot her.

One day I was near Oxford Street again and went out for a trawl round the boutiques, although the really trendy ones are in Kensington. At least they used to be. I saw a girl doing the usual picking up items from the floor where customers had flung them and putting them back on hangers. I was leafing through some peasant blouses and she put one back on the rack and I saw it was Artemis, my old colleague from the shop.

"Hi, Artemis!" I said. "How are things?"

"Oh, just bombing along," she said sulkily and pushing out her bottom lip. She always looked a bit like that.

"Good that you got another job, though?"

"Yeah." She looked a bit shifty. "If you don't mind, I've dropped the 'Artemis' and gone back to Sandra. Artemis was just a name they gave me. And Nomi was really Naomi – I don't know why they changed it, something to do with numerology. It was a freaky scene altogether. You'd better pretend to be buying something."

I picked up a pale blue peasant blouse and asked her if they'd got a size 6 and she pretended to look for one.

"I like these," I said. "They look better without embroidery." She found my size and handed it to me and I felt I ought to buy it.

"I went to see Lawrence," I said.

"Did you? That was brave."

"It must have been horrible, the trial and that. Poor you."

"Oh, I got let off with a caution."

"Thank goodness, anyway."

"What are you up to?"

"Temping as usual – and working as a child model."

"That sounds pervy!"

"I mean modelling kids' gear."

"Yes – I can see you might. Well, hope it goes well. I'd better look busy."

She didn't seem to want to chat any more, and I went off to pay for the blouse. It was funny, we used to be so-called friends and go to the cinema. But I suppose they had been told to be friendly to me because they planned to pass me on to the coven at Harpsden Manor all the time.

I bought some cigarettes and chocolate and some fashion magazines and took them to the prison. They brought Lawrence out and he still looked pale and thin, but smiling.

I pushed the stuff and the magazines across the table.

"Thanks, darling! I need to keep up with the scene if I want to go on working in the schmutter trade. We don't see many girls in here – only in girly mags. And they don't wear many clothes."

He flicked through them a bit.

"All a bit straight, aren't they? Kind of 30s revival. Bonnie and Clyde."

"Yes," I said, "Nobody wants to go off and live in a forest any more, do they? Or the distant past."

"Cold and damp."

"So I hear. I hope you'll be able to get a job when you – leave."

"Just like school! Well, I can't wait to see the back of this particular Borstal."

"I bumped into Artemis – she was working in a boutique near Oxford Street."

"Oh, good for her!"

"She wasn't terribly friendly, but after all, I did shop you to the police."

"You've got all the parlare, haven't you?"

"It's the company I keep."

"Could have been worse, darling! Anyway, I'm working on my good behaviour and spending a lot of time in the library."

"Good, I wondered if you needed something to read."

"You're never without a book, are you? I've been catching up on Dickens. Why not give him a whirl?"

"OK – where should I start?"

"Bleakers is good – Bleak House, you know. Or Our Mewch. Have you seen any more of our mutual friends lately?"

"No, only Artemis, and Naheed. She was lecturing about astrology."

"She was OK. Perhaps the rest have all gone abroad. And good riddance."

"The rest?"

"Yes, Dorinda is out. Naheed told me. Dorinda wasn't really involved. They probably parked the stuff in her flat in a Ming vase. She just provided a front with those séances of hers. Or perhaps she hypnotised the screws. Wish I knew the secret."

"I'll keep an eye."

"You do. Let's hope they've gone beyond our ken."

"I hope you do get a job in the schmutter trade – does it mean clothes? What language is that?"

"Yiddish. Like keeping shtumm. It means the rag trade. Several of the boys have done a stretch or two. Probably for smuggling snap fasteners or something."

The guard came to take him away, and insisted on flicking through the magazines in case I'd hidden anything in them. So we said goodbye.

****

Then it was my birthday and Mike was taking me out to a posh restaurant – we've been there before. It's called Chez Philippe in Fitzrovia and the menu is in French and everything. I wasn't sure what to wear. Lawrence was right, there is a 30s, 40s revival still going on, but the dresses look like child's party frocks on me. In the end I wore the dress I'd bought in Oxfam with no jersey underneath, and a long cream scarf. The dress is almost knee-length and ought to do for Chez Philippe.

We tried to choose different food from last year and had paté and toast to start, followed by sole with mashed potato balls and French beans. There was still a little dance floor so we got up and fooled about a bit then danced closely. Then we went and sat down again and had pudding – torta della casa, i.e. posh apricot flan with whipped cream.

There was a man walking around with some long-stemmed scarlet roses in a bucket and Mike bought me one. Then he took a little box out of his pocket and said "I never got you an engagement ring but I hope you don't mind doing everything backwards." And he handed it to me and inside was a diamond ring.

"I couldn't be more happy!" I said and put it on next to my wedding ring. It had one tiny diamond.

"Because it's almost our wedding anniversary as well, you know," he said.

"Happy anniversary!" We held hands across the table.

57

I went home carrying my rose and hoping everybody on the bus would notice the sparkly diamond. And for the moment I forgot about malevolent beings or wicked people who might be out to get me. I looked up diamonds later and "diamond" means "indestructible", and is under the Sun and Venus.

***

I rang the Stella Orrin agency as usual and they've got another job for me! Hurrah. I rang the secretarial bureau and they sighed but they said they'd probably find me a few days for the rest of the week. Then the girl (the "temp controller") cheered up a bit and asked me what it was like modelling. "More fun than typing letters about insurance. We had to blow bubbles and clown around. You do know I'm trained in audio now?" She said she'd put it on my card.

I turned up at Stella Orrin on the day and the kids were the same mixture of dark and blonde and red-haired. Christine and Paula were there – the little blonde girl and her sister. Christine came and sat next to me while we were waiting. She was reading Honey magazine and we flipped through it together.

"Who wears these things?" she asked, looking at a picture of a girl with clown's makeup wearing long stripy socks in chrome, cobalt and scarlet. It wasn't a "Honey" type of day as it turned out. Instead we were all togged up in floaty, feminine, flowery dresses, with platform shoes that were hard to walk in, and there was a backdrop of a meadow full of daises. The little girls even had white frilly aprons.

"Of course my hair used to be that colour," said Christine, looking at Paula in her getup. "I suppose I could dye it but it always looks wrong."

"It's a nice colour now," I said. "Dark blonde."

Her hair is pale brown, what people charmingly call "mouse". But it went with her round face and wide mouth. They were still adjusting the backdrop and putting a green cloth on the floor, and setting out some olde-worlde chairs and tables.

"How's your acting job going?" I asked.

"Well, it wasn't exactly acting, more kind of modelling again. It comes and goes."

She sounded a bit embarrassed and I wondered if she'd made it up in the first place. Or perhaps she thought demonstrating ironing board covers wasn't cool.

"I'm at college, really. Term will be starting again soon."

"Oh, which one? What are you studying?"

"Regent Street Polytechnic."

"I've got a friend there, she's doing history, and I know another girl doing sociology."

"I'm doing history too: 15th century Florence, the Medicis and Machiavelli and that whole bit."

"And I've signed up to do an evening course there. Course – it sounds better than 'class', doesn't it?"

Then I remembered where I'd seen her face before – when I was looking at Rowena's horoscope and I saw the foyer of the College with people milling about.

"There's a good social life," said Christine. "Have you been to the canteen? And there are discos at the weekend."

"Are they OK? I've been to a couple in the Kings Road but they were very loud and dark."

That was in my boutique days. I wanted to ask her if she lived at home or a hostel or shared a flat but then I was called, and we posed around in the floaty dresses and pretended to have a picnic at the tables with hunks of wholemeal bread and cheese and apples. The little boys were wearing cord knee-breeches and waistcoats.

The stylist said the clumpy shoes looked wrong, so we swapped them for flat ones, and they took more pictures. Then they cleared away the furniture and got out a skipping rope. I'd forgotten what fun it was. Then we did some clapping rhymes but I couldn't remember the ones the Scottish girls had taught me, and we fell back on "I went to the Chinese restaurant, to get a loaf of bread bread bread". That made us all laugh and the photographers were pleased.

The boys couldn't wait to get out of their costumes, but Paula said she wished she could keep her dress.

"I don't think it's really my style," I said, hanging mine up tidily. It had a flounce, and small green flowers, and a lace-trimmed yoke. Yuk!

"What is your style?" asked Paula seriously.

"Oooh – these days I try to look sophisticated and grown-up! Like a personal secretary!"

"What's that?"

"You work for one person and have to answer the phone and take messages, I think," I said.

Christine came up to help Paula do up her dungarees.

"Is that your job?" she asked me.

"No – I like temping and I don't think I'd be any good at being a proper secretary."

"You probably have to keep secrets as well."

"I hadn't thought of that! What secrets would they have?"

As we were going out through reception, one of the stylists stopped me and said: "I hope you'll be free in the next few weeks – we've got an assignment I think you'll be suitable for." I said fine and please to remember me. Christine and Paula went off to catch a bus south.

"Look out for me at college!" said Christine, and I said I would. I wondered if she knew Ginevra and Rowena. It would be nice to have some girls to go to the Wimpy with again, or a movie sometimes. And wasn't there an ice-rink somewhere?

Mike was working that evening which was annoying because I was dying to tell him about the lacy dresses and the fake picnic. I had some Heinz ravioli that tasted a bit like convent cocoa, and a cup of Nescafe and a banana for pudding.

Then I got out my crystal ball from its black velvet wrapping and set it up in the window with two candles beside it, and turned out the lights. (Sometimes we have candlelit dinners.) What I see can be quite haphazard, but sometimes it's stuff people don't want anyone to know. I wondered where Gilles and Dorinda were, and what college would be like, while I watched fog swirl around inside the crystal. The mists parted, and I saw the Polytechnic foyer again, and the kind of students I'd seen before. A mixed bunch, like at the modelling shoot, with an Indian girl in a pink trouser suit and a long scarf, and Japanese girls in kilts like my fellow students at secretarial school. And some English girls and boys, and tweedy men.

I saw Rowena in a baggy denim dress, and Christine walking quickly carrying a briefcase and looking rather serious. I seemed to be hovering over the foyer and she walked towards me and vanished out of the picture – in real life she'd have been going out through the front door. Then the mists came down again and parted to show the grey, metal-framed window of an office. It was raining and the rain made the window blurred and I could just see lights beyond, and office chairs, and big indoor plants, and a couple of people moving about. They were just dark shapes. The window vanished behind the rain, and then the mist, and then I saw a hilltop, and a tree, and a single star, and then nothing.

I thought I'd better put the crystal away again, which I did, by candlelight. It seemed mean to spy on them all, and anyway, if I wanted to do that I could just turn up at the college. I'd be meeting the students soon, I hoped. At the convent you were somebody if you had visions, like St Bernadette, and people tried to have them, but they wanted to see the Virgin Mary, or just darkness and brightness like St Julian. I think that would frighten me more than anything.

CHAPTER SEVEN

For the rest of the week, it was back to Magister Enterprises. I asked the woman in charge of the typing pool if I could give the modelling agency the number in case they wanted to ring me and she said OK. It wasn't Olive today, but a pale woman in brown.

There are always security guards in the foyer, which has a beige marble floor and a girl or man behind a desk. On the second day I noticed one of guards had a long ponytail, and when he turned round I saw it was Alan, one of the hippies from Harpsden Manor. He looked different in a uniform navy bomber jacket and polyester trousers. He was about the only person I talked to at Harpsden apart from Gilles and Ursula – the others were stoned all the time. He caught my eye and I went up to him.

"Hi!" I said.

"It's Anna, isn't it?"

"That's me. Alan? You were always reading."

"Did you ever embark upon Tolkine?"

"I'm afraid I didn't – I've taken to Margaret Drabble."

We were talking in undertones, but the other guard was looking out through the big plate-glass windows onto the carpark.

"Welcome to the straight world, eh?"

"It's OK. I think I prefer it. What happened to you, did you -?"

"I didn't go away on a long holiday, like some of the others. Or I wouldn't have got this job, I expect! Despite the Old Pal's Act."

"How did you manage it?"

"I wasn't there when the fuzz arrived. I moved flats a few times. And all I did was deal a bit to friends. And only weed. How about you?"

"I didn't even know all the drug-dealing was going on. Not really."

"It all got a bit heavy. And I was never involved in the more freaky end of the spectrum."

"The black magic and stuff?"

"Right. Not my bag. Been here long?"

"I'm just temping – I come and go."

The other guard turned round ponderously and looked over at us, and I bade Alan goodbye and made for the lifts.

"See you in the canteen some time!" he called after me.

I took my seat in the typing pool and a girl with a black bob and big glasses came in and handed the new supervisor a load of tapes. After a morning spent typing about more projects with weird names (Elegos and Malphas today, with people wittering on about resorts and golf courses), I went to the canteen at lunchtime and got my usual rolls, and looked round for a space. I didn't see Alan, though there were some other security men. Then I saw some of the Scottish girls from the pool and there was a space at their table and boldly asked if I could join them. They said yes and moved some glasses and cutlery so I could put my tray down.

"What happened to Olive," I asked. "Is she on holiday?"

"No," said one of them. She's called Clemency and has brown hair tied with a bow at the back of her neck. "We turned up one day and she was gone. She never said anything."

"She was an old trout, but a bit young to retire," said Kirstin – she's the one with the bubble cut who knows a lot of clapping rhymes.

"What about Marian, I met her in here one day?"

"I haven't seen her around for a while either. And Alison and Davina went back to Lossiemouth. They took the payout and left the scheme early."

"We've had quite a few farewell dos."

""Farewell, farewell, my own true love"
"Farewell, farewell," cried she," sang Kirstin.

Clemency chipped in with:

"As they were walking up the street
Most beautiful for to behold
He cast a glamour o'er her face
And it shone like the brightest gold."

"That's lovely," I said. "Where's that from?"

"Oh, I can't remember just now! It's from the same song. We learned them all at school."

"It's the one about the girl who leaves her husband for the devil!" said Kirstin.

"It's all in a book called the Child Ballads," said Clemency.

"Not suitable for children at all!" said Kirstin.

"Anyway, it's time to go back to the grindstone," said Clemency, so we went and crowded into the lift.

"I'll miss Olive's jumpers," I said.

"She got them all at jumble sales – or a trunk in her granny's attic!" said Kirstin.

They were really friendly. I must find out what the rest of them are called.

***

Now all my old enemies are on the loose again, I wondered what more I could do to protect myself. I'd spotted a spiritualist church near the bottom of the Heath and the mixed bathing pool, and I checked when it met, so one evening when I was on my own I went along. It might be worth trying. I was curious as much as anything – I didn't know Spiritualists actually had churches. But people always say that, don't they? "I was just curious, I just dabbled in the occult, and then..."

The spiritualist church was small and modern-looking, in dark red brick with white edges. There was a little railed-off garden in front with rose bushes. I went through the gate in the railings, past two black Labradors who were tied up to the railings, one on either side. They looked at me with yellow eyes.

Lots of people were going in – mainly women, so I followed them and took a seat near the front but not too near. I'd come from work, so I was wearing a dress and my hair up, and my fake glasses. Well, they make things look a bit sharper and they're useful in the cinema. I had a long pale pink scarf too. There was a girl in front of me in a suede two-piece outfit with fringes, and a large smiling woman in trousers on my left, and a very pale woman on my right with black hair in a rigid style. Instead of an altar, there was a stage which we were all facing, with some chairs at the side and one in the middle, with arms. It was fancier than the others and looked a bit like a throne.

To my surprise, they called out the number of a hymn and everybody opened hymn books and sang:

Gracious Spirit may thy presence
Shed a healing ray
Turning all their nights of darkness
Into glorious day.

I sang along as best I could – the tune wandered about like most hymns. Then a woman came out from the wings and said: "We are very lucky to have with us this evening the very gifted medium Potnia Theron." At least it sounded like that. Another woman walked out onto the middle of the stage. She was a bit stocky and had short, untidy iron-grey hair and was wearing an emerald green blouse and a charcoal trouser suit with a sleeveless top. The harsh overhead light cast dark shadows over her cheeks and under her chin.

The first woman sat down on a chair at the side of the stage, and the medium began throwing out names and saying: "Can anybody take a Charlie?"

Some people responded, and she would give them some soothing platitudes about how happy George or Charlie was in Summerland. And then she'd say something like "Did he pass with his heart?" or "Think carefully before moving house", or "Have you looked behind the clock?"

If the person looked blank, she'd say: "I'll leave that with you. It may not make sense now, but you'll find out what it means later." She picked out the girl in the fringed suede and told her not to let her head be turned by flattery. Then she pointed at the woman on my left and said "Now this lady – or gentleman?" The woman smiled back at her and said "I'm female!"

The medium said "I beg your pardon", and said she was getting a feeling of oriental influence, and did the lady have any relatives from India? That fell a bit flat. But then the medium shut her eyes and put her hands to her head, and the chairwoman or whoever she was said "Quiet, everybody, Potnia is going into a trance. We're very lucky."

Potnia swayed slightly and began to speak in a different voice: "And these are the bodies belonging with the names: the first is Athoth, he has a sheep's face... The second is Harmas, called the eye of flame...

When the Light mingled into the darkness
the darkness shone.
When darkness mixed with the Light,
the Light diminished,
No longer Light nor darkness but dim.

This dim ruler has three names:
Yaldabaoth is the first.
Saklas is the second.
Samael is the third."

She staggered slightly and sat down in the chair behind her. She rested her head on the back of the chair and her arms on the arms and seemed to sleep for a few seconds. I glanced at my neighbours – they were both looking earnestly at the stage. I looked back at the medium. Her head was tilted back now, facing the light, and I realised she was Dorinda, who I'd last seen with dark hair and makeup, and wearing a succession of kaftans. I supposed she had to make a living somehow. Lawrence had said she faked her trances, but I wasn't at all sure. I huddled down in my seat and held my scarf over my mouth in case she saw me.

She opened her eyes and looked into the dimness of the hall and seemed to pull herself together.

"I'm getting Francis – can anyone take a Francis?"

I didn't move.

"He has a message – he's saying, 'Keep it up, you're on the right lines.' Does that make sense? Can you take that? He says 'Look behind you'."

She smiled – this was more like her normal act, I guessed. Then she handed out a few more messages, but I noticed her hands were trembling. Then the chairwoman got up again and thanked her, and we all sang another hymn:

Grant us thy peace, O God of peace and love
Who dwelleth in the shining realms above
Grant us with thee forever to abide
Where is no night or falling eventide

Till that day breaks
And earth's dark shadows cease
O God of peace and love grant us thy peace.

The shining realms above – was that Summerland? I didn't like the idea of daytime all the time. Isn't that how they torture people? Peace is OK, though the hippies used to hand out too much peace and love. The lady with black hair on my right was crying quietly into a hanky. We got up to leave and she rushed on ahead of me. I turned to the large lady on my left and asked "What is Summerland?"

She smiled and said: "It's the highest sphere, according to Swedenborg!"

"Oh, so there are lower spheres? In the afterlife?"

"That's right. There are many planes apart from the earth plane. I'm sure there are books you can read – there's a good library at the College of Psychic Studies. It's nice to see a young person with an enquiring mind."

The College of what? First I'd ever heard of it. I remembered I'd be at a proper college soon and they'd have a library. We all moved quite swiftly out. The dogs were still there. I patted one of them on the head to see if he was real — he rolled his eyes at me. I walked on towards Highgate Road. I back over my shoulder, and saw "Potnia" in the distance, leading the two Labradors and chatting to the chairwoman. I speeded up and almost ran to the junction, nipped over the road when there was a gap and walked south so they wouldn't see me at the bus stop. Then I side-stepped into College Lane, the little alley that runs behind the houses down to Kentish Town.

Mike was at home watching telly. I told him where I'd been.

"Yes, I've noticed that place," he said. "What was it like?"

"Mainly some woman telling people their loved ones were happy and sent their love, and not to move house without thinking about it carefully."

"Are you hungry? I'm starving. We keep an eye on people like that – some of them get a lot of money out of the gullible. You know they even go through their bins so they can find some detail they 'couldn't possibly have known'?"

"It was mainly just guff that could have applied to anybody. And hymns! And no, I won't go back, once was enough. I was just curious. I'm starving too, and I don't think there's much in the fridge."

So we went and got fish and chips. For some reason I didn't like to tell Mike the medium had been Dorinda. I wished Frank would meet me in Lyons and not be so cryptic if he wanted to tell me something. And what was all that Dorinda was waffling about in her trance? And how long will I be stuck on the earth plane, and do I really want to move on?

CHAPTER EIGHT

I'd got in the habit of ringing the Stella Orrin agency and leaving the phone number of where I was working, and they rang me again and said there were a couple of out of town things they needed me for next week and they hoped I was free. I said yes to both – the money's better than temping and once I've done the shoot I get time to muck about.

For the first one I turned up at the Soho office and the same kids from the floaty dresses shoot were there, and their chaperones. Once we'd all gathered, they ushered us into a mini-bus that was parked in the alley and off we went out of London. We stopped a couple of times at service stations, and fortunately nobody was sick. The sun came out, and I sat behind Christine and Paula and they talked to me over the back of the seat. It was like going on a day trip from the convent – we went to exciting places like shrines where we bought luminous plastic crucifixes. This time we sang songs for the kids like Row, Row Your Boat and One Man Went to Mow.

After about an hour we arrived in a hayfield. There were lots of other vans and lights and equipment, and picnic tables and chairs. We got dressed in the same old lacy get-ups and big straw hats with streamers and they took pictures of us sitting at the tables with the boys handing us plates of cake, and then they got us to run about in the long grass, and skip and blow bubbles again, and blow dandelion clocks and play ring-a-roses. We got the giggles which was just what they wanted.

Then we put on our own clothes again and had some real sandwiches and the sun sank a bit. We got into the minibus to go home, and Christine and Paula and I sat at the back, and Paula went to sleep with her head on Christine's knee, and we talked quietly and looked out at the scenery.

"I miss the country sometimes," I said.

"Did you live there?"

"Yes, near Haslemere, and then we lived in the town for about a year, but there were woods behind our house."

"How romantic!"

"Are you doing the shoot tomorrow?"

"No, we're not called for tomorrow."

We said we'd see each other at Regent Street Polytechnic, if not before.

I turned up at the agency next day and found I was the only person in reception. Fortunately I'd brought a paperback of One Pair of Feet, which is about being a nurse during the war.

Soon Janice appeared and said: "Hi, Anna! Are you ready? I'm going to drive you to the shoot."

"Just me?"

"Yes, just you today, the others have got their own transport. You've got a book – good, there might be some waiting around. I've got a thermos and biscuits!" She showed me in her shopping bag. She was wearing a cotton check shirt and jeans. We went downstairs and found her car and drove out of London again, east this time.

"I suppose the client wasn't really convinced we were having a picnic in the studio."

"That's right – yes, the shots in the field were a lot better. They liked them, thank the Lord. You know I tend to forget you're not really 12!"

"Well, keep it in mind!"

We got to a small town which was rather pretty, with antique shops, and she said we were nearly there, but we drove through it and out the other side and through fields again, into a wood and then came to a gate across the road. The minibus driver got out and opened it and we went through and he shut it behind us again. After some more woods the road came out onto a small green with villagey houses on the edges. There was a tree in the middle, with a bench round it, and scattered about were the usual cars and vans.

The photographers greeted us. I went to the chemical loo in a trailer and when I came out a woman with a clipboard took me and another lady towards a mobile dressing room in a camper van. Janice was sitting on the bench smoking a fag and having a cup of tea.

"I'm Sandra," said the one with the clipboard, "And I'm running the show here today!"

We smiled and nodded as if to say we wouldn't be any trouble. She was wearing jeans too, and a sleeveless top with a cardigan slung round her shoulders.

"And I'm Linda," said the other woman.

"I'm Anna."

"OK, I'm your mum for today!"

"I should explain I'm really grown up. I'd better take my wedding and engagement rings off."

"Wow, I wasn't expecting that!" she said and laughed. She was pretty and had shoulder length dark-brown hair in old-fashioned flick-ups, like mums tend to in adverts.

"Here are your clothes," said Sandra. "I'll leave you to it and see how the fellas are getting on."

"It's very quiet here, isn't it?" I said, looking out of the slit-like window. "Nobody about."

"Perhaps they asked them all to stay indoors – or go out for the afternoon. You can make a mint hiring out your house and garden for location shoots. And it's quite a quaint place."

She took off her own shirt and skirt and put on the ones on her rail, which were almost identical but pale blue.

I almost fainted when I saw what was on my rail – beige knee-socks, black strap shoes, a white blouse, a green gymslip like something out of an old-fashioned school story, and a straw hat with a green band. I put them on and tied the gym slip with the scarf-belt. There was even a stripy tie and I remembered how to do it up. We did a twirl for each other.

"I'm so glad I made the sacrifice and sent you to private school!" said Linda.

"Yes, the education is far superior!" I said.

Sandra popped her head back in, shouting "Hope you're decent!" and ushered in another girl who brushed our hair. She put mine into two bunches coming forward over my ears. The less we see of my pointy ears the better.

Then she back-combed Linda's hair a bit and brushed the flick-ups into place and sprayed lots of hairspray around. She made up Linda's face with blue eyeshadow and pale pink lipstick.

"We'd better go and meet my 'husband'," said Linda. "He seems nice. And I've got a son as well! I had him very young, you know."

We went down the steps of the van and joined a man and a boy who were standing about looking a bit sheepish.

"How nice to meet you!" said Linda to the man, shaking his hand. "How long have we been married?"

The man had black hair and a tanned face and was wearing slacks, a shirt and a blue jersey. His 'son' had black hair too and was quite tall and dressed in school uniform too with a blazer. He smiled at me.

"Simply ages – unless we had these two out of wedlock!" said the man, who said he was Derek and the boy was Gary. We introduced ourselves.

"Shall we get on with it, people?" said Sandra. She got us to stand in front of various houses and cottages, and made me put my hat on the back of my head. The gardens were a bit bare and dry, with mainly grass down to the road and a few beds with bedding plants. They kept us busy standing in groups looking relaxed and grinning broadly. While our "parents" were being snapped opening garden gates and walking up paths smiling broadly, we lurked in the road.

"They usually want more Nordic people for shoots like this," said Gary. "But we could really be brother and sister. Perhaps they want to appeal to a wider audience."

"Yes, perhaps."

"English people don't usually have black hair."

"No, I don't know where I get it from."

"My gran is from the Philippines," he said. "That's my mum over there."

He waved at her and she waved back.

"Is that your mum with you? She doesn't look old enough."

"No, it's just someone from the agency. I'm actually 20."

"Go on! You're having me on! They must have fed you on gin and cigarettes."

"No, I'm just naturally short."

"I'm 15, that's why I still need to bring my Mum. She doesn't mind being my chauffeur, it's quite fun usually. Have you passed your test?"

"Driving test? No – I've never learned to drive. In London you don't need to. We don't have a car."

"We?"

"Me and my husband. I've taken my rings off."

"You're winding me up! So why are you modelling? I want to be an actor, or a pop star. How about you?"

"I'm happy just working and doing interesting stuff like this."

Then it was our turn to stand by a front door and smile at each other, and then at the camera. Then they moved a car into shot and Linda and Derek pretended to be getting out of it. They'd given her a beige handbag like the Queen's.

While they were getting the pose right, Gary ran up the path of the house we were standing in front of, and tried the door-handle, but nothing happened. He called through the letterbox "Anybody at hooooooome?"

"Sh, there might be. They've been told to stay out of the way."

He peeked in through the front window.

"Don't!" I said. "If I lived here I'd find that really annoying."

"Oh, don't be so – grownup! Come and look – there's nobody at home."

I quickly peeked in as well. The room was empty. It didn't even have a fireplace, and there wasn't a door in the doorway. The walls were plastered grey, but not painted. There were flowery curtains in the window – where it showed.

"It's just a set!" said Gary.

"Come back down here, kids! That's enough larking around!" called Sandra. "Sorry Anna, you're not a kid, I know."

We joined Linda and Derek by the car and we all got into and out of it a lot. "They must use this place for lots of things," said Gary. "Perhaps they've hired it from a film company."

Then we had sandwiches and cups of tea, sitting under the tree and it was all very jolly. Gary disappeared off somewhere. When he came back, Sandra said: "Please try and stay put, Gary."

"I just went for a wander," he said.

"Oh, OK," said Sandra, and went on talking to his mum about knitting patterns.

Gary took my hand and pulled me aside behind our changing caravan and whispered: "I nipped round into the back garden and there's a whole different village on the other side."

"Perhaps it's a new development. Council houses," I said.

"The gardens are different. There are palm trees, and purple creepers – but they're fake. And all the houses are empty, too. No wallpaper, no furniture. This place is weird."

Then they called us together and said it was a wrap and they didn't need us any more, and we went into the caravans and peeled off our uniforms. I said goodbye to Gary and he said:

"See you again some time!", and everybody drove away. Janice and I drove back to London, stopping off at a pub on the way. She had a half of lager and I had a Coke and she smoked a cigarette and told me gossip about the people who worked at the agency. There was somebody who could "bring the conversation back round to herself in three easy moves".

"And just make sure you're never alone with Helmut!"

I said I would.

"I'm sure you can look after yourself."

"I've been OK so far! And my husband's a policeman."

"No, really? Does he wear a uniform?"

"No, just a suit. He's a detective sergeant."

I got home and told Mike I'd been out in the country in a village like the one in the Prisoner.

"I think it was a film set," I said. "The houses were empty and the plants were fake."

"Or one of those villages where they do army exercises," said Mike. "The police have got some."

"Can we go out into the real country again soon? Or to a beach?"

So we got out some maps and tried to decide on places to go. "I'm due some holiday some time," said Mike. "Shall we hire a caravan for a week, somewhere like Camber Sands?"

"That sounds like bliss. Have we still got that brochure I stole from work?"

"No, I think I chucked it away. Do they want it back?"

"They'll just be one short. It looked a bit like the pictures in the brochure – the village did, I mean."

"I'll ring this Camber Sands holiday village and see if they've got space."

***

I went to the library one evening and got out some records: the Irish Country Four, and one with African men in lurid kaftans on the cover. The music was nice, though, despite the kaftans. They had a copy of the Child Ballads – they're not children's songs, he was a bloke called Francis Child. There was some music printed with the words, so I got a penny whistle from an Irish shop in Camden Town to work out the tunes.

I found the songs about glamour, and glamourye, which seems to be a kind of magic that hypnotises people into seeing things that aren't there. I love that it's always "the wan water", and the girl who cut her skirts to the knee and her hair "a little abune the bree". Was glamourye how Gilles hid the exit from Harpsden Manor, and how he escaped from prison? He just hypnotised everybody and persuaded them he was a psychiatrist, or something? Perhaps I'd have found the exit if I'd searched for long enough, but I was looking for somewhere to climb over the wall via a handy tree. Because the real exit would have been locked, wouldn't it, like the front gates? I never saw anyone come in or out, but the cleaning ladies went home at night and the hippies appeared and disappeared. It was a good thing I found the stream before too long.

Mike told me we'd been invited to a social with his colleagues. He said they were all quite conservative, but I've been trying to be more conservative for years. Months, anyway. I'd got my modelling cheques, and the allowance from my parents, so I went and bought a mauve sleeveless dress with a slightly flared skirt, and fake pockets with gilt buttons. I thought they might not go for the 30s-peasant-Edwardian look, and I was right.

When we got to the place, with was some kind of club or institute that probably belonged to the police, all the other girls and ladies were wearing shift dresses and two-pieces, some in lurex or brocade, some with frills round the neck and hem. Their hair was all a bit "done" even if long, and set on rollers which I can't do. Some of them had elaborate updos – I wondered if they were just pinned on. They wore rather thick orange makeup, too. I hadn't done anything to my hair. Mike held my hand, and introduced me to people, and said did I remember Fred and Stan. Fred's the older one, and Stan's a thin, ratty bloke with slicked-back hair. The men (and Mike) were wearing suits.

"What can I get the little lady to drink?" asked Stan. I said I'd have a bitter lemon and Mike had a half of something. There wasn't a band, but there was a DJ playing rather corny old records. The place had a bar, and tables and chairs, and wood-effect panelling, and pink curtains.

The men started talking about work, and football, and I found myself with the girls.

"What's that you're drinking?" I asked one for something to say.

"A snowball!" It was in a triangular glass – perhaps conical is the word, and had a cherry on a stick in it.

"I don't really drink, just the occasional glass of wine."

"I bet they don't serve you in pubs!"

"I don't go to them all that often."

"It's advocaat, cognac and lime juice, with lemonade."

"What's advocaat?"

"Egg yolks and... what is in advocaat, Shirley?"

"Brandy, isn't it?"

"Anyway, that's why it's orange."

"And I'm Shirley, and this is Elaine and this is Fern."

We carried on chatting. They were nice, and explained this was the policemen's club, a bit like Rotary. I didn't dare ask them what Rotary was as I didn't want them to think I was completely dim.

"You know it's a funny thing about gangsters' wives," said one.

"What?"

"They look just like us!"

They all roared with laughter at that.

"So when did you get married?" asked Fern. "You must have eloped!"

"We just went to a register office. A couple of years ago."

"So you did elope! What about your parents and family?"

"We haven't got any."

"Oh, that's sad! We had all my aunts and cousins, and a marquee and sausage rolls and eclairs."

"I suppose we could have invited friends," I said. "But there wouldn't have been enough to fill a marquee."

"They get terribly hot," said Shirley.

Mike came over again, with Fred and Stan.

"Hello, young lady!" said Fred. "Haven't seen you for a while. Not since you helped us out over that drugs case. First time I met you, you looked a bit like a drowned rat!"

"How flattering!" said one of the girls.

"And now you're married and all! Have you seen any of our old friends lately?"

"You mean – from then?"

"Yes, our old chums, yours and mine."

"Well, I did see Artemis – she's working in a boutique again."

"One of the young girls? Most of them got off with fines. But the new Act – the new law - will tighten things up drugswise and we'll be able to put our acquaintances away for longer."

"And I visited Lawrence, my old boss, in prison."

"How was he?"

"Not very happy, but he was talking about getting a similar kind of job when he gets out."

"In fashion, not drugs, I hope!" And he roared with laughter.

"He said quite a lot of people in the – schmutter trade had criminal records."

"Probably for dodgy dealing, cabbage, all that kind of thing."

"Cabbage?"

"Making extra garments from designer fabric and selling them down the market with phoney labels."

I couldn't quite see how that worked. Again, I didn't feel like mentioning that I'd seen Dorinda, for some reason. How would I explain why I'd gone to a spiritualist church?

"Oh, I did see Naheed, she was giving a lecture on astrology."

"The Indian lady? They seem to have had her fooled, along with a lot of other people, with all that occult nonsense. It was just a front, like the clothes shop. But it's the big kahuna we're after – you know, the one that got away, Lemaitre."

"How did he get out? Lawrence made it sound quite mysterious."

"We had a lot of people on the carpet over that. Just rubbed their eyes and he was gone? Thought he was a visiting psychiatrist? I don't think. No, I don't know how the trick was worked. If you see him, don't ask."

"Don't speak to him – tell us," said Mike.

"And we'll talk to him all right," said Fred.

"Yes, of course I will. I mean, I won't." I said. Fred and Stan went to talk to some other people, and the ladies asked me if we had a holiday booked.

"We were thinking of Camber Sands," said Mike. "I must see if we can book something."

"You'll be lucky – you've left it a bit late," said Shirley. "I always book ours in January."

I asked her where she was going and she said two weeks on a Greek island. "It's a package, they do everything and you don't have to speak Greek or Italian or anything! And it's got restaurants and a pool."

I said it sounded lovely. A waiter came round with canapés and vol au vents. I ate a lot of little biscuits with prawns and parsley on. I was glad Mike was hovering near me.

"So do you have a job?" asked Shirley. She was tall, and a bit older, with blond hair scraped back and then built up in a kind of structure on top of her head. She was wearing pale blue and silver brocade.

"I work as a secretary, and sometimes as a model."

"A model! Ooooh, how exciting! But aren't you a bit – "

"Small? I model children's clothes. Do you have children?" I got in quickly, as she looked a bit taken aback. So they started telling me about their children, and saying that I'd be having some soon.

"But not too soon," said Fern. She had long hair with a backcombed top and an olive dress with jewels round the neckline. "Have a bit of fun before you get tied down!"

"Oh, I don't know," said Shirley. "Why not have them young, then once they're at school you could do anything – run your own business."

I said I'd think about it.

"It would put paid to the modelling, though," said Fern.

"Your children could be models!" said Shirley. "I'm sure they'd be good-looking like their parents."

"This flattery will turn my head!" I said, and they laughed.

The DJ started playing more lively music and some of them dragged their husbands onto the floor to dance and we looked on.

"Come on, it's the chacha!" said Shirley.

"I did this one at the convent," I said to Mike. "Do you know how?"

We walked onto the dance floor, where someone had turned on a thing that sent rainbow-coloured lights moving over the ceiling.

"It's just like a disco!" said Fern.

"It's nicer than any disco I've ever been to," I said, and we launched into the chacha. We couldn't help sending it up a bit as usual, but nobody minded. I didn't know Mike was so good at proper dancing.

"I learned ballroom dancing when I lived in a suburb," he said while we were sitting at a little round table drinking Diet Coke with ice. "Let's not live in a suburb after all. There are nicer places. We'll find one. But let's go to the seaside anyway."

"Yes, do let's."

"But you know, if you see Lawrence again – look out for Stockholm Syndrome."

"What's that? I'm not as clever as I think, you know. I didn't know what advocaat was."

"Eugh, advocaat! Anyway, Stockholm Syndrome – there were these people held hostage in a bank robbery in Stockholm, and they ended up getting very matey with the people holding them hostage – they kind of went over to the robbers' side. That's why it's called that. Or else it comes in reverse – just when you're safe and the cavalry arrive, you attack the bank robber."

"Oh, I see. I'll watch out for it. Sometimes it's hard to tell who the good guys and who the bad guys are."

"Exactly."

I think it was the first party I'd ever been to that I actually enjoyed all through. And they kicked us out at 11pm.

Mike did some phoning round and we got a weekend in a B&B near Camber Sands and so we went and it was really sunny. We had fish and chips on the beach and sat in the dunes, and walked along the beach for miles, and swam in the sea, and said "This is the life!", and in the evening went to a bar at the campsite. When we got home I said it was the best holiday I'd ever been on. I used to go to the seaside with Mum and Dad, usually in England, once in France, but they didn't like mingling with other people so it was a bit lonely, though I did once play Grandmother's Footsteps with some French children who didn't speak any English at all. Anyway, soon it'll be term time and my course will start.

CHAPTER NINE

September 1970

One lunchtime I asked the Scottish girls at Magister's if they were going to the canteen and could I come with them. It would have been awful if they'd said "No" but they said "Yes, come along. It's Dead Man's Leg today!" and laughed. That's suet pudding and custard in case you didn't know.

The girl with the black bob came in with some more tapes and gave them to the new "Olive", who's called Joanna. They chatted for a bit in undertones, and I heard Joanna call her "Melusine". I remembered the name from a fairy story book we had at the convent: she married a count, but she turned into a snake every Saturday. She had 12 remarkable children (one had tusks, and one had a paw-print on his cheek), and she eventually flew out of the window and was never seen again.

Melusine was wearing a black pinafore dress over a grey poloneck, and black boots. I wonder why she wears old-fashioned bright red lipstick with such a smart outfit? It was put on rather clumsily, too, outside the "lipline", which fashion magazines tell you not to do. I hope she didn't notice me staring at her.

Joanna called up me and a couple of other girls, and handed out tapes to us in envelopes labelled things like Haborym and Picollus. She handed me a Haborym envelope and said "You can cope with this, I'm sure. Your spelling's very good, I've noticed."

"Oh, thanks! Why do they have such funny names?"

"Oh, they're just nonsense kind of code names," she explained, and we took them back to our desks. As before, I got part one of Haborym, and other people got part two and three: the usual people yakking about rate of return and somebody explaining, and throwing figures around. We work away all morning, apart from when a lady brings round a tea and coffee cart and you get a milky coffee in those pale green cups and saucers you find at village fetes.

At lunchtime me and the girls got the lift to the canteen. There seemed to be fewer of them than before. We queued up and I got rolls as usual, and a bowl of salad, and the others got plates of mince and potatoes, or pudding and custard. We found a table by the window with a few other people on it, security guards and men in brown coats.

We chatted for a bit and ate our lunch and eventually I said:

"Marian told me you all live in a hostel. I used to live in one near Hyde Park. What's yours like?"

"Hyde Park? Ours is further out in the sticks! It's OK."

"It's a bit like being at school."

"Ours had cubicles carved out of a big room."

"Ours is purpose-built – we get little cells of our own!"

"And do you have a commonroom and a telly?"

"All mod cons! All the luxuries! And where do you live?"

"In a flat in Kentish Town with my husband."

"Oooh, when did you get married?"

"About a year ago."

"Child bride!"

"That's me."

"Didn't your parents mind?"

"They're not around."

"Oh – I'm sorry to hear that." She put on a sympathetic expression.

I said: "There aren't so many of you as before, is somebody on holiday?"

"Donna went back to Kinlochbervie, and Fiona went home to Kincorth. We don't stay long. There are always more who want the McRobbie experience – as it used to be."

"It's thinning out at the hostel, though," said another girl. "I wonder if the scheme's being wound up for good?"

"Let me get your names straight before you all go north!"

Clemency and Kirstin I knew, and the others are Flora, Jean and Lorna.

"Trouble with being a temp – sometimes you don't get introduced to anybody, sometimes you get introduced to everybody but you can't remember anyone's name! I looked up those ballads you said you learned at school, Clemency."

"Oh, they're lovely aren't they, so poetic!"

"Load of old tripe!" said Kirstin.

"Did you find the one about the woman who marries a seal?"

Clemency began to sing and after a bit I joined in.

The earthly nourice sits and sings
And ay she sings, ba lily wean,
Little ken I my bairn's father
Nor yet the land he travels in.

"How does that bit go?" I asked. "I haven't quite got the tune..."

She sang another bit.

I am a man upon the land,
I am a silkie in the sea,
And when I'm far frae every strand,
My home it is in Sule Skerry."

"I get it now I think," I said "My home it is in Sule Skerry..."

"You've got a nice voice," she said. "Have you ever thought of going to a folk club?"

"I don't know anybody who goes," I said. "Aren't they mostly in pubs?"

"Yes, but upstairs in another room so it isn't too noisy and smoky."

"I think there are some in Camden Town. I'm sure I'd be too shy to get up and sing though."

"Oh no, you'd be fine!"

The security guards at the end of the table had gone rather quiet when we started singing and I hoped they wouldn't say something sarcastic as men tend to do. But they didn't. One of them even said: "That was very nice, girls! Come and sing to us again some time!"

They looked quite friendly, but there were some on another table who looked rather grim and gurly, as they say in Scottish ballads.

As we went back to the lift I asked: "Who's that woman with the black hair who delivers the tapes? I never see her in here."

"She's from the top floor," said Clemency. "They're very security-conscious up there, or something. It's all confidential. We're not supposed to gossip."

"Perhaps they have their own dining room," said Flora.

"They never used to bother," said Kirstin as we crammed into the lift. "About confidentiality, I mean. Then they gave us the chat. Perhaps you didn't get it as you're just a temp. I didn't mean that in a nasty way."

"What was that about going home early and getting a payout?"

"Oh, it's all part of the scheme," said Flora. "Why not take the money and give someone else a go?"

Clemency must have said something to Joanna, because she called me aside during the afternoon and said she needed to give me the regulation chat about confidentiality, and I promised not to gossip. She was perfectly nice about it and said she expected it was the same wherever I worked and I said, "Yes, of course."

***

The next morning I woke up burbling about some dream I'd had. Something is always something else in dreams, or somebody else.

"You're making no sense," said Mike. He went to put the kettle on and made some tea and we ate cornflakes sitting by the window.

"It was one of those anxiety dreams," I said. "I was supposed to be a medical student, but I only went to one lecture a week. And I was supposed to find out the timetable from the other students, but I was too shy."

"Sounds like you're worried about starting your course soon. Do you think you'll do more than one evening a week eventually?"

"I suppose I might. Some of the other courses sound fun. I'm not nervous at all, I'm looking forward to it, and I know people there. Not just Ginevra and Rowena, the girl I met at the modelling gig goes there too."

"The one with the sister?"

"Yes. But maybe I just want to play at being a student. I've been designing costumes."

"I thought they wore a uniform!"

"Really?"

"Dirty jeans, long hair, CND medallions?"

"None of the ones I've met look like that. Remember those friends of Ginevra's? And then somebody began singing in a high voice, and I joined in, and you should never tell people your dreams."

"Eyes I dare not meet in dreams. In death's other kingdom."

"What's that?"

"T.S. Eliot."

"I suppose you did him at school. I'm so uneducated. And anyway we were singing in the canteen at work. That must explain that bit. And they said my voice was good and why didn't I go to a folk club."

"There are lots in Camden Town. Shall we check them out one night?"

"Yeah, let's."

"There are blues and jazz bands too – let's go one night. You won't go on a student protest, will you?"

"What are they all protesting about anyway? What do those symbols mean?"

"Nuclear disarmament. Peace."

"Well, I'm all for peace."

I wondered if death's other kingdom was Summerland, where it's never dark. I hoped I'd never end up there, even if I do want to move on at some point. I must try reading Mum's book again. Perhaps if I wrote it all out and tried to read the ye olde handwriting and work through from the beginning I might find the spell I was looking for among the "leechdom" as it calls it – the one to counteract the longevetee potion.

***

I went to the canteen again with the Scottish girls and it was all a bit different. The servers had a different uniform, with brown and orange stripes and little trilby hats. Suet pudding was off, and the girls were furious. Instead there were bowls of pasta salad and green stuff sprinkled with cress. The girls crossly got lasagne, chips and peas. The friendly guards and postmen were nowhere to be seen, it was all other office workers. I wondered if they ever paired off with the Scottish girls.

While we were eating yoghourts and trifle in plastic dishes for pudding, the fire alarm went. We grabbed our bags and all filed down the stairs — you're not supposed to use the lifts when there's a fire. We were led through the forecourt and out onto the pavement and people counted us, and some of us lit cigarettes and leant against walls. Kirstin had brought her trifle and a spoon and carried on eating it. Eventually one of the security guards came out and said "You're OK to go back in! Somebody thought they saw black smoke, but there's nothing wrong."

"No smoke without fire!" said Kirstin, and we trooped back in again, and soon it was time to go home.

I wondered if I should do some more invocations, or if the ones I'd done were still working. Perhaps I'd better just remind my protectors that we were still in danger. When we'd had dinner – macaroni cheese - I found a poetry book we'd had at school and flipped through it while Mike watched telly. There was nothing much on, so Mike turned it off after a bit.

"Is that a school book?" he asked.

"Yes, it is."

"Any Eliot in it?"

"I don't think so."

He got down TS Eliot's poems and I said I'd read them next.

"I've finished Catch-22," he sighed.

"Would I like it?"

"It's all about the war. Quite gruesome."

"Girls read it at the convent because there was stuff in it about brothels. They wanted to know what 'whores' were."

"I'll have to move on to Alastair Maclean."

He put a stack of records on my old record-player.

"Let's go to a movie at the weekend. Or a pub with a blues band."

"Yes, let's."

"D'you fancy Love Story?"

"Sounds rather soppy."

I'd found a poem that might make a good incantation – or a good song. It starts:

"This is the key of the kingdom.
In that kingdom there is a city.
In that city there is a town.
In that town there is a street..."

And so on till you get to a basket of flowers, and then it runs backwards again. It's a string of beautiful sounds, anyway.

"Or Mash is on, but that's all about war too. The Korean war actually. There's a folk club on Thursday at the Auld Shillelagh – shall we go?"

"Might be a hoot. But I'm not singing, I warn you."

So we went out at the weekend and saw The Aristocats. I probably should be reading up more about Greek myths, but when I've got a spare moment I write out another bit of Mum's recipe book. I still had the Child Ballads (I keep extending it and nobody else seems to want it), and looked through it for a tune that would fit the Key of the Kingdom. I found one that would do with a bit of adjustment, so I bought some music paper (ruled with five lines) and wrote it out with the words underneath and put it into the exercise book where I was writing out the recipes. I leave mum's book at home in its hiding place, but I take the exercise book with me in my shopping bag.

We went to the folk club on the Thursday and it was rather smoky and full of men in very thick jerseys made of flecked wool with a lot of cable stitching. There were some women and girls as well, who tended to have long skirts and straggly hair. They seemed pleased to see us and we sat at a table with some of them and had drinks and sang along with the choruses of some sea shanties. I don't know why they sound so mournful when the tunes are stirring and the words are either funny or probably rude.

"I expect they do this in suburbs," muttered Mike to me.

"You should know."

"Not in mine."

"The hippy gear might not fit in."

"Perhaps the suburbs have moved with the times. How about Ongar?"

Men with beards got up one after another and sang songs about pit disasters and whaling tragedies.

"Do we have any other floor singers?" asked the bearded woolly man who was introducing everybody and doing the honours.

"Now's your chance." Said Mike. "I gave him your name."

"You didn't!"

"No, I didn't, would I?"

"Anybody?"

"Oh, go on," said one of the girls we were sitting next to. Somehow I found myself getting the song out of my bag and going to the stool where people had sung from. I looked into the crowd – they were hard to see, thank goodness, because there was a bright light on the "stage".

I said: "I haven't really practiced this, and I've only just put it together." So I sang the whole thing.

This is the key of the kingdom.
In that kingdom there is a city.
In that city there is a town.
In that town there is a street.
In that street there is a lane.
In that lane there is a yard.
In that yard there is a house.
In that house there is a room.
In that room there is a bed.
On that bed there is a basket.
A basket of flowers,

A basket of sweet flowers.

Flowers in a basket,
Basket on the bed,
Bed in the room,
Room in the house,
House in the yard,
Yard in the lane,
Lane in the street,
Street in the town,
Town in the city,
City in the kingdom.
Of that kingdom this is the key.

They clapped at the end and I said "Thank you". I walked back to my place and the women with straggly hair smiled, and the girls gave me another clap and said they liked it, which was kind.

"That was a nice song," said Mike.

"But you should have said where it was from," said the girl sitting next to us.

"I got the tune out of the Child Ballads and bent it around a bit," I said. "And the words are a clapping rhyme or something. Anyway, it's by Anon!"

"Those great poets, Anon and Trad! I thought the tune sounded familiar."

"Anon writes the words, Trad writes the tunes," said another lady.

The emcee wound up the evening, and everybody else shuffled out and the man on the door said he hoped we'd come again. We went home in the dark – the days are drawing in, with that back-to-school feeling.

CHAPTER TEN

I made a date with Ginevra to meet her and have tea/supper before my class and before she went home. Her mother looks after Richard when she is at college. I got there a bit early and looked at the timetable on a noticeboard. There were a lot of other evening classes which made Greek mythology look quite scientific: astrology, ley lines, dowsing, spiritual healing, aura reading and something called Earth Energies.

Then Ginevra turned up and took me to the canteen where we had cups of tea and dry fruit cake with cherries, and slabs of cheese which we ate in a sandwich with the cake. Rowena came and sat with us, dressed in rust as usual. I looked around for Christine but didn't see her – though I did spot Naheed from the back in her green sari, sitting next to a grey-haired woman. It was nice having girlfriends again.

"There's the lady who gave that astrology lecture," I said.

"Yes – isn't she a friend of yours?" asked Ginevra.

"I did know her before, yes. She was a friend of some friends of mine. Did I tell you I was a model now?"

She looked surprised like people usually do. "A child model – modelling children's clothes."

"That must be fun," she said, a bit doubtfully.

"It is so far."

"How did you get into it?" asked Rowena.

"I was approached by a lady in the street – yes, yes, I know, they usually lure you into cars and give you drugged sweets and you wake up in Buenos Aires, but honestly it's on the level."

We chatted some more and they gossiped about fellow-students, and writers I'd never heard of, and then Ginevra went home, and Rowena kindly showed me where my class was and then went to the library.

I sat and took notes on some shiny new file paper and we looked at slides of the gods, and a sacred spring, and the oracle's cave, and some digs where they'd found layers and layers of mounds, and a lot of dogs' skeletons. The teacher seemed to jump about a bit in time and place, but I didn't mind. Perhaps we could go on holiday to Greece next, people were always saying how cheap it was, but not to a resort where you never went anywhere but the beach.

At the end of the class I gathered up my notes and put them in my shopping bag – I must get a folder or something a bit more studenty. Perhaps I'll dig out my old satchel. Everybody seemed to be leaving and I could see Naheed and the grey-haired woman up ahead. I called out "Hello, Naheed!" as we all spilled out of the front entrance and down the steps.

They turned round.

"Hello, Anna!" said Naheed, and added in a lower tone, "You remember Dorinda, don't you?"

"I'm calling myself Potnia, now," said Dorinda. "Nice to see you. Come with us while I pick up the dogs."

I suppose I could have said I had to rush for the bus and go home and make Mike's dinner, but he was working late. And anyway it would look rude.

"Were you at Naheed's class?" I asked.

"I'm teaching a course myself – psychic development and Gnosticism," said Dorinda – or Potnia.

"And what are you studying?" asked Naheed.

"I'm just doing the course on Greek mythology."

"Oh, you will find that most rewarding! I remember you were interested."

We turned left into a mews, and there were the dogs, tied up to some railings. They were lying quietly on the ground, but they got up when Dorinda approached. They were the biggest labradors I'd ever seen.

"They're very well-behaved," I said rather weakly.

"They are – with the right treatment," said Dorinda. "And with people they like."

She took their leads in one hand. "Do you have to rush off home?" she asked. It was quite a warm evening and she was wearing a patterned overblouse in brown and green, and baggy brown trousers.

"No, my husband's working late. And I had high tea with some friends."

"Come and have a cup of coffee or something – there's a Kardomah round the corner."

"I'd love to – won't they mind the dogs?"

"They know me."

"But I must love you and leave you!" said Naheed, and went off to get the tube. I wished she hadn't gone. Why was Dorinda being so friendly? We went to the Kardomah, where the waitresses made cooing noises to the dogs and brought them bowls of water which they lapped noisily. Then they lay down again near Dorinda's chair while she looked at the menu. She ordered tea and scones, and I just asked for some tea.

"What a coincidence meeting you!" I said, for something to say.

"There is no such thing as coincidence," said Dorinda, looking me in the eye in a meaning way. She seemed to have lost the habit of smiling, and altogether looked older, as if she'd "let herself go", as the magazines say.

"Yes, I've changed, haven't I?" she said. "You haven't. There was no way of getting my hair done – in that hotel where I was staying, you know." She smiled grimly.

"I had to tell Mike something – my boyfriend – about where I'd been and why I didn't come home. He was worried about me and was looking for me. I couldn't help that he's a policeman."

"At least it seems you haven't got any relatives – we checked." Just then her scones arrived, with pats of butter in silver paper. I wondered why they cared – except that if my parents had been around they'd have got the police looking for me too, like Ursula's did.

"Pot of tea for two!" said the waitress, plonking it down.

"Look here," said Dorinda, buttering her scone. "I'm neutral. What's done is done. It was the drugs the police cared about. We could hardly hide all the plants growing in the hothouses."

"There were hothouses?"

"Perfect for cultivating cannabis."

"I never found those."

"Do you know, I believe you? They were screened behind trees, and a wire fence that was always padlocked. Look, it doesn't matter now, all that. There's no need to be afraid of me. I think you can help me."

"In what way?"

"It's Gilles. He got out of prison, thanks to some wizardry of his own, but did he come and get me? He did not! He never even contacted me when I was released. He doesn't want to know me any more!"

"But you're free now, anyway," I said, rather lamely.

"My sentence wasn't very long. I just hosted parties, but they found some stuff in my flat. I bet Gilles got some of those layabouts to plant it there! I read a lot, you know, while I was away. It's come in useful teaching this course. He's got me to reckon with now. And he's not going to forgive you in a hurry."

"No, I suppose not."

"We'll be much stronger together."

"What do you want to do? I mean, is he still in England?"

"Oh, I know where he is. I found out that much. He has done very well for himself. And he's very well-protected. He must have been preparing, you know, in the – in the monastery. It wasn't going to hold him long. He has other schemes now. And another girl. He takes a back seat and she does the talking. But you are stronger than they are, much stronger. You and I – we can conjure -"

"Look – I really don't want to get involved in all that again," I said.

"Aren't you afraid of Gilles? Don't you hate him? Don't you want to hurt him, for what he did to you?"

"I think I got off lightly." I leaned forward and spoke quietly. "And if you conjure up anyone to help you, won't they be more frightening? And will they go away again?"

"I know what I'm doing. But if I can use you..."

I gathered up my bags.

"Dorinda," I said. "I'm sorry you feel hard done by. And it must have been grim, I'm sorry about all that. But..." I desperately tried to think of the right words. "I must follow my own path."

"And it's not the left-hand path," she murmured.

"No!" I said.

"Well, don't come crying to me if you need MY help!" she said rather tartly. "And don't expect ME to tell you where Gilles is now!"

I tried to scramble out of the booth where we were sitting. One of her dogs was in my way. I was wondering if I should step over him when he reared up on his front feet and growled.

"Not this time, Belphegor!" muttered Dorinda, and the dog got up and backed away.

"Isn't he adorable?" said the waitress, coming up behind him. Dorinda pulled his lead.

"They don't like you," said Dorinda. "They can tell if anyone's hostile. Down, Anubis!"

"Well, goodbye, Dorinda," I said.

"It's Potnia, now."

"Potnia, then."

"Don't forget the offer's open."

"But I thought you said — ?"

"You might need me. But they told me you were a hard nut to crack – the Haslemere lot, you know."

"Gerald, and Mrs B and Mrs Wheatley? And Charles?" I said, remembering the commuter belt coven. Some of them weren't so bad.

"Yes, we're still in touch. Apart from Charles. They knew you quite well, didn't they? There's quite a lot I could pass on to any employer of yours. Nobody can ever really leave, you know."

I thought of that nude ceremony round the bonfire in the woods.

"Where are you working, by the way?" she asked.

"I'm a temp – I'm never in one place for long."

"If Gilles finds you he'll want you again, you know!"

Two long-haired ladies in hippy gear wanted to pass me and I stood aside for them. I was glad they were between me and the dogs.

"I can't go on standing here in the gangway," I said. "I'm sorry – I'm sorry for YOU – but there's no more to say."

"All right," she said, grumpily. "Goodbye, then." She stirred her tea glumly.

I walked out, looking over my shoulder in case Dorinda and her hounds followed me, and bumped into the hippies, who were hanging about on the pavement, sweeping it with their bedgraggled hems. I said sorry and we disentangled ourselves, and I got on the bus and went home and made myself a tuna sandwich and watched telly. If I'd played Dorinda along I might have found out where Gilles was and told Mike, but she'd seemed to want to hang onto that knowledge as a bargaining counter.

***

I was working near the BBC on my lecture night, so I could walk to the college and sit in the library working through the reading list or have a cup of tea till it started.

95

I got there and the hall was full of people coming in and out as usual, and standing chatting on the steps. I thought I saw Christine, clutching a load of files and walking quickly with her head down. I was about to say hi, but she went into the Ladies. I strolled into the canteen to see if I could see the others and there they were, sitting together, so I got a cup of tea and went over and said "How was your day?"

"We've been at a lecture on Durkheim," said Rowena. "How about you?"

"I'm an audio typist, now. Trained and everything. I've been typing some boring letters somewhere near Warren Street."

"Oh, poor you!" said Ginevra.

"I hope it's not always as boring as that," said Rowena.

"No, at Magister Enterprises I get focus groups and it's real people chatting. It's as good as a play."

"What about?" asked Ginevra.

"Well, I'm not sure, it's all rather disconnected. They talk about investing, and flats in Greece, and developments in – come to think of it, they told me it was confidential and not to discuss the firm's business. Well, if I knew what it was I wouldn't!"

"But I suppose you get to see different places, and meet people?" asked Rowena, rather wistfully.

"Yes, sometimes they tell me all about their love lives, and what they're having for dinner, and what colour they're going to paint the bathroom. Modelling is more fun and less hard work."

I was in the middle of telling Ginevra about the shoot in the field when I saw Christine come in hugging her files to her chest. I smiled at her and she came over to our table.

"Hi, everybody!" she said. "Can I put these here while I go and get a cuppa?" And she put her stuff down and went off to the counter.

"That's Christine – she's studying Renaissance Italy," said Rowena.

"Yes, I know her from modelling."

"What a coincidence!" said Ginevra.

"There's no such thing as coincidence," said Rowena solemnly.

"I didn't know you did modelling too," Ginevra said to Christine when she sat down with a cup of tea and a doughnut.

"I'm just an occasional chaperone," said Christine. "I was a model, but now I'm too old! I chaperone my little sister, or sometimes my mum does."

"I waved at you just now in the hall but you didn't see me," I said.

"Oh, didn't I? I'm so sorry."

"Never mind, you were rushing into the loo and I was surrounded by tall people."

"Have you talked to the agency recently? They're looking for people to do another Victorian-type shoot."

"Oh, I'll call them."

Rowena and Ginevra went on talking about their lecture, which seemed to be about primitive tribes in Africa. I tried to eavesdrop a bit while Christine was gossiping about the Stella Orrin agency. What did tribes have to do with sociology? I thought it was about slums and youths and people having too many children.

"The last job I did was out in the country somewhere again," I said to Christine. "There was a nice boy there – Gary, have you met him? – and we were the kids and two adults were our parents and I had to wear a ghastly school uniform..."

Soon we all separated, me to my lecture, Ginevra home to her family, Rowena to the library and Christine out to the pub with some other students. "Are you coming to the disco on Friday?" she asked the others. "You could come too, Anna! They play golden oldies."

"Can I bring my husband?"

"I always forget you've got one of those! All the more reason to get out sometimes."

"We did go to a party at some kind of club with his work colleagues – it was fun and we did the chacha."

"How square!" laughed Christine. "Our golden oldies don't go back that far, only to Tamla Motown."

"Good, I think I like that sort of thing."

"I'll see you there. Oh, wait for me, Benny!" and she ran after some students, mostly boys, who were just going out of the door. I noted down the disco details from a poster on a noticeboard and ran to my lecture. There was more about digging up remains in Greece. I wonder how you become an archaeologist? There are lots in Agatha Christie, but then she was married to one.

When I got home Mike was there and we made a quick spaghetti carbonara – he fried the bacon.

"Do you want to come to a college disco on Friday?"

"Why not? You only live once! What are the students like?"

"Quite international. And serious, you know, like the ones we met."

"Beardie weirdies."

"Exactly. But, you know you said to say if I saw any of our old friends?"

"Yes. We need to keep an eye."

"Well, I did see Alan. He was at Harpsden Manor, the one who was always reading. I chatted to him a bit, back then I mean. He was about the only one who ever said anything! Or did anything apart from sit about and stare into space."

"It has that effect, apparently. Pot, I mean."

"What, makes you really boring?"

"So I hear. At least drunk people get into fights."

"I don't know which is worse. Anyway, though, he's OK, he's got a job. He's a security guard where I work sometimes –

Magister Enterprises. I think he said it was the old boy network but I'm not sure what he meant by that."

"Well, good for him getting a job. It's not easy with a record. I don't remember an Alan, but there were so many of them, we couldn't get them all. And for a lot of them we could only prove possession. Still, it all goes down on your sheet."

"And – I did – we pour the egg on now, don't we?"

Mike went to the sink to drain the spaghetti in the sink and I beat the eggs. He put the pan back on the heat and I sloshed the eggs in and he mixed it all around while they cooked, and I put out some plates.

"What were you saying?" he asked as he spooned the spaghetti onto the plates.

"I did, I did see..."

It was funny, I felt as if I couldn't get my words out. He was crumbling the bacon and putting it on a plate. He put it down in front of me and we sprinkled it on the spaghetti.

"Just a moment."

"Are you OK?"

"I will be in a minute."

"The spaghetti'll get cold."

"Yes..." I shut my eyes. I could see a thicket of tangled trees and brambles and nettles. I saw myself slashing at them, and struggling through, with the thorns scratching my legs. "I wanted to tell you..."

"What, what?" He put down his fork. "What is it?"

"I saw her, twice." I had broken through now, whatever it was she had put in my way. I thought of those not very friendly dogs. I thought of winged lions instead, and the stone lion who rescued me and Ursula from the Halloween Party and gave us a lift home.

"Who?"

"Dorinda. She's calling herself something different. I'm pretty sure she wouldn't like me telling you. She was the medium at the spiritualist church."

We started eating our spaghetti, which wasn't bad once we'd ground some pepper over it.

"And she's lecturing at the college – I saw her last week, but not this evening, thank goodness. She brings her dogs and ties them up outside."

"I thought you were going to say – "

"What?"

"Never mind. Well, that's not a crime, unless the dogs are dangerous?"

"They look rather fierce. And they're huge."

"So she's got a job, too, then? If mediuming is a job."

"Lecturing, anyway, about developing your psychic abilities."

"Rum sort of college, isn't it?"

"That sort of thing is getting more mainstream. Everybody says so."

"It sounds rather old-fashioned to me. Were there many young people at the spiritualist church?"

"Well, no. Just one other girl and me."

"So did Dorinda talk to you?"

"At the college, a bit – she was with Naheed, the Indian lady, you know, the astrologer. She wanted to be friendly, and said she didn't hold a grudge, but I – well, I was a bit frosty."

"Did she say she'd seen any of the rest of the outfit?"

"No – it sounded like she'd fallen out with them, actually."

"OK, we know where to find her if we want her, then. She probably won't give any more trouble. She was just providing the front with all that spiritualism stuff. It gave them an excuse to meet. We must cook this again some time."

"I wanted to try Boeuf Stroganoff, but you marinate it in red wine and we never have any. Shall we go to the disco, then?"

"Why not?"

We finished the spaghetti, washed everything up, and went to bed. A disco! Well, that was something to look forward to. It couldn't be worse than the ones I'd gone to with the girls from the boutique.

CHAPTER ELEVEN

The Stella Orrin Agency actually called me and booked me for another shoot in the country. Whoopee! Good thing I don't have a real job, I'd never get all this time off. I bought some dark blue and gold mugs with the money I hadn't earned yet.

We went to the college disco and it was all a bit like a children's party, with balloons and streamers. I wore a dress and my hair down and Mike wore a stripy shirt and no jacket. There was beer in huge tins which was a bit tepid, and lots of fruit juice, and crisps and nibbles in paper bowls. Ginevra wasn't there, but Rowena was, and we yelled to her across the loud music, and conversed with some of the other students who were friends of hers and failed to hear their answers. They usually screamed "What are you studying?" and "Is this your first year?"

They played some quite nice music that you could dance to, the Supremes and the Jackson Five. I've lost interest in pop rather, all the singers have beards now and the songs don't have tunes. I suppose it's all psychedelic, or is it progressive? Mike says it's all the blues really. Anyway, we just bopped around. Rowena, who was wearing a long dress a bit like a nightie, stood at the side and jived about a bit. I hoped she was OK. Then she was asked to dance by a very tall boy with dark hair and specs who'd told us he was doing chemistry and soon they were close dancing and snogging. Hooray for her.

Christine arrived rather late with several boys, and leapt about enthusiastically. She close danced with Benny, who's Chinese I think. There were some Indian students there too, but they seemed a bit shy. Quite soon we decided we'd had enough so we said goodbye to Christine and left. Rowena was in a clinch with the chemistry student. As we were going home I said to Mike: "It's such a relief being able to leave parties whenever you like, and not to wait to be picked up by your parents." We sat next to each other on the top of the bus and I leaned my head on his shoulder.

I saw Christine again in the canteen my next lecture day – she was with Benny and some other boys so Ginevra and I sat down with them. Benny was looking neat in slacks and a sleeveless jersey, but the others were wearing flared jeans with bits of old curtain let in at the bottom. The boys were rather annoying, and whatever I said, they would give some plonking reply. Apart from Benny, he seemed sweet. His hair is short and sticks up.

"Did your mother fix your trousers for you?" I asked one of the boys.

"My costume is tailored by elves from the tenth planet," he said, and giggled as if it was terribly funny.

They laughed at Benny, too, saying things like "Has it all gone Wong?"

After a bit they wandered off, apart from Benny.

"What are they studying?" I asked Benny.

"How to do up their shoe-laces," he said, so I supposed he didn't mind.

"It's like going to school on the train, before I had friends," I said.

"Remember we're old and married," said Ginevra. "This lot are mostly 18."

"That's only two or three years younger than us."

"It makes a difference at our age."

"Oh, you poor old ladies!" said Christine. "What about me?"

"We'll talk to you if you try to be very mature," I said. Perhaps I'm learning how to do sarcasm.

"The disco was fun, wasn't it? Are you sad you couldn't come, Ginevra?"

"I never really went to discos much, and then I met David," said Ginevra.

"I got that job," I said to Christine. "The shoot in the country."

"Oh, good for you! They said Paula was too young – they wanted 12 to 14 year olds."

"When you've just said how ancient you are!" said Ginevra.

"You were born old and never grew up!" said Benny.

I hoped he was wrong about not growing up. He and Christine went off after a bit – they were going to see a horror film called Trog, about some scientists who find a live Early Man.

"I couldn't say it was all a mistake and I had to get married," said Ginevra. "Though I wouldn't wish it was any other way. I expect I'll have lots more kids – Vatican roulette isn't very effective. Just as long as I don't get pregnant before the end of the course."

"Vatican roulette?"

"Yes – the rhythm method. I'll explain it to you if you ever need it. You know we aren't allowed to use contraception, or perhaps you don't mind?"

"I'm not doing anything – just waiting and seeing."

"Twenty is really a bit young – we're meant to plan our families now. We had a seminar on reproductive rights."

"Don't look so worried! Ianthe would be shocked – she doesn't want us to get married or have kids. What does she want us to do instead?"

"Have careers," said Ginevra sadly.

"You make it sound such fun!" We laughed. "What would happen if people stopped having babies? Tell me about these seminars – I've got to go off to my class soon."

"They're all very keen on abortion and if I try and say anything about it they jump on me."

"Oh, how mean!"

"I'm lucky I have an extended family. But don't they have mothers?"

"Their mothers have careers! Don't take any notice of them. I know, I know, it never worked with the boys on the train. I just used to get upset."

So we left too – she to go home to her little boy, and me to the class, where we learned about the Master and Mistress of Animals – Potnia Theron, and Pan, who is also Cernunnos, the horned god, and Herne the Hunter. So that's where Dorinda got her new name from! And why she goes everywhere with her black hounds, if that's what they are. And Pan is the son of Hermes, and his name doesn't mean "everything", like I thought. They said we'd have to write an essay by the end of term – I have no idea how.

***

Next week it was the shoot – we turned up at the agency and Janice put us in a minibus and off we went. I didn't know the others – all girls, younger than me – so I spent the time looking out of the window at the countryside once we'd got out of the suburbs. We stopped at traffic lights by little parades of shops: dry cleaners, and places that sold ballet shoes and tunics, and hairdressers with fancy names, and then set off again and left them all behind. Imagine being stuck somewhere like that, though.

We arrived at the "location", and they got out sandwiches and cans of coke for people who hadn't brought their own lunch. We ate them sitting at some tables in the car park and I felt a bit awkward being on my own, even though Janice was there.

When we'd eaten our late lunch or early tea and put the paper and tins in a bin Janice rounded us up into the big van with the clothes in it. We all came out looking like Alice in Wonderland, down to the stripy socks. Droopy, frilly dresses and sashes again. The photographers were setting up in a grassy field with tall trees round it, and the sun was going down a bit and the trees were casting long shadows.

I saw Helmut crouching down snapping some weeds. He waved at me.

"Hi Anna! Have a look at this!" and he beckoned me to look through the viewfinder. "Look at the sun coming through that dead plant! That's what we want."

So he posed us in ones or twos behind the weeds. There were other men hanging around, I supposed they were stylists, or people from the ad agency or the company that made the clothes. They got us to hold our hat-brims, or take the hats off and hold them in one hand, and they tried to get us all to do a dopey, far-away expression.

Then it was my turn to be photographed on my own and the others went and sat at the table in the car park again, or on the fence. Nobody seemed to mind about the dresses getting dirty.

"Think of nothing, Anna!" said Helmut. "That's it. Now think about your worst enemy. You are planning a horrible fate for her. Smile nastily."

"No, thanks," I said.

"I'm sure you can think of something. Perfect! You have that otherworldly look. Unheimlich."

"What's that mean?"

"Yes, yes, like that, look grumpy. You are sick of standing here in this field. Now look over there and you see something in the distance. Perfect. Now take the hat off, hold it by the brim and look off to the right again. Now chuck the hat over here."

One of the other men took it. Eventually Helmut was happy, and we trooped back to the caravan and dressed in our own things again, and got back in the minibus to go home. I made a bit of an effort and talked to the other girls about O Levels and Top of the Pops.

"It was rather a strange shoot," I said to Mike later. "Everyone was about 12 apart from me and they wanted us to look gloomy instead of madly happy like they usually do."

"What were you wearing – you were wearing clothes I hope?"

"Old-fashioned gear. Granny Takes a Trip. More like the dressing up box than real clothes."

"It sounds a bit weird."

"And what have you been doing?"

"Oh, the usual stuff. Paperwork, legwork, looking for mispers, interrogating people in council estates, identifying John Does."

"Who are they?"

"Unidentified bodies."

"Now THAT's creepy! What are mispers?"

"Missing persons."

"Well, I hope the next shoot is back to rainbow colours, hot pants and pigeon toes."

"Pigeon toes?"

"Yes, they think it looks childish to stand with your toes turned in."

"That's even creepier."

So we watched some telly and drank tea out of the dark blue mugs.

CHAPTER TWELVE

Back at Magister's Kirstin stopped by my desk on her way back from the tea cart and told me in an undertone that Jean had gone north.

"Nobody's been replaced," she added. "They're just getting in a lot of temps. They come and go – they're not as good as you."

This week's projects are Marax, Orobas and Phenex, and it's people rabbiting on as usual, with someone chipping in and telling them not to talk over each other. Lorna was sent off to deliver something and was a time getting back. Joanna was a bit short with her, but Lorna explained: "The way they've moved everything round – I went to the wrong floor!"

At lunchtime, they got up to go to the canteen and beckoned me to go with them.

"They're phasing in electric typewriters, now!" said Kirstin. "Huge pot plants on every floor, and suet pudding's off the menu!"

"They have golf balls instead of type bars," said Lorna. I said they sounded rather fun.

"Golf balls belong at St Andrews!" she said.

"Perhaps they want us all to lose weight," said Clemency gloomily, looking at the salads.

On my way out in the evening I saw Alan, reading surreptitiously as he stood just inside the front door in the foyer.

I greeted him discreetly and asked: "What's the book today?"

"Apewlius!" he said. "About this guy who gets turned into a donkey by a witch."

"I remember a story about a magic cabbage that turned people into donkeys," I said.

"No cabbages! He has to eat roses." He shoved the book back into his pocket as another guard came out of a concealed door by the desk. "Pretend you're asking the way – here comes Mr Gremory."

"Oh thanks! Left, right and left again!" I said loudly and went out of the door and Alan winked at me.

When I came in again the next morning he was on the door again and nobody else was around.

"Who's Mr Gremory?" I asked. "Don't you mean Gregory?"

"No, Gremory, as in memory. He's our boss. Oh, look out, here he comes again."

"Thanks, I found it OK!" I said in a high voice and scooted towards the lift. As I got into it, and faced front as other people got in, I saw Mr Gremory taking a chair behind the desk. He was shortish, and had a white face with acne scars, and red-rimmed eyes. He caught my eye and said "Cheer up, it may never 'appen!", and the lift doors closed. I hate it when people say that.

***

When I get to college I go straight to the canteen as the others are usually there. I haven't really chummed up with the other people doing my course, though we do have ten minutes for tea in the middle. This time just Christine was sitting at a table reading on her own, with folders and file paper shoved into a bag. She waggled her hand at me and I brought my cup of tea over.

"What's the topic of the day?" I asked.

"The Madness of Crowds," she said. "It's about turning lead into gold."

"Does it tell you how?"

"Sadly, no."

She shut the book and pulled out a Woman's Own from the bag. "Let's look at our horoscopes."

"Mine always says that Mercury is retrograde in my sign. But he can't do me any harm."

She read out some stuff about "changes of scenery" and "enjoying your own company". It made it all sound attractive, even being on your own for a weekend, which can be dreary. I suppose if you've got no choice, it might help to pretend it was fun.

She read out: "Feeling inspired? Time to write that memoir!"

Then we moved on to the knitting patterns, and recipes for scones, and French bread pizza which sounds quite easy.

"Has Paula been doing any more modelling?"

"No, it's been quite thin on the ground. How about you? Didn't you get that gig?"

"It was another scene in a field in the country. They wanted us to look moody, and hung about while the sun went down. It was quite fun but a bit cold and there was nobody much to talk to."

"Let's go on another shoot – they should be doing spring stuff now. It's cool when you can chat. And it's like a little world where nobody knows who you are," she said dreamily.

Just then Rowena and Ginevra came over with trays and fairy cakes. Rowena's tall chemistry friend came and joined us too – he's called Harvey. He was wearing a brown corduroy jacket and black-rimmed glasses like my semi-fake ones – I take them off for college, and take my hair down too, so I can be student me.

Benny turned up as well, wearing a pale grey polo neck. He smiles all the time. "Here come the headbangers!" he said as the boys with long hair and home-made flares came and crowded onto the end of our table.

Christine shoved Woman's Own back into her bag and became much more animated and laughed a lot. I suppose that's what you have to do with boys. I'm glad I missed out that stage.

"Anyway," I said to Rowena and Ginevra after we'd all said hello. "I've got to write this essay. I mean, help! I haven't written an essay since school and I was hopeless at it then. I think I missed being told how when I changed schools."

"Oh, it's easy!" said Benny, smiling and creasing up his eyes. "The title always seems to be asking you what you think, but they never want to know that. They want to know what you conclude from the evidence, or what other authorities say. Read some books and lift it from there – it's just to show you've read the books."

Rowena chipped in: "You say at the beginning something like, authority A says blah, but authority B thinks blah. Then at the end you say, because of blah, blah and blah, I think Authority A is more likely to be right."

"Of course, you don't always get opposing theories," said Benny. "But often you do, because there has to be a Great Debate about anything."

"Well, they never told us that at the convent!" I said. "They just said they were right. They never even mentioned other ideas about anything."

"I hope you didn't believe them!" said Benny. "I didn't know you went to a convent."

"For a bit, then I went to an ordinary day school," I said. "The nuns were frightened of anybody who disagreed with them. This is much more fun. But what are headbangers?"

"People like that lot!" he said, jerking his head at the end of the table, where the bell-bottom boys were kicking each other and eating sausage sandwiches. "Heavy metal freaks."

"It's a kind of music, isn't it?"

"What do you listen to?"

"Old music like Motown. I even like folk music."

"There's a Folk Soc here!" said Rowena.

"Perhaps I'll try it some time. I like being a fake student."

The "headbangers" left, and so did Christine and Benny.

"You wouldn't think she was an A student," said Rowena leaning forward confidentially. "Every week she seems to have a different boyfriend, and she's always in the student bar with that crowd."

"The heavy metal crowd?"

"Yes. They're all doing Geo and Env."

"Some friends of mine are doing that," I said, thinking of my old friends Murray and Elspeth, now in Norwich. "I don't think they'd get on with those types."

"That's right," said Ginevra. "Christine comes top in exams and gets amazing marks for her essays. She must do it all at home – you never see her swotting. And she's quite quiet in seminars – just takes a lot of notes."

"Perhaps she's hired a lookalike to do the exams for her," said Harvey.

They started comparing marks, and discussing their tutors, and I drifted off rather, but of course it matters to them and they want to be teachers or whatever.

I went to my class and the tutor gave us a choice of essay titles. One of them was "Magical beliefs in Apuleius's Golden Ass". That must be the book Alan was reading, so I picked that one. A short reading list came with it, with books by Plotinus and one called Arcana Mundi. The Golden Ass must be out in paperback – there's a bookshop near Magister's and I can buy a copy tomorrow.

****

I flourished The Golden Ass at Alan as I came in from lunch. It's quite good, but I keep reverting to Agatha Christie and girls who completely change their appearance with a cloche hat and a couple of bunches of curls. I've been working my way through Mum's book, too, when I've got a moment, and copying it out. Apparently dandelion roots are used for divination, and give you prophetic dreams, and also "provoketh urine". Pomegranates cure old wounds, when boiled in vinegar. St John's Wort frees the air from demons. At the end of the book there are some scribbled notes:

"Sonnet 66" – then there's a drawing of a skull and a poem:

Behowlde youre selves by us
Sutche once were we as yow
And yow in tyme shalbe
Even duste as we are now.

Then it says: Seek the Reversall. Tithonus.

I've looked all through the book, and I can't find anything labelled "Reversall", but there are some loose pages shoved in, and there's a particularly brown, old, tatty one like a dead leaf, just headed "R".

I guessed Sonnet 66 must be by Shakespeare, so I looked it up in the college library. It goes: "Tired with all these, for restful death I cry", and then it lists a lot of things you might be weary of.

I asked the librarian if she knew what "Tithonus" meant, and she said it's a poem by Tennyson, so I looked HIM up, and he was given immortality by a nymph, but she forgot to give him eternal youth as well. The poem goes:

The woods decay, the woods decay and fall,
The vapours weep their burthen to the ground,
Man comes and tills the field and lies beneath,
And after many a summer dies the swan.

That's rather beautiful – decaying and falling is just what Hampstead Heath is doing now. The next line must just mean "and it's pouring with rain".

Tithonus asks:

Why should a man desire in any way
To vary from the kindly race of men?

I agree with him. It would be much better to be just like everybody else. But I don't want to actually die, not right now. What if the potion is poisonous? But then, if somebody just wants to die, they don't have to use magic. The potion Mum gave me, disguised as a cold cure, is for "longevetee", not immortality. Well, I'm glad I worked that out. And the Reversall ingredients don't look poisonous. I'll see if I can get them together. There are some weird spices, but I can probably get them in Soho.

We watched the Midnight Movie (they're black and white and ancient) and this week it was The Maltese Falcon. I liked that line about are you just pulling strings and hoping it'll all work out somehow? And the Fat Man telling the whole plot to Humphrey Bogart.

I read more of The Golden Ass and wrote some notes about the magic spells and being rescued by Isis, and the book called Arcana Mundi. A young boy saw Hermes in a glass of water, and some bloke called Plotinus says of course the gods don't answer prayers, it's just that the whole universe is connected like the vibration of the strings of a lyre, or something. Yes, you pluck one string and another one sounds, like on a guitar. I put that in my essay too. I'm not so sure that's how it works, but I didn't say so. "It is only natural for the soul to be directed by the tune and the sound of the incantation," says Plotinus.

Mike says we're invited to a Halloween party with his colleagues, at the same club where they had the party before. I wonder if I can find my old costume from two years ago?

CHAPTER THIRTEEN

I looked for my old Halloween costume but I think I must have thrown it out, and the witch's hat got bashed up. So I bought a black A-line midi-skirt and shortened it. I'm sure there's room for a sewing machine here, I wonder how much they cost? I got a low-necked black T-shirt and a black crochet shawl, and bought another witch's hat and some eyeliner and purple lipstick. Mike bought a skeleton outfit in the witch's hat shop, and some furry tarantulas. I sewed one of them onto shoulder of my T shirt. I've still got my black strap tap shoes.

We turned up at the club, and the lights were dimmed and there were a lot of silly decorations, and purple crepe paper over the lights. I recognised Shirley, in a witch outfit, and Elaine and Fern and Stan and Fred. The ladies admired my costume. Some waiters passed round trays with bridge rolls with green fillings, and chips and cheese dips with faces made out of olives, and there was a giant cake in the shape of a spider and everybody laughed a lot.

Fred got me a Coke and said "Staying out of trouble, I hope?" We played some silly games like trying to eat buns hanging from strings, and Shirley (she's Mrs Fred) won a tacky luminous skeleton. The DJ was playing spooky music like Dancing in the Dark and I Wanna Be Evil.

We hopped about and made fools of ourselves as usual. Mike looked good in his skeleton outfit, being slight anyway. But the mask got too hot and he took it off. I shed my shawl and hat, too. Shirley went and sat at a table and started telling fortunes with a pack of cards.

"Lucky you not needing a wig!" she said. "I learned card reading from my gran, she was a seventh daughter. Shall I tell your fortune?"

I sat down at the table where she had set up her stall, and paid a shilling into the police charity fund, and she told me to beware a dark woman, and that I would travel over water.

We didn't have much chance to chat with anybody. The men danced with their wives, Fred with Shirley and Stan with Fern, and then we swapped, and I danced with Stan, who was dressed as a ghost in a sheet with eye-holes.

"Ghosts walk at Halloween," he said, "Why shouldn't they dance too?"

"Well I haven't seen any," I said.

We swapped partners again and I got Mike back. "I thought I saw your friend from John Lewis with the untidy hair," he said. "Sitting over there at a table with her friend. He looks like a postwar spiv. I wonder how they got invited?"

I danced with Fred next and he hugged me rather close so I said I needed to go and powder my nose. The ladies' room had a witch stuck on the door, and there was a devil on the gents'.

When I came back I looked into the dark corners and saw Frank and Elsie sitting at a table near the DJ. Some couples were close dancing next to them. I got another Coke from the bar and danced through the throng and sat at their table with my back to the room.

"Hi!" I said, "Nice to see you!"

"It's our night out," said Frank. "We thought we'd revisit old haunts."

I drank Coke through a straw and pretended I was looking at the pattern of the disco ball on the wall.

"Don't forget most people can't see us," said Elsie. Her brownish grey hair was up on the top of her head in a swirl, and bits were falling down as usual. She was wearing a beige dress with a draped bodice and a few silver sequins. I wonder where she keeps her clothes? Fred was wearing a shabby black suit as before – I suppose it is a bit old-fashioned, with wide lapels, but they're trendy again - and his longish black hair blended in with the spooky theme.

"Did you get my message?" asked Frank.

"You said to look behind me, and I looked over my shoulder and saw Dorinda. She wanted me to help her attack Gilles, but I don't want to do harm to anybody. Apart from anything, I don't think it's safe, somehow. I know I'm being selfish, but I don't want it to rebound on me."

"Quite right, dear," said Elsie. "We don't want to add to the evil in the world. Quite the opposite."

"Anyway," said Frank. "Keep looking behind you, and around you. You're doing OK. We must meet soon for a longer chat."

"We've just dropped in," said Elsie. "Lovely party, isn't it? Reminds me of the old days at the Locarno ballroom."

"Call us any time," said Frank. "And now we must be on our way – we've got a busy schedule."

"OK," I said. "Goodbye, then."

I got up carrying my glass and wiggled back through the dancers and found another table on the other side of the room, near the opening into the bar. Mike was dancing with Fern, and when the record was over he came over and sat down.

"Was it them?" he asked.

"Yes, but they had to go." I looked over at the table next to the DJ, and it was empty.

"They must know somebody here," he said.

"I expect they do."

"If she's not a shoplifter, what does she do?"

"I think she's kind of retired."

"Come on – we can foxtrot to this one." So we did.

"We ought to find somewhere to practise," said Mike.

"Elsie said she missed the old Locarno Ballroom."

"Hammersmith Palais is still open."

"Let's go some time!"

I went to Soho in my lunch hour one day and bought some sea salt in Fratelli Camisa, the Italian shop, and some pasta and tomato paste. And some frankincense, myrrh and orris root powder in an Indian food shop. I got some sandalwood incense sticks too. There's a potion in the book for making your hair grow, but I don't think I need it. Which is a good thing, since it requires three gallons of rainwater. There's a spell for getting rid of tedious guests. You do some stuff with brooms and forks, and say:

Get thee hence beyond my door
For I am weary to the core.

But we hardly ever have guests. I needed some iron filings, so I went to the magic and joke shop opposite the British Museum and got one of those sets with a funny face and some iron filings under plastic, and a magnetic wand so you can give the face hair or a beard and moustache. When I got home I played with it for a bit, then put all the stuff I'd got so far in a shoe box and put it away next to the crystal and the Tarot cards.

I can get essential oils in one of those "head" shops that cater to hippies – I think they mainly sell stuff to do with dope smoking, and I suppose it's not illegal to sell pipes, or incense to mask the smell. Ground-up eggshell I can make myself, and I can find white and black pebbles somewhere. I've got a lavender bag which Mum made – lavender is used for summoning the dead, and also Hermes and Hecate. I wrote "Yardley Lavender water" on my list.

***

Lorna is going back to Monifieth and we threw a little party for her in the Magister canteen, which now has even more plastic greenery draped round the counter and the windows.

"They don't let you bring alcohol, but I got some Schloer apple juice," said Kirstin, pouring it out into plastic cups. "We can pretend it's champagne."

"Every week now they change something," said Lorna rather sadly. "And the hostel's practically empty."

"I heard they were going to shut it," said Clemency. She's a bit older than the others.

"Our ghosts will walk those empty corridors," said Kirstin. "Our footsteps will go tap, tap, tap on the brown lino." She passed round a plate of Jaffa cakes. "We ought to stick a birthday cake candle into one of these, or something."

"But we'll be back home in Scotland, not in the beyond!" said Jean.

Clemency took a Jaffa cake and started singing:

Came ye by the salmon fishers,
Came ye by the roperee?
Saw ye there a sailor laddie,
Waiting on the coast for me?

We joined in with the chorus:

I know where I'm going,
I know who's going with me,
I know who I love,
But the de'il knows who I'll marry.

Mum used to sing it.

"I know where I'm going," said Lorna. "Back home! Perhaps I'll find a boyfriend at last. A sailor laddie. Or someone who works on an oil rig."

"There's nobody here but men in suits with families," said Kirstin. I looked over to where a lot of porters and drivers and postroom men were sitting on two tables pushed together.

"Them? They've all got families, too," said Kirstin. "But what about that one with the ponytail? I saw you chatting to him. And you a married woman!"

"He's a friend – I knew him before."

"What did he do then?"

"Oh, nothing much. I think he was on the dole."

"Nice friends you have!"

"Did I tell you I went to the folk club?" I said, changing the subject. "There were a lot of men in thick jerseys who sang songs about whales! And some sad sea shanties."

Even "I know where I'm going" is rather sad – it's the way it ends in the air, tune and words. As we went out one of the porters said "We'll miss you girls! We always get a free cabaret."

"Miss us?" asked Clemency as we waited for the lift. "Does he know something we don't?"

"This building is supposed to be haunted too, you know," said Kirstin. "The way people keep seeing smoke. We spend more time out the front than actually working."

"They have to have drills, though, don't they?" I asked.

"They took all the panels off on the fifth floor, looking at the wiring."

We got out at our floor and trailed back into the office.

"And then there's that thing that's just a dark shape!" said Kirstin.

"You're just making things up now," said Clemency.

"I'm sure I saw it one night outside the lift," said Kirstin, pretending to shiver. Joanna was looking at us a bit disapprovingly, so we settled down and got back to work.

***

When I got home Mike was sitting on the floor listening to Simon and Garfunkel and reading The Hobbit.

"This is a good story – you can read it after me," he said.

"We listened to Simon and Garfunkel in the common room at the convent. We had an old radiogram and we had them, and The Hollies, and Dvorak's Sixth Symphony. I practically learned it by heart."

"I got some Carole King 45s at that shop by Camden Town tube. Shouldn't you give these Irish folk songs back to the library?"

"I keep renewing them – I don't think anybody else likes them."

He put the Irish record on and we listened to songs about the Crimean War and hare hunts while I opened a tin of soup and toasted a baguette and set out some Brie on the breadboard.

"Why wouldn't the secretaries at work want to go out with the security guards?" I wondered aloud.

"I don't know. It's a mystery beyond our human understanding."

"They were complaining – I think they'd all come down south to find a boyfriend, and all they met were met in suits who already had families. But there are loads of men in the building, and some of them are quite young. There are boys who push round trolleys of files."

"Perhaps they wanted to meet somebody professional."

"Well, they all seem to be going home."

"I expect they'll marry Scottish farmers," said Mike.

"Or men from oil rigs."

"That would be convenient – they'd be away all the time."

So we had the soup and ate the bread and cheese.

***

I've got most of the ingredients for the Reversall, and none of them look poisonous. I went to the Chinese medicine shop in Camden Town and got some wolfsbane, and I got Dr J. Collis Browne's Chlorodyne from Boots, because it has opium in it. Mum used to keep it in the medicine cabinet.

I got asafoetida at an Indian shop, and valerian at a health food shop (it makes you sleep). You don't add the iron filings, I was relieved to see, just put them in a little dish, and do the same with sulphur and sea salt. I can see I'll have to go to Hamley's and get a chemistry set for the sulphur. Hyssop I can get from the garden centre at Ally Pally (Alexandra Palace, if you're not a Londoner). It is a plant of Mercury, as are several mentioned in the recipe. So invoking Hermes will do no harm.

But where can I do it? I can't just cook the stuff up and swig it – I have to draw a pentacle, and put all this stuff out in saucers, and light a candle. I need to find a little temple somewhere. Or somewhere with some statues.

I thought about how lucky I've been, and all the nice people I've met, even if I haven't seen them for ages. I wrote to Elspeth – she and Murray will be graduating and getting married soon. But what if I couldn't go on seeing them, because they'd get older and I wouldn't? I tried to imagine them both with wrinkles. You couldn't get fond of anybody. You'd have to keep disappearing. And I don't think Mike would want to live on far into the future with me, until we were living on Mars in in 2170. I don't think I'd like it much either. I like life the way it is. And I don't really care if I can't go on modelling. They seem to use people up quite quickly, anyway.

Mike finished the Hobbit and I'm reading it now – I held it up for Alan to see as I turned up at work. I went to the college in the evening, but I was early, so I walked through John Lewis and lingered around the haberdashery – it's open late one night a week. I bought some Wundaweb for sticking up your hem when it falls down, and then went out the back entrance and cut through Cavendish Square gardens.

Christine was sitting on one of the benches under a lamp, talking to somebody. It looked like the dark-haired girl from Magister's – Melusine. She's a bit scary, and besides, I didn't want to interrupt. Perhaps Christine was looking for a part-time job if her "acting and modelling" had only been a summer gig. It seemed an odd place for an interview.

I was still in the dark bit behind some shrubs, so I lurked behind a spotted laurel and hoped Melusine would go away soon. Christine was writing something down, perhaps an address, and Melusine was looking in her pocket diary. She was wearing a trench coat with the collar up and a beret, like a spy. After a bit she got up and walked towards Wigmore Hall, the other way from college.

I thought I'd better not rush up to Christine and say "Who was that?" She was cagey about her other job, and actually she never talked much about her life. She got up and made off towards the college and I counted to 20, then followed her. I lingered in the hall, and I could hear Dorinda's voice lecturing in one of the rooms. I looked in through the glass panel in the door – it was dark inside and she was showing slides, so I sneaked in at the back.

Dorinda was saying: "When you think, you open your brain to a drop from the Ocean of Thought... The pure light surrounding the Invisible Spirit... ***A veil exists between the world above and the realms that are below; and shadow***

came into being beneath the veil; and that shadow became matter; and that shadow was projected apart..."

She had about ten students, sitting at the front and frantically taking notes. I stood it for a few minutes and then snuck out again. Come to think of it, she always used to talk like that. It didn't sound much use for casting real spells.

CHAPTER FOURTEEN

The following week, Mike was on night shifts. Alone in the flat, I cooked up the potion, let it cool, then decanted it into a mineral water bottle. Then I washed everything up and opened the windows, even though it was cold, because it smelled a bit odd. I put all my substances into little bottles with screw tops – I got them at John Lewis, they're for putting makeup in when you go on holiday, shampoo and bubble bath and stuff like that. I packed them all in my school satchel which I've still got, with the recipe, which I'd written out on file paper.

I took it all with me to work and put it under my desk and said it was some shopping. I asked Joanna if I could leave a bit early and she said that was OK.

Kirstin said: "Got a date?"

"Just an appointment," I said.

"Oh, of course you're a married woman, aren't you – or perhaps you've got a bit on the side?"

"My husband's on the night shift!"

"When the cat's away, eh?"

Joanna shut her up, and she looked wearily at the clock. The last hour is tough. Can I stick doing this for much longer? I was glad to be leaving early. Anyway, I got a bus to the British Museum, which was still open and full of schoolchildren, and mingled with the crowds. I was wearing black tights, and a green skirt and cardigan, a pale green shirt, and a double-breasted navy winter coat. I'd done my hair in bunches over my ears, which looks neat enough for work.

121

I wandered about, looking at little clay pots, and primitive marble figures, and Greek vases, and then I milled around in the Egyptian Hall with a lot of kids in navy macs and school hats. They were darting about filling in worksheets and making a row. They began to thin out, and their teachers rounded them up, and the staff or guards or whoever they are started shooing them off and shouting that the museum was about to close.

I hid behind a huge granite beetle where there's an alcove with a fresco of Anubis, the Egyptian lord of the dead. He looks like one of Dorinda's dogs. Click, click, click, they turned off the lights, until there was just a glow coming in through the windows. I took off my shoes and put them in my coat pockets. I could see the men coming round with torches and calling out: "You done in the Elgin Marbles, Jim?"

They flashed their torches around and were coming towards me, so I dodged round a stone arm and an obelisk and crouched behind a kind of stone bath.

"All clear in here, Bob," said a voice. "I'll do another sweep-round at midnight."

"I'll leave you to it, mate. Have a quiet night. Look out for King Tutankhamun!"

I wondered if he said that every night. So I had until midnight. I padded in stocking feet into the Greek and Roman room and found a statue called the Farnese Hermes. I stood in front of him and said quietly:

Son of Zeus and Maia
God of change and doorways
Mover between worlds
Aid me in my task
See me safely through
Guard me from all harm

Absolutely nothing rhymes with "worlds", and I don't think they did rhyming in Ancient Greek times anyway. I went back into the Egyptian Hall. I could still just see thanks to the street lights shining through the tall windows. Egyptian gods are the same as the Greek ones, I've discovered, just with different names, and with animal heads. Thoth is a baboon, but he's also the Egyptian Hermes. The Greeks thought their gods had come from Egypt – or did the gods have to hide out there and disguise themselves as animals?

I put my satchel down in front of a black statue of Bast, the form of Artemis/Diana with a cat's head, huntress, goddess of the Moon and protector of young girls. There are several of them in a row. I drew a pentacle on the floor with chalk, and set out some coffee saucers I'd bought at Reg's junk stall in Camden Town for a few shillings, and poured the substances into them. I took off my coat, and undid my hair. I put out the black and white pebbles, and set down the candle in its candlestick, and lit it. That made the shadows much darker. As the flame flickered, the gods seemed to move slightly and smile or frown. I looked around, and saw someone standing next to the statue of Thoth, a grey shape in the darkness. I froze, but then I realised it was only Hermes himself from the other room.

I got out a woven hippy belt from Kensington Market with fringes at the ends, and tied it round my waist in an Isis knot with a loop sticking out. The recipe doesn't give any invocations, but I said to Bast:

Great goddess of the moon
Break the enchantment soon
Fourscore is my span
Like any woman or man

I stood in the pentacle, unscrewed the cap of the mineral water bottle, and drank the potion. It was very bitter, but I swallowed it all. Then I bowed to Isis, poured the substances back into their bottles and put everything back into the satchel. I undid the girdle and used it to rub out the pentacle. Then I snuffed out the candle and put that away too.

I looked down the end of the hall and Hermes was still standing there. I saluted him, and he bowed, and walked off behind Thoth, back to his proper place.

There's a bench with a back near the stone sheep, so I went over to it. I put my shoes back on and lay down with my coat over me and my head on the satchel. The saucers and bottle clanked a bit. I should have brought something to eat, but I wasn't hungry, just terribly sleepy. I supposed that was the valerian. The bench was hard, but soon I fell asleep.

Then someone was shining a torch in my eyes and saying, "Hullo, what have we here?"

I struggled to wake up – it was one of the uniformed staff.

"Well, then, what happened to you?"

"I was in the ladies, and when I came out, everyone had gone and the doors were shut. I wandered about a bit, but there was nobody here, and it was dark and spooky, so I thought I might as well go to sleep and wait for the doors to open in the morning."

What an idiot! I could have hidden in the ladies all night, probably, but I'd been so sleepy. And it was friendly among all the statues.

"Never mind, come with me, I've almost finished here. Nobody around but mice – and the old gods, of course. They won't hurt you. Come along to my cubby hole and we'll brew up."

So we went. The cubby hole was through a door and down some stairs and in a basement and there was another man in it boiling a kettle on a gas ring, who said "Hullo, ullo, ullo!"

"They don't often leave one behind, do they? I thought they counted them," said the one who'd found me. "My name's Jim, by the way, and this is Sid. Now let's have a cup of tea and a doorstep and we'll work out what to do next."

They showed me a loo, which was full of brooms and dusters and smelled of floor polish, and I washed my face and hands and put my hair back in bunches. I came out, and they presented me with a mug of tea and a plate with thick ham sandwiches.

"Are you sure you've got enough to go round?" I asked.

"Oh yes, and we've got some Penguin biscuits too."

We munched the sandwiches and drank the tea which was sugary and dark brown. I was famished and accepted a Penguin biscuit.

"So, was you in one of them school parties?" asked Sid.

"That's right," I said.

"Won't somebody be missing you by now?"

"I'm boarding, and I expect the other girls will cover for me. It's one of those posh schools for delinquent girls. We do it all the time."

"Sure we shouldn't call the police, Jim? No, no, only joking, love. You sound older than you look – how old are you?"

"I'm 16."

"Oh well, perhaps you'll grow! My Eileen did that all of a sudden, her mum had to let her hems down."

"Perhaps I will!"

"So you see – we're OK!" said Jim. "He's got kids older than you!"

I felt all right and I didn't think I was dead. I'm sure I couldn't have drunk sweet tea and eaten ham sandwiches if I'd been dead.

"OK," said Jim. "We'll say no more about it. We won't put it in the report, will we, Sid? And we'll let you out the back before anyone else turns up. You're safe in our hands!"

"We'd get a black mark! I hope you don't," said Sid. "We'll say no more."

So I lay down on their rather grubby sofa and went off into a deep sleep again. I still kept the satchel under my head just in case. They woke me up later – they'd put another coat over me – and I tried to wash some more and brush my teeth with a finger and some soap which tasted as nasty as the potion. They'd made more tea and some toast, and I ate and drank it quickly, then they took me up the stairs and out again past Thoth and Bast and the giant arm and the obelisk and through some storerooms to a little side door.

They let me out in the cold morning air, and I said: "Thank you ever so much! You've been incredibly kind, and thank you for all the tea!"

They said: "Don't mention it. Sure you'll be all right getting back into your school? I expect it's in Kensington or somewhere grand like that."

I said I'd be fine and I'd get the bus and just mingle with the others, and walked off into Soho in the cold dawn and had some black coffee in a café and read the Hobbit until it was time to go to work. Bilbo is getting braver and talks to dragons now but something awful is going to happen, I can tell. I remembered I'd forgotten to tell Mike I loved him before taking the potion, just in case it went wrong, but I felt OK so far.

I tried scrying in my cup of coffee, just to see if I could still do it or if everything had changed. The café was full of men in donkey jackets from building sites, or Covent Garden veg market. They all faded a bit, and I saw clouds and a night sky with stars, and the huge black cat-headed figure of Bast, standing on a grassy plain with trees. Then I saw Melusine from work, sitting in a big office with a view over London. She was drawing or writing on a giant chart spread out over a huge desk. Then a door opened and a man came in, but black smoke quickly covered the whole scene, and all I could see of the man was white hair and dark glasses and then the whole thing went dark and was a cup of coffee again.

"You all right, love?" asked one of the men. I must have looked rather dazed. "You look a bit young for a night on the tiles, although in Soho anything goes. Shouldn't you be at school?"

"I'm 20!" I said. "I left school ages ago. I'm just on my way to work but I'm a bit early."

"I believe you! Thousands wouldn't. What are you reading, interesting book?"

"Yes, the Hobbit."

"What's one of them?"

"He's a kind of dwarf, it's like a fairytale with dragons."

"And you said you was grown up!"

"Well, I'd better be going, goodbye!"

I passed a Boots and bought a toothbrush and some toothpaste. How nice people are, apart from the man in the café. I hate it when they say "interesting book?" I mean, would I read a dull one? I still had time to spare, so I nipped into a Woolworths and bought a white school shirt. I changed into it in the ladies at work and also brushed my teeth to get rid of the lingering taste of soap, and brushed my hair and did it in plaits.

"You look a bit tired!" said Kirstin when I came in. "You can't fool us – that's an overnight bag!" I put it down under my desk and it clinked – she'll just have to wonder. I looked at my face in my handbag mirror – was I getting older already? But I looked just the same.

The temp agency rang me but it was just to find out if I was happy in my "placement", and I said everything was fine. I counted the hours till I could go home and have a bath and put all my stuff away. Fortunately I can trust Mike not to go through my things, like I don't go through his. When I got back he'd just woken up and so we had bacon and eggs, breakfast for him, supper for me. He stayed up and watched telly. I wanted to stay awake for the Midnight Movie which was The Quatermass Experiment but I was dropping with tiredness and went to bed and slept dreamlessly.

CHAPTER FIFTEEN

Mike had the weekend to recover from being on the night shift and he said apart from drunk and disorderlies they spent the time sitting around drinking tea and doing paperwork and the crossword and looking through files of mug shots and memorising faces, bios and MOs. That stands for "modus operandi" and it's how a criminal operates. We went to see Airport and it was rather good and found a pub in Tufnell Park with a blues band which wasn't bad either.

On the Monday, I put my hair up again with the giant plastic hairpins. They've got some of the new electric typewriters with a golf ball. I hope I get a go on one. We were sitting there typing away on our ancient machines when Joanna, the new boss, got a call and looked a bit flustered. She was busy checking through some transcripts to see if they made sense and the spelling was OK. She looked round the room and her eyes lighted on me and she beckoned me over.

"Would you mind running an errand for me?"

I said no I didn't mind, it would be a break from the monotony.

"Could you take these transcripts up to the top floor? Turn right when you get out of the lift, and right again, and ask for Melusine. I'm sure you know which one she is, she has short dark hair and glasses."

"Yes, I know her, she comes and delivers tapes sometimes, doesn't she?"

"That's right. Straightaway if you don't mind."

She handed me a thick envelope and off I went. The envelope was marked Shax. Were they working their way through the alphabet? Or were they all Greek islands? I got out at the top floor and looked out over the rooftops – but I couldn't see far as it was dull and misty. There were big pot plants, almost trees, and thick grey carpets much cleaner than the downstairs ones.

I turned to the right as instructed and pushed through some heavy glass doors and there was Melusine sitting at a huge teak desk, just as I'd seen her in the coffee cup. It was just her in the office, and a huge window, and more trees in pots. The big plan she'd been working on was pinned up on the wall, or perhaps it was a different one, with dates, and coloured pins, and flags with code names. She was reading through some papers and frowning.

I said, "I've brought the transcripts".

"Thanks, just put them down here," she said harshly, without looking up, pointing to a spot on the desk. I put them down and turned to go, but then she said: "Wait a moment – come back here a minute."

She put down her pen and looked at me through her heavy glasses. Her fringe needed cutting – it was falling into her eyes.

"Take off your glasses!" she said. I was rather stunned, but I did.

"I suppose your hair is quite long, isn't it?"

"Yes – is it coming down?" I felt it anxiously.

"No, it's fine. I think I know you now. Mr Magister has been looking for you ever since he saw your picture in the brochure."

"In the brochure?" I asked stupidly. She opened a drawer of her desk and scrabbled in it for a bit then pulled out a brochure and slapped it on the desk.

"Have a look."

It was labelled "Valefor Village", and there on the cover was me in school uniform, Gary, the nice adults and the fake houses. They didn't look fake in the photo – it looked like a real model village.

"They made me wear that awful hat," I said.

"I suppose you do modelling in your spare time." She looked at me, not smiling. She had a monotonous voice, like someone filing through an iron bar.

"Yes," I said. "I've been modelling children's clothes. But most of the time I work as a temp. I've been here off and on for a bit"

"Come next door," she said, putting the brochure back into the drawer.

We went through her office into an even bigger one on the corner of the building, with black leather sofas and a huge desk with hardly anything on it apart from a giant onyx desk set.

"Look!" said Melusine, pointing at a picture on the wall. There were some other pictures, black and white photographs of tower blocks, and cranes, and old-fashioned streets, and there in the middle was a sepia photo of me, in a flowery dress, standing in a shaft of evening sunlight in a field under a tree, looking glum.

"I remember that shoot," I said. "We changed in a car park and they told us to look miserable."

"You look under-age, but I suppose you must be 18 or 19."

"I'm 20." Did I look 19 already?

"This was on sale in some arty shop and Mr Magister bought it. And then he saw you in the brochure. He looked through all the pictures they took that day and then he told me to find out who you were and contact you. He usually just signs off on things like that."

"Well, you don't have to bother now."

"Oh, I found out who you were through the agency we used for the brochures. I told Mr Magister that the agency had a policy and didn't give out models' details, and to liaise through them. He told me to keep trying. He probably meant bully them, or burgle their files or something."

"I don't understand."

"I wasn't going to find you for him, was I? I'm sick of looking at your face on the wall day after day. Now you've turned up, you can go. Don't worry, Mr Magister is out and won't be back for a while."

"OK, I'm off."

We went out of Mr Magister's office and back into hers and she escorted me to the door. "He's obsessed with that picture. You don't think I'm going to tell him where you are, do you? I'll tell him a girl came up here and went through confidential files, and nobody in the firm will book you again. Stay away."

She hadn't raised her voice during any of this this.

"Look, it sounds like I'd better keep out of his way, anyway, doesn't it? Don't worry, there are other firms I can work at. I'll ring the temp agency."

"You do that. So will I. Goodbye."

I pushed my way out through the heavy glass door again, and pressed the button for the lift. She stood looking at me through the door until the lift came. I went back to my desk and rang the agency. I wondered if there was something worth reading in the confidential files. When I got through, I asked them if they could book me somewhere else next week.

"But I thought you were happy there – can we discuss it? Hang on, there's someone on the other line, I'll have to call you back."

I typed away for a bit and then the woman from the temp agency called me back.

"Well, it's odd, I've just had a call from someone at Magister's I haven't spoken to before, and she said they aren't happy with you and you read some confidential documents. I'm sorry, but they're very hot on all that."

"Well, I didn't go through any filing cabinets if that's what they said."

"It is a bit strange. Was there some trouble – is that why you rang? Did you upset somebody? I'm sure you didn't mean it. I'm going to call Joanna and have a word with her and see if we can sort it out."

So I hung up, and the phone on Joanna's desk rang after a while and she had a muttered conversation, and then she beckoned me over.

"That was your agency asking if we were happy with you, and I said you were one of our best audiotypists. I think there've been some crossed wires somewhere! You're happy here, aren't you?"

"I've been perfectly happy up to now. I mean, everybody's friendly and the work's interesting and the food's nice!"

"Look, shall we sleep on it and we'll talk in the morning?"

I said OK. I supposed she was going to ask some questions. I can always avoid the creepy Mr Magister who has my picture on his wall – the girls are around, and Alan's usually in the foyer, and there are crowds of people and the top floor feels like a long way away. It was only Melusine who didn't like me, but I couldn't imagine her liking anybody. She must be jealous. I wonder what her job is? Something important, to have that big office.

Going-home time rolled round, but I was a bit late leaving as Joanna asked me if I could finish the tape I was working on and there was only about half an hour's worth to go. Most of the other girls went, and Joanna stayed at her desk for a bit, reading stuff, then she left. I finished the task eventually, and rang Mike to say I was just leaving and sorry I'd be late.

"Never mind," he said. "We can get a takeaway or open a tin. Take care in the fog. Look out for Jack the Ripper."

I got my coat and took the lift downstairs and the building was pretty empty. There were different security men in the foyer, nobody I recognised. They must be there all night. I went out into the forecourt where the street lights were making haloes in the thick fog. I could hardly see the street, but it seemed quite empty and quiet. It was about half past six by this time.

I turned to the right, to walk along the pavement bit next to the entrance to the underground car park. You can't walk straight out, there's a shrubbery in the way. There was a tall man with white hairin a dark overcoat standing there getting car keys out of his pocket. I passed quite near him, and just then there was a growling and snarling, and two black dogs ran through the open gates from the street towards us. Their fangs were bared and they looked bigger than normal dogs. I crouched back into the spotted laurels and they made straight for the man. One of them leaped up and clenched its teeth round his arm, and the other one worried his legs. He dropped the briefcase and staggered back.

Banks of white mist rolled up and over us like a cloud fallen to the ground, and I felt cold rain on my face and there was a smell like coal fires. I couldn't see the street at all any more. We were alone in the white mist. The man raised his arm to try and shake the dog off, but the beast held on, standing on its hind legs.

The man began to chant:

Agares, Amdosius, Amon!
Barbatos, Baalberith, Bifrons!
Crocell, Dantalion, Decarabia!
Focalor, Forneus, Furcas!

The dogs still held on, and if he fell over they would start chewing him to bits. I jumped out of the laurels and ran towards them, calling out:

Canis major, canis minor!
Potnia Theron stands before thee!
Let him go now, I adjure thee!
Or into pieces I shall tear thee!
Avaunt, Belphegor! Avaunt, Anubis!

I held out my hands and the hounds let go of the man's arm and leg and fell back, whining and yelping. They cringed down on the concrete and crept towards me, still grinning. I pointed to the gates and they galloped through them and disappeared into the white mist, which folded around them and followed them and vanished too, leaving just normal fogginess and drizzle.

The man was panting and picking up his briefcase. My invocation worked — I must have used "adjure" correctly and not mixed it up with "abjure".

"Are you all right?" I asked.

"Anna!" he said. "You answered my call just in time."

"Mr Magister!" I said. "Magister, Lemaitre. Of course it's you, Gilles. But are you really all right?"

You may wonder why I was so friendly after all I've told you about him kidnapping me and keeping me in his chateau so that he could raise evil spirits, but he was always rather charming and we'd even been friends in a way, though enemies as well. He did command some demons to attack me in the underground carpark, but I escaped with the help of Hermes.

"They've just bruised my arm and torn my trousers. I'll be all right. This coat is very thick."

"Of course you know Dorinda hates you now – those were her dogs, weren't they? She even brings them to college and people think they're sweet."

"To college?" He was getting his breath back. His face was the same, but more lined, but he looked even thinner and his thick hair was now white. It suited him, rather.

"Yes, she's lecturing about the Occult."

"I wonder what she's been studying, or whom she's been consulting. I've been keeping a low profile."

"And she found you anyway. But what do you mean you called me? I didn't hear —"

"I have been summoning you for weeks - months. We can't stay here, they'll be shutting the gates soon — can I give you a lift anywhere?"

"Thanks, but no thanks!"

"All right, I understand. But I need to talk to you. Shall we walk round the square?"

"All right. Not for too long."

We walked out through the gates and along the pavement to the square, which is surrounded by Georgian houses and odd churches. We started to go clockwise - Gilles was walking slowly and limping a bit.

"So how did you summon me?"

"I performed the Conjuration of the Shadowy Vortices, with the help of - friends."

"I've been temping at Magister's for months."

"I saw your picture in a gallery, and they used you as a model for our brochure - I knew you would be here soon."

"I didn't know the pictures in the field were going to come out quite like that - I thought it was another fashion shoot. I'm not surprised to see you, anyway. I've been expecting to bump into you ever since I heard you'd got out of prison. I've been watching for you over my shoulder."

"The past is the past. I don't want to harm you."

"Dorinda is furious you got out and left her there and then never got in touch. She wanted me to help her attack you. And she said you'd found somebody new and she's terribly jealous."

"I told Melusine to try and find you through the model agency, but apparently they have rules. I thought the art company might be less scrupulous."

"I've met Melusine — she doesn't seem to like me any more than Dorinda. She told the temp agency today I'd been going through confidential files, and she's got me the sack!"

"Don't worry about her. She'll do what she's told."

"But why were you summoning me in the first place?"

"Dorinda will try again. And there are other things..."

A few people came up behind us, walking briskly because of the cold and the drizzly rain and the fog. Gilles flinched as they passed, and drew closer to me.

"What things?"

"We should be safe here," he said, looking back. "They don't like coming too near churches. And besides, you are stronger than they are."

"People keep telling me that." We were passing the Eglise Protestante, and there's a Catholic one on the other side.

"Don't worry about Melusine, her powers are solely of the mind. She helped me take over McRobbie's and set up Magister Enterprises."

"I've never worked out what it actually does."

"It is Melusine's brain child."

"It's odd – I saw her in Cavendish Square talking to my friend Christine from college. Christine never mentioned her, but I supposed it was about a job."

"Christine – you know her? Yes, she did a little job for the firm."

Was this the mysterious "acting job"? Perhaps she's in another of the brochures.

"And I suppose the police are looking for you, too, Gilles."

"And you could quite easily tell them where I am. But before you do that, let me put something to you." He looked at me thoughtfully, as if he was working it out.

"I'm listening."

"Your friend Christine - you wouldn't want anything to happen to her, would you? You see, if you mention to anyone that you've seen me, and who I am, and where I am, things would unravel, and she'd be caught in the net."

"Oh dear, what was the job she did? Something illegal? I suppose I shouldn't ask. All right, then, I won't, if it would get her into trouble. And it's probably silly of me, but I'm sorry for anybody who goes to prison."

"I read a lot there, even the works of that vile sentimentalist Charles Dickens."

"So did Lawrence! Dorinda said she read a lot too."

"I've tried offering you riches, and you weren't interested, I remember. But you can always change your mind. I offered you a life with me -"

"I'm married now."

"Really? Congratulations," he said politely. "And what does your husband do?"

"He's a detective sergeant."

"That could be awkward for both of us. And you wouldn't want your friend Christine to come to harm?"

"No, I wouldn't. If you're involved in something illegal, I don't know about it. So can I go home now?"

"No, wait!" He stopped and held out a spidery hand, but he didn't touch me. "You wanted to know why I summoned you."

"I'm curious."

"It wasn't just to protect me against Dorinda. Or to ask you to run away with me. While I was in prison I performed the Evocation of Nothingness and called up a djinn – an afreet. A creature of smoke and fire. It threw sand into their eyes and assisted in my escape."

"I knew you'd used magic to get out. You cast a glamour over them. So anyway, it worked."

He looked at me and said quietly, with a bitter smile: "One can call abhumans from the outer circle, but can one persuade them to leave again? I see something dark always in the corner of my eye. It wasn't prison that turned my hair white. And it takes human form. It poses as one of the staff."

"And you think I can banish it? I can't promise anything." This was a far cry from the kind of spells I used to do – getting people's boyfriends back and cursing unpopular teachers. "Now can I go? And it looks as if I'll have no work next week."

"Don't worry about that – I'll deal with Melusine."

"She won't like me being in the building."

"I told you not to worry. But you don't want anything to happen to Christine -"

"No, I don't."

"When Dorinda attacks again, she may attack the whole building. You've made friends here?"

"The Scottish girls in the typing pool."

"And with a djinn haunting the place..."

A thing of fire and smoke...

"And if you refused to help Dorinda, she will bear a grudge."

"You mean she'll be after me too?"

"Exactly. And what does your husband think about all this? The policeman?"

"He doesn't know about most of it."

"Naturally, he doesn't know you're a witch, and you wouldn't want him to."

"No."

"Well, it's up to you."

I had another idea. "What about Lawrence? Can you get him out of prison? He's quite unhappy."

"You'd like that? I'll see what I can do. And you won't tell anyone you've seen me? It's a bargain?"

"It sounds fair."

"And you'll help me exorcise the afreet? The djinn?"

"I'll do some reading. But I can't attack Dorinda, only protect us from her."

"Pity." He smiled again.

"You see – it might work."

"Yes, I do see. Meanwhile... a truce?"

"A truce."

He took a card out of his wallet and handed it to me. "Here are my private numbers."

I didn't offer him my number, but I took the card and put it in my purse. We had traversed three sides of the square now and the main road with taxis and buses and shops was up ahead. I stopped, and he held out a hand. We shook hands, and I walked towards the main road while he turned back towards the Magister building. I supposed they could let him in again to get his car. There were a few spots of blood on the pavement – the hellhound must have bitten him.

"And see a doctor!" I called after him. He turned round, raised a hand, and walked on.

I walked off to get a bus home, mentally going over everything that had happened. It's blackmail all round, of course, but what can I do? I suppose I'll have to tell Mike everything one day, but not until all this is over, one way or the other. And is it safe to attack a djinn – what happens to it once you've exorcised it?

CHAPTER SIXTEEN

When I got home, Mike was watching telly.

"Sorry I'm late," I said. "I had some stuff to finish – it means I get paid for an extra hour, though!"

"Is it still foggy out?"

"It is a bit."

He left the telly on, and got out some bread and eggs and started frying them. I slumped in a chair and watched Z Cars for a bit.

"You're a bit quiet," he said.

"I'm tired. The work's interesting, but you don't get much time to relax. Perhaps I'll see if I can get another modelling gig – then I'll have the rest of the week free if I'm lucky."

"Let's go out into the country," he said. "Even though it gets dark so early. I've got some time off end of next week. What about that place where you used to live?"

"Haslemere."

"You could show me round it."

"It's only about three-quarters of an hour on the train. There's a museum, and some old buildings, but I never really noticed them. And it has woods. They're beautiful in winter too."

It seemed like a long time since I was at home, or in Nature, or in a wood in winter. I was thinking about djinns. And I thought I remembered the Museum had a booklet on hellhounds. We ate the fried eggs, and then had tinned pineapple, followed by instant coffee.

I went to work the next day – the forecourt and the spotted laurels looked just as usual. Perhaps Melusine would get me the sack and I could forget all about it. I smiled at Alan covertly, as his boss Mr Gremory was lurking around talking to another guard.

In the typing pool I said good morning to everybody and we settled down to pound keyboards. After about half an hour Joanna came over to me and I took off my headset.

"Don't worry about yesterday," she said in an undertone. "The top floor rang through again and it was all a misunderstanding. I'm sure you didn't look at anything you shouldn't have."

"I just delivered the envelope and chatted a bit to Melusine."

"I said we liked you and you worked well and fitted in."

"Gosh, thanks! I think my typing must have improved."

"It's fine. They're bringing up some of the new typewriters – I'll see you get one of them. And I've spoken to the agency."

Then the tea lady came round and we all slacked off for a bit and ate digestives.

"The tea doesn't taste the same out of these," grumbled Clemency, looking at her new teacup – red and white plastic with a space-age handle. I dialled the Stella Orrin agency and Janice said: "I'm glad you've called – I was going to call you. There's a shoot next Thursday – you're quite in demand after those arty pictures."

I said I'd be there, and went to talk to Joanna.

"I don't want to take advantage, after you've been so kind – but can I have Thursday and Friday off? I'm juggling another job, but it's only occasionally."

"No, that should be fine." She looked at her calendar and made marks on it. "Actually we'll be quite quiet at the end of next week."

In the afternoon, Mr Gremory and some of his minions came in with the new machines on trolleys. The other fellows did all the work — taking old typewriters away and doling out new ones — while he bossed them around and bantered with the girls. The new machines are big and heavy and the ribbons go in differently, but they're much less hard work to type on.

"I don't think I'll ever get used to this," said Kirstin, practically crying, after we'd tried them out for a bit. Joanna came over to her.

"I'll see if we can get a bit of training," she said. "They've got them on other floors and the girls there should be used to them. It's just changing the ribbon that's a bit tricky."

She's all right, even if she isn't as stylish as Olive. Olive wouldn't have liked newfangled typewriters — perhaps that's why she left.

I went to college in the evening and met Ginevra and Rowena, who were sitting with Harvey the chemistry student and an Indian boy in glasses.

"How's your essay getting on?" Rowena asked me.

"Oh, I'm just copying bits out and going on about witches and Lucius praying to Isis."

"I'm sure that'll pass muster!" said Harvey. "This is Amit – meet Anna."

"Are you studying chemistry too?" I asked him.

"I am studying esoteric philosophy. And I am going to some very good lectures given by Miss Theron. And you?"

"I'm just doing Greek and Roman mythology once a week."

"That must be very interesting too. I have taken many notes in Miss Theron's lectures, but I find it hard to make sense of them. While she's talking it's a different matter! It all seems coherent then!"

"The early alchemists were the first experimental chemists," said Harvey. "Though they said they were looking for imaginary things like the Philosopher's Stone."

"It was not imaginary," said Amit. "All that about crucibles and elements is symbolic, you see. They were looking for their heart's desire, or so I believe. But to Miss Theron it is all about spiritual development and moving to a higher plane. What did the Greeks have to say on the subject?"

"Well, this book I'm writing an essay about has witches who turn people into animals and fly."

"You don't get what you want in this life, but if you're lucky you get what you need," said Rowena. "If you got what you wanted you probably wouldn't like it. The journey not the arrival matters."

But I noticed she and Harvey were holding hands under the table.

"The nuns used to tell us not to dabble in the occult," said Ginevra.

"Don't dabble – jump in with both feet!" said Amit, smiling. And we got up and collected our files and books and went our various ways.

***

Work was quiet, and men came in and hung up Christmas decorations, and they put up a tree in the foyer, with silver and gold decorations. We went to the canteen and tried out the salads – white rice, peanuts, raisins and sweetcorn, with chopped-up peppers for colour. I bade goodbye to the Scottish girls on Wednesday night and said I'd see them on Monday.

"Going on a little holiday?"

"Just a day out, and working at my other job."

"Tell us all about it!"

"Will do."

Actually I haven't told them about the modelling, though they might always recognise my picture on the brochure. Except we never get to see the finished product of anything we do — I suppose it all gets whisked to the top floor. I wonder who else works up there? There's space for more offices.

***

On the Thursday I turned up at Stella Orrin with my hair down, and Janice was waiting for me to drive me to the shoot. We chatted a bit on the way, though it wasn't very far. When we got there the location turned out to be a house done up with dark wallpaper and potted palms, and old watercolours on the walls in gold frames, and a conservatory on the back. The owners were there in the kitchen, and they gave us coffee and biscuits, and showed me a bedroom where I could change, with a small rack of clothes and shoes.

Janice came up there with me, to tell me what I was supposed to wear.

"Where are the others?" I asked. "Shouldn't we wait for them?"

"Oh, no, it's just you today. I told you you were popular."

And she got out another long dress, plus a white pinafore a bit like the ones the smaller girls wore at the convent, with frills on the shoulders. I togged up, down to the black stockings and strap shoes, and we went downstairs. Mrs Homeowner was hovering in the hall, and came with us into the living room, where Helmut and the usual types were setting up the lights and stuff.

"We spent every weekend for weeks restoring the cornice and the ceiling rose!" said Mrs Homeowner, pointing it out. "And then someone said we could hire it out for photography and filming. We put back the stained glass in the front door, too, and found some lustres for the mantelpiece."

"You made a good job of it!" said Helmut. "I think we're ready to start if you don't mind leaving us to it."

She went out – I think she'd have loved to stay and watch. But at least Janice was there, co-ordinating, because otherwise it was just me and the fellas.

"Would you stand in front of the mantelpiece, Anna?" said Helmut, and we got going.

The fireplace was huge and made of black marble, and they moved some potted palms to either side. It was a bit gloomy, but Mrs Homeowner must have had fun doing it all up. The "lustres" were candlesticks with glass dangly bits, and Helmut came rather near me to adjust them so that they caught the light in the right way.

We moved round the room, and I stood in front of the window, where there were some ferns in a glass case, and pretended to look at an old photo album. Then I changed into a different getup, and we went into the conservatory – more plants. And into the garden, which was bare and wintery with berries on the shrubs. I tried to identify them, while my feet got colder.

"Enough!" said Helmut after I'd been standing for ages in a big woolly shawl and a plaid frock with smocking, and we went inside and had some more coffee, and some Kitkats and crisps Helmut and the boys had brought, and I changed back into jeans and a jersey.

"I thought Janice might be your mum!" said Mrs Homeowner.

"Thanks very much!" said Janice.

"Don't you have to be chaperoned by a family member?"

"Not Anna!" said Helmut. "She is quite a young lady."

I got my wedding and engagement rings out of my purse and put them back on. "I don't think I'll look 14 for much longer, though."

"Cash in while you can!" said Helmut. "Are you saving for a holiday?"

"A house – eventually," I said. "What's a nice place to live that isn't too dull?"

We had a nice chat with Mrs Homeowner, who had her hair in a bob and a big colourful jersey. No wonder, her house was pretty cold except in the kitchen where there was an (authentic) Aga. I admired her wallpaper and she said it was William Morris, and she asked me where I lived now.

"Kentish Town," I said. "I like it, but we haven't got a garden or a balcony."

"I've got some friends with a terrace house in Chiswick," said Mrs Homeowner.

Soon we went back to London and I went home and Mike asked me how it had gone.

"It was just me – in ye olde clothes again, in a house all done up like a set for a BBC historical drama," I said. "A very nice lady owned it and she talked all the time and made us coffee."

"Perhaps she was lonely," said Mike.

"I don't think I'll go on looking 14."

"It would be odd if you did. Anyway, your brain is grown-up!"

"I'm glad you think so!"

I looked in the mirror – no crow's feet as yet.

"We need to get up early tomorrow," said Mike, "Because it gets dark about four."

CHAPTER SEVENTEEN

We got up pretty early, and as we were going out I saw a letter for me on the shelf in the hall that I'd missed yesterday — it was Elspeth's writing. We got the tube to Waterloo and bought return tickets. It was only just getting light, and men in black overcoats and bowler hats and umbrellas were pouring off the incoming trains and down to the underground.

"Good luck we're going the other way," said Mike. We went to a newspaper stall and Mike bought the Times and I got a Woman's Own.

We just had time to get some more coffee so we went to the tea hut in the middle of the platform — all the other cafés seem to have closed — and got milky coffee and doughnuts, and slurped and ate, getting sugar on our chins, then ran for the train. As we expected, it was quite empty and we rattled off and looked out at Battersea, where all the houses are small and terraced, with only schools sticking up out of them.

"Look, Watson!" said Mike. "Schools! Lighthouses! Beacons of the future! That's what Sherlock Holmes said. Perhaps he was right."

"I didn't know he cared."

"He was always waffling on about life and quoting German poets."

"Detectives have to have a gimmick, don't they?"

I opened Elspeth's letter and read it in bits as the train went out of London and I looked out for the cemetery and the mosque. Mike read the paper.

After a bit he said, "I wonder if houses are cheap in Battersea? I'll ask around."

"Good idea." I was in the middle of a long description of a field trip Murray and Elspeth had been on, to see folded sedimentary rocks and old volcanoes in Scotland, staying in youth hostels and having silly jokes. It sounded fun, especially the being out in the open air bit. And cooking rice and cabbage and cheese in the hostel.

"Who's your letter from?" asked Mike.

"My schoolfriend Elspeth – she's doing geography at East Anglia. Or something to do with development or the environment – they've been up in Scotland looking at rocks."

"Like going on a long walk but looking for clues."

We looked out of the window for a while, then Mike said:

"It'll be Christmas soon. We'll have to go to the staff Christmas Party."

"Great!"

"You won't want to go to church or anything?"

"No, I don't think so."

"We might go and sing some carols, though. Actually the police choir will be doing a carol concert."

"Let's go to that."

"They have audience participation. You can be Good King Wenceslas's page."

"We're nearly there," I said. "This is Milford."

The view was starting to look more wooded and countrylike, with bare trees and brambles and Old Man's Beard, and we passed a corrugated iron shed and then we were at Haslemere and we got out.

"We could walk, but let's get the bus," I said.

"I wanted to see where you used to live, is it far?"

"No, it's just off to the right past that chapel on the corner."

We went and looked at our terraced house and front garden, and I saw a few shrubs Mum had planted.

"That path leads into the woods, they backed onto our back garden. But let's get the bus into town now." I didn't want to look into the windows and see other people's sofas and chairs.

"OK, we could come back in the summer."

We got the bus for a few stops and got off near the refined dress shop and Madgwick's radios and another little chapel, and walked up the high street.

"It's all very historic," said Mike, looking at the half-timbering. "I suppose some of it's real and some is fake?"

"I suppose so. How can you tell? I'd like to go the museum, and wander round the shops and then we could have lunch."

"That place looks nice." He pointed to Howard's café, opposite the museum, set a bit back from the road.

"It is."

We went into the museum and looked at the nature table which had a lot of dead grass and moss, and then on into the bit with the stuffed animals. We gawped at the fluorescent rocks under ultraviolet light, and the models of early people in their diorama with painted mammoths in the distance, and took the sides off the beehive to look at the bees, and said hello to the Egyptian mummy. I pointed out a few gods in the hieroglyphics.

"There's Thoth, the god of wisdom."

"Baboons are pretty wise."

"And that's Horus, the hawk. Now, which one is Osiris? Here he is with a hook and a flail. And I think this one is Nephthys, Goddess of rivers, death, mourning, the dead and night."

"You like all this stuff, don't you?"

"I even go to the British Museum on my lunch break."

Thoth/Hermes the god of tricksters must be inspiring me to tell all these blatant lies. But one day I won't have anything to keep quiet about, I hope. We went out to the front again, where there are dolls in national costume, and into the little shop, and the lady at the till recognised me.

"I expect you left school a long time ago! You wanted to know about saints and sacred springs."

"Yes, I've been working for ages, and this is my husband!"

"Well, well, fancy that," said the lady. "What can we interest you in today?"

I was turning round the stand with pamphlets and booklets on it. There was one of the history of buttons and I picked it out and twiddled the stand some more.

"I'm looking for the one about the Hound of the Baskervilles."

"That's a good Sherlock Holmes story to start with," said Mike, who was looking at the postcards. "This place has got a theatre!"

"And a cinema," I said.

The lady came over and picked out a booklet. "This one has the Hound in it."

It was called Black Shuck and Barguest, and I bought it, and the button one. Mike got some postcards of some half-timbered buildings in the high street. We went out at the back to the garden, which is huge, and looked at the view of leafless trees in the valley. Then I dragged Mike off to look into Mr Mason's woodyard, but there was nobody there I knew, and then to Barbara's riding stables. There were a few people around sweeping up and doing things with straw bales, and some of the horses were sticking their heads out of their loose boxes. We patted their noses, then we crossed the high street and dropped into Miles's the hardware store and Mike went all round it.

"I'm sure there's something here we need," he said. "Doesn't it have a nice smell? Couldn't we put a deck chair somewhere?"

"Do you mind if I go on to Howard's – you know, the café we saw?"

"No, go ahead, I'll be along in about ten minutes."

So I went back up to Howard's and went in and there sitting at a table was my old friend Charles, wearing a three-piece tweed suit and eating dainty sandwiches and reading what looked like school essays. I went and joined him.

"Hi, Charles!" I said. He looked up and saw me and got awkwardly to his feet.

"Anna! How lovely to see you! Are you back home for the weekend? Do sit down."

"It's not home any more – my parents moved away."

"Ah, I remember."

"We didn't live here long, but it feels like home."

"To me too – I commute to school, didn't want to move."

He teaches geography, and you'd never know he used to be a local wizard. A waitress came up, but I said I was waiting for someone and she went away. Charles looked inquiring.

"I left my husband in Miles's, he'll be here in a minute, but before he comes —"

"So you got married? I thought you were terribly modern and didn't believe in such things."

"I always thought it was a good idea, it's just that you don't have to. And lots of my old friends are married or engaged."

"Perhaps respectability is returning."

"Perhaps. Look, now you're here, I wonder if you can help me with something you might know about?"

"Anything I can do." He looked serious.

"We'd better talk quickly. What do you know about djinns?"

"Djinns, afreets — I'd have to look them up."

"What I really want to know is how to get rid of one."

"Oh dear, that could be serious."

"It's not for me, it's for a friend."

"Really?"

"Yes, really. He called it up when he needed help getting out of a tight place." I couldn't help shuddering at the thought of the thing hiding in the air-conditioning or the rubbish chutes of the Magister Building.

"But it's quite close at hand," said Charles.

"It is. But I said I'd try and exorcize it or whatever you do."

"Is this a suitable friend, I wonder?"

"Oh, not suitable at all." I remembered Charles probably knew Gilles – hadn't he been at the bonfire at Halloween? But if I explained, Charles might want to tell the police where he was, or something. I thought it better to keep quiet.

"Write to me here." He took a notebook out of an inner pocket, tore out a page and quickly wrote an address on it and passed it to me. I put it in my purse.

"And if you'd write your address and number here..." He handed over the notebook with its little pencil and I wrote our address.

"So you're Anna Savage now? I'll do some reading and let you know. Is it urgent? I'll do it this weekend. Marking can wait."

I saw Mike looking in at the window, and then he came in. Charles stood up politely again.

"Mike, this is Charles, he teaches geography," I said, and they shook hands and sat down.

"And what do you do, Mike?" asked Charles.

"I'm a detective sergeant."

"That must be interesting. So you're living in London now?"

"Yes," I said, "Kentish Town."

"A pleasant area I hope?"

"Not bad," said Mike.

"It's near the Heath," I said, "But somebody was stabbed in the chip shop queue the other day."

"It doesn't happen every day," said Mike. "But we thought Battersea looked nice, from the train."

The waitress came over again and I picked up the menu.

"Well, I must be going," said Charles, putting the essays into a briefcase. "It has been lovely to see you again, and to meet you, Mike. Goodbye, Anna. Immediate thoughts — try giving him something to do. Idle hands, you know!"

And he went and got his overcoat from the hat stand by the door.

"What a polite bloke! What were you talking about?"

"Oh, problems at work."

"You never say there are any."

"Just some difficult colleagues."

"Good thing you can always move on! What shall we get – soup, sandwiches, or scrambled eggs?"

"Soup AND scrambled eggs, I'm starving even after those doughnuts."

"Sorry I was a bit long, I went on down the street and found a record shop and bought a few 45s. Some old Beatles I never got, and Dionne Warwick's Raindrops Keep Falling on My Head."

He looked around for the waitress, and I said: "I suppose some people keep moving on and reinventing themselves and changing their names."

"They're usually conmen. Where's that girl gone?"

"I wouldn't want to do that. You'd have to keep leaving people behind."

"They do – trouble is, people see through them. Oh, there she is. Miss!"

She came over and we ordered soup and egg on toast and ate it — they still put cress on everything — and looked at the records and leafed through the booklet about Black Shuck.

"Black dogs have been reported from almost all the counties of England, the exceptions being Middlesex and Rutland," read out Mike. "Where did they go wrong? 'A straunge and terrible wonder' — I can't read this old writing."

We had some coffee, and paid, and then walked down the road past Woolworths where there's a path that goes behind Barbara's stables and into some fields and woods and we communed with nature for a bit and got muddy feet. Then the light was fading and it began to rain lightly, so we came back, had a quick cup of tea in Mary's Cake Kitchen and got the bus back to the station and home. I read some more of the Black Shuck book — it warned you not to stare into their "strange, pretercanine" eyes. They are also called Gytrash or Wish Hounds, but there wasn't much about protecting yourself from them or their owners. You can try shooting them with a silver bullet, but they just pass straight through.

****

"Well, that was a nice day out," said Mike as he scrubbed the mud off our shoes in the sink with old newspapers.

"Wasn't it?"

"Who was that old geezer? Did he teach at your school?"

"No, he was a friend of a friend of Mum's — that was how I met him. They belonged to some kind of group."

"That's the trouble with the country — what would you do with yourself? You'd have to join groups. He seemed nice, though."

"Yes, not all of them were."

"Sherlock Holmes said the same — there's more crime in the smiling and beautiful countryside than the worst slum."

And he looked in the bookshelves and got out some Holmes stories for me. When I first met him, I didn't even know he read books. So many people don't. I asked him what he wanted for Christmas and he said The Lord of the Rings in three volumes.

CHAPTER EIGHTEEN

I got a letter from Charles, with some helpful and some unhelpful advice. Tie three of your hairs round a bullet? You'd have to have a gun, and it would be awfully fiddly. I didn't see how I could get hold of viper flesh, wolfsbane or elf bolts, but he said they were only suggestions. Fire, juniper, tar, cold iron, opium and cowbells would be easier. But apparently you can recognise djinns by their greenish cast of countenance and fiery eyes.

It's not so far from Magister's to Soho, so I went out one lunchtime to the Indian shop and bought some hippy temple bells which they still had in boxes, and some sparkly green and pink plastic bangles. I showed the bangles to the Scottish girls when I got back because they always want to know what anyone has bought.

One of the ingredients was incense, so I asked Joanna if I could have a long lunch-hour to do some shopping and she said OK. Perhaps I can take liberties as long as Gilles needs me.

I got the tube to Victoria, fortunately it's quick, and looked for the Catholic Cathedral, which I'd never been to since I stopped going to church. On the way there I saw a little shop with a window full of dog collars and priests' shirts and soppy statues of saints and the Virgin Mary. Inside was more of the same, and a man behind a counter looking out through festoons of wooden rosaries.

"Do you have any Cathedral Incense?" I asked him. It's what mum used to have. She occasionally threw a handful on the fire.

"Yes, indeed," said the man who was quite young with curly hair, and he went and looked on the shelves. The shop was rather like the joke shop by the British Museum — full of unlikely things and pictures of people in old-fashioned clothes. I looked at St Rita flying up a staircase.

"Is this what you were looking for?" he said, holding out a tin. I looked at the ingredients — frankincense and myrrh, which are real plants, or rather resins from plants. Frankincense is a tree called Boswellia elongata and myrrh is a bush.

"You harvest myrrh by wounding the tree and bleeding the sap," I said.

"Goodness!" he said. "I never knew that. It's quite symbolic, isn't it? Anything else you need?"

I wanted some holy water, but I don't think you can just buy it. I put the incense in my satchel and thanked him and asked him how to get to the cathedral.

"Further up Victoria Street on the right!"

I went that way and found it. The cathedral is quite impressive from the outside, and very stripy. I went in and there was the usual smell of stone and incense, and the sound of people's footsteps echoing, and people whispering — they do that in Catholic churches. There were big wooden confessionals along the walls, and banks of candles twinkling in the gloom.

Fortunately there weren't many people about. I wandered around a bit and looked at the mosaics — they are shiny and new with a lot of gold, but they stop halfway up, and the ceiling is far off and dark. I strolled casually back to the front door where the holy water stoups are (they're basins in the wall). I made sure nobody could see me, and filled a bottle I'd brought and put that in my satchel.

Then I moseyed around a bit more, looking into the side chapels and checking out the bookstall (more pious pictures, but in a more modern style). There was a priest in a cassock hovering near it and he came up to me.

"Everything all right?" he asked, smiling. He had rimless glasses and looked quite young.

"Oh, everything's fine," I said. "I've never been inside so I wanted to see what it was like. I like old places."

"This one is quite modern," he said. "1903."

"It's got a lot of atmosphere, though."

"You know, if you need to chat, there's always somebody here."

"Really? That's nice to know."

"I saw you fill a bottle with holy water — it's all right, people do that from time to time. Especially Italians."

"It's for protection."

"I hope it works!"

I thanked him and said goodbye. All Catholic priests have to be exorcists. Charles said they banish demons to the Red Sea, but don't have power against afreets. I went back to work and Alan was behind the desk and for once nobody else was around.

"Hi!" I said, and he said "Hi there".

"They let me go and do some shopping. What are you reading now?"

"She."

"She?"

"Just She – who must be obeyed." He showed me the cover, of a semi-naked woman standing in some flames. "Dead good. Lost civilisation, woman who lives for four thousand years. Look out, Mr Gremory is lurking — he always has time on his hands."

"I don't think I'd like that – living for four thousand years, I mean."

"Me neither."

Mr Gremory came out of a secret side door (you can't really see it's a door from the outside), and I ran for the lift.

***

Just after tea, when the ladies with trolleys had gone, Joanna got a call at her desk. She talked for a bit and then beckoned me over.

"They want you on the top floor again," she said. "Someone will meet you at the lift. Straight away!"

So off I went. I was a bit nervous, but it wasn't Melusine this time, but Gilles who met me at the lift, wearing a dark suit.

"Hello!" he said. "Come this way!" and he unlocked a different door and ushered me through it. We went along a passage and then it opened up into a big room with black leather settees and windows all down one side. The curtains were drawn back and there was a brilliant view of London and buildings with lit windows. There was a bar, and copper lampshades hanging from the ceiling, and low teak tables with Swedish glass bowls, and it all looked something out of a magazine.

"Have a seat," said Gilles. "Can I offer you a drink?"

"I don't really drink, thanks, and we've just had tea."

"Something soft?"

"OK. Fizzy mineral water."

He poured me out a glass at the bar and put a slice of lemon in it, and poured himself a drink of some kind and sat opposite me on a low black leather armchair. All the furniture was square, with a few chrome bits, and the carpet and curtains were mustard.

"What do you think?" he asked, gesturing at the flat. I supposed there must be a bedroom and bathroom somewhere.

"The view is fantastic."

"This is a Gabo," he said, pointing to a small metal whirligig on a plinth.

"Nice!" I said. "Very different from your old place."

"Gothic even down to the gargoyles!" he laughed. "It's still mine. I'm not sure what to do with it. Surround it with model dwellings? What do you think?"

"It would be a shame to build over that garden. And would the council let you?"

"I'd just have to bribe them!"

"So anyway, why did you ask me up here?"

"Well, you're my employee. And I gave you a little job. How is it progressing?"

"I've done some reading, and I asked a friend. Oh, he can keep a secret."

"But is he likely to know anything useful?"

"Yes, he's a wizard, or at least he was before he gave it up." I didn't want to mention Charles by name, since he was now trying to be an ordinary geography teacher.

"As long as he didn't burn his books."

"I don't think he did, because he said he'd do some reading and he's told me a lot of stuff. I've got some of the necessary..."

"Ingredients? Equipment?"

"Yes. I got some mercury out of a chemistry set, and some sulphur. Girls at the convent used to keep blobs of mercury in their pencil cases, but apparently it's quite poisonous."

"Better handle it with kid gloves."

"I got some little glass bottles for putting home-made perfume in. Anyway, I'm not quite ready yet."

"I thought the 31st of January would be a good date. It's a Thursday. You probably understand its significance."

"Do I?"

"It's Imbolc."

"Oh, of course! One of the witches' festivals."

"The passing of the goddess from the crone to the maiden. But tell me more about your researches."

"I did some reading in the college library, and there are a lot of Egyptian demons. There's one called 'He who drives off those who would demolish'. But if you set a demon to catch a demon... And the wizard says Catholic priests can't exorcize djinn — they are too powerful."

"I can call spirits from the vasty deep!" quoted Gilles ruefully.

"But the wizard did say one thing that might come in useful meanwhile. He said, 'Give it something to do'."

"And what did he mean by that?"

"I thought he meant like when the demons say 'What shall we do next, O Master?', and you tell them to go and count the sands of the seashore, or find the centre of a labyrinth, or pick up flax seed."

"That's an idea. Well, thank you for your progress report. Let me give you the tour."

He showed me a switch that dimmed the lights, but it was only so that we could look out of the window and pick out landmarks like the Houses of Parliament. He had a super hifi and radiogram and lots of LPs, mainly classical.

"We only listen to pop music," I admitted.

"I believe you can get classical 45s," he said. "You know, you could still share all this with me. My offer stands."

"I told you I was married."

"What's marriage these days? Nobody takes it very seriously."

"Well, I do. I'm not very modern."

"I thought jealousy was out. Or is it 'possessiveness' now?"

"You're just teasing me. And Joanna will be wondering where I am. Besides, it's nearly time to go home."

"I suppose you want to be safe," he sneered.

"Don't you?"

"What do I want? I want everything. And it's working — look around you." He gestured at the sculpture, and the bronze floor-to-ceiling curtains. "I mean, what's the point of magic if it doesn't get you what you want?"

"Dorinda would say it's all about moving to a higher plane. And Rowena would say if you got what you wanted you wouldn't really like it. But I think Dorinda's students are a bit disappointed."

"Of course you don't give anything away to students at evening classes. But don't go just yet. Let me just show you this gizmo..."

He pressed some buttons and a cinema screen arose out of a sideboard.

"That is clever," I said.

"You sit here." I sat on the leather settee while he flipped another switch. He came and stood behind the sofa. I remembered I'd kicked him on the shins once – I hoped he did. The screen lit up and a film started playing, of a room full of people and somebody giving a kind of lecture in front of another screen. It was Melusine, and she was talking away about a seafront development, and showing the people slides of flats and swimming pools and beaches.

"So that's where we get the tapes from," I said.

"Yes, presentations and focus groups," he said. "You see what I mean? Look at all those potential investors just longing to move money from their bank accounts into mine."

On the screen Melusine's voice sounded quite warm and interested and she was even smiling. "But she's different," I said, puzzled. "Perhaps she's putting on an act."

"Don't worry about her. I've told her to leave you alone." He stopped the thing and the film faded and disappeared, and the screen sank back into the sideboard. He was still standing behind me. "I see it all the time, now," he said. "In the corner of my vision. And now it has red eyes, like points of light."

"How horrible!" I said, getting up and turning round. "But I really must go now."

"Let me know how you get on. You have my private numbers. And what's yours?"

"You don't think I'd give you my home number?"

"Perhaps not. Let me show you out." He led me out the way we'd come and stood by me while the lift came which fortunately didn't take long.

"One other thing," I said.

"Yes?"

"That the wizard said — you can spot them when they're disguised by their fiery eyes and greenish complexion."

"Ah, indeed."

"And don't forget about the ropes of sand."

"I won't."

The lift came, I got inside and he stood looking at me while the doors closed.

I told Mike I was writing another essay, which gave me an excuse to go to the poly at the weekend, and I began to put together a ceremony and some invocations. There was some stuff about banishing souls into nothingness, but that seemed rather unfair and cruel, even for a creature of evil. And besides, it might rebound. I looked up wolfsbane, and the book said it grew in mountain areas and was really called aconitum and was terribly poisonous, but it was used in Chinese medicine under the name Fu Zi.

I dropped into the British Museum, which was full of schoolchildren as usual, and visited the gods I had invoked before: Hermes/Thoth and Bast, the black, cat-headed avatar of Diana. I muttered a quick invocation:

Great Moon Goddess, hear my plea!
If there's danger, come to me.
Hail to thee, O power feline,
Bound to master menace canine.

I looked out for the friendly staff, but perhaps they're always on the night shift. We've got to do another essay, and I'll pick the Egyptian gods if I'm allowed, or perhaps look into the way they're all Greek gods really, and why. I've still got that novel about Ancient Egypt by a woman who thought she had lived before. I'll read it again. It's the kind of thing Alan might like.

CHAPTER NINETEEN

It's almost the shortest day, when demons walk. "The Goddess in her dark aspect calls back the Sun God, the Ancient God of the Forest, who returns from the shadows" — or so it said in one of the books on our reading list.

We went to Mike's staff Christmas party at the club, and the same people were there. They'd set up some long tables with red checked tablecloths and we ate turkey with all the trimmings and pulled crackers and wore silly hats. We went to the police choir's concert, too, in a church in the City, and they were really good as naturally they had a lot of tenors and basses. The audience joined in on some of the carols. I like In the Bleak Midwinter and God Rest You Merry but I do get sick of Ding Dong Merrily on High.

I got cards from Ginevra, and Murray and Elspeth, and I got one from Ianthe, and I sent them all trendy cards from Paperchase in Tottenham Court Road. Ianthe said she was going to be in London over Christmas, and did I want to meet up, because her parents would be in Denmark.

I bought some holly and conifer branches from a flower shop, and stuck them up around the place. It symbolises life – it gets darker and darker, but the evergreen trees show that darkness can't conquer light. I bought some candles as well, and lit them after dark, and put them in the windows. Mike got some tinsel and draped it around the bookcases.

"What about a tree?" he asked. "There isn't really room."

"I'll look for a miniature one."

"What shall we cook for Christmas lunch – how about a chicken?"

"I think I can do that."

"I'll get a cook book as one of your presents, and give it to you early. We don't absolutely have to have sprouts, do we?"

"No, let's have frozen peas instead. And I'm sure you can get instant gravy."

"Shall we invite people?"

"Who could we invite?"

"Who do you know who's on their own?"

"Perhaps Ianthe – she'll be in London, and her parents are in Denmark."

"Is she the frightening one who lives in Oxford?"

"That's her – she's not frightening really. Just rather Women's Lib."

"Oh well, ask her anyway!"

"I will. And can I ask Alan? He's never talked about his family and perhaps he hasn't got one."

"Who's he?"

"You remember, he was one of the Harpsden Manor crowd, but he turned up at Magister's as a security guard."

"Right, he should be reintegrated back into society. We can start by asking him to Christmas lunch."

I got a miniature tree from Woolworths – a fake one in a pot. While I was there I got a plastic chandelier as well, and Mike put it up in the living room. It's an improvement on the woven straw lampshade that came with the flat. I rang Ianthe and she said she'd love to come. She'd be staying in a hotel and going to some Women's Lib meetings and political cabaret.

"Not to a panto?"

"Oh, no I won't!"

"How will you get to us – there won't be any buses or tubes?"

"There'll be taxis."

"Oh, good."

I asked Alan if he was doing anything for Christmas and he said no, so I asked him too and he said it would be a blast.

****

On the day Mike and I gave each other some small, silly presents, then we put the chicken in the oven and basted it from time to time, and parboiled the potatoes and then put them round the chicken, with chipolata sausages. I'd got a Christmas pudding and some double cream, and we had a bottle of Asti Spumante in the fridge and another bottle of white wine and some beer and Coke. We pulled out the table and put a tablecloth on it, and the miniature Christmas tree and some candles and green branches in the middle, and laid it and put chairs round. There was just about room in the flat for four people.

They turned up in good time and we gave each other cards and presents, and all had a glass of Asti Spumante, which was fizzy. Alan was wearing ordinary long hair instead of the pony tail, and a denim jacket. He'd brought a guitar, which he stashed in a corner, and gave me a book called Monkey by Wu Cheng En, and I gave him a paperback of the Epic of Gilgamesh.

"I hope you haven't already got this one," I said. "It's about a flood even before Noah. We did it at college."

"If you want to learn about ancient civilisations you can't leave out the East," he said.

I gave Ianthe Murder Must Advertise, and she gave me The Female Eunuch, which had a picture on the front of a swimsuit made out of a woman's body. I gave Mike the Lord of the Rings. Then I opened my present from Mike, which was in a huge cardboard box, and it was a new record-player. I hugged him and thanked him.

"I'll plug it in after lunch – we can put the old Dansette under the couch."

I put on the peas and did them quickly, and added some butter, and made some instant gravy, and Mike carved the chicken. He'd worked out how long to cook it and it really did taste OK. Then we ate the Woolworth's pudding with double cream, and toasted each other in Asti.

"Here's to 1971!" said Ianthe.

They all said the food was great and actually it wasn't bad.

"I'm thinking of trying this macrobiotic diet," said Alan. "Apparently it really frees your mind. But you have to eat a lot of brown rice."

"Brown rice? Like brown bread? Where do you get that?"

"There's a really good shop near here, in Brecknock Road. It's called Bumblebee!"

"I'll look out for it."

I made some coffee. The sun was shining outside, even though it was cold, so we decided to go for a walk. So we put our coats and hats and walked up College Lane to Parliament Hill.

"It's not like being in London," said Ianthe. "We might be in, I don't know, Godalming or somewhere quaint."

"The days'll even start getting longer now," said Mike.

"Yes, you always forget how dark it gets, don't you?" she said. "Did you ever do any modelling, after all, Anna?"

"I did – it's been quite fun, and you get to go out to the country in a minibus."

"It's a bit cold for that now."

"So what's the Female Eunuch about?"

"Women's oppression. Germaine Greer says women should live without men in communes in Italian farmhouses and bring up their children together."

"So where are they going to get the children? And what happens when they run out of farmhouses?" asked Mike.

"I don't go along with everything she says," answered Ianthe. "She thinks we ought to wear no pants, make our own eyeliner and give up brushing our teeth, as well!"

We got to Parliament Hill and there was a bit of light left and we made it to the top where there was a little crowd of people who said "Happy Christmas!" to us, and we all watched the sun go down together. Then we ran down again, and walked briskly back to our flat. We cleared away the lunch, and I made some tea while Mike plugged in the new record player and Alan looked at our books. We had tea and Christmas cake – a chocolate log with a robin on it – and then Alan got out his guitar and we sang a few carols like O Little Town of Bethlehem, and a few folk songs we knew, like Greensleeves.

Then Mike tested out the new record player, and it worked perfectly, and we listened to records for a bit. I lit the candles on the windowsill, to symbolise the return of light and longer days.

"Just tobacco, guv!" said Alan, lighting a Players Number 6.

"They've tightened up the law," said Mike. "Better keep on the right side of it."

"OK, officer. Did you ever read the Hobbit?"

We said we'd loved it, and Ianthe said but wasn't it all about a vision of a non-existent Merrie England?

"It's more about finding an ancient treasure," I said.

"And battles," said Mike.

"And Bilbo finds himself," said Alan. "They say he's a thief, so he is a thief."

"I feel sorry for Gollum," I said.

"But don't they all go 'There's no place like home' in the end?" asked Ianthe.

After a bit she said she'd phone for a minicab, and offered Alan a lift. They thanked us and went off together.

"I like your friends," said Mike.

"They are nice, aren't they?"

"I can't see them waltzing off into the sunset hand in hand, though, can you?"

We tidied up, and listened to more records, and watched Christmas specials, which were pretty awful, and went to bed.

CHAPTER TWENTY

I went and found Bumblebee, the health food shop, and got some brown bread which Mike said was like cocoanut matting, but it was better toasted with lots of butter and honey. We went back to work, and it was cold and miserable, and even snowed a bit.

I seem to be at Magister's permanently now — perhaps Gilles tells them to book me. Alan thanked me for the Christmas lunch and said it beat hanging around in his bedsit. "And I like your red-haired friend!" he added. "She's a laugh."

The tapes keep coming, and it feels as if I've transcribed the same one over and over again. I suppose they keep getting different people together and asking them the same questions and telling them the same stuff. Or are they just trying to find me something to do?

The typing pool is a bit like our classroom at the convent where we used to have to sit and "study" for two hours after tea. We either read or did the work we'd been set, and weren't allowed to talk. It was dire. And it still gets dark at about four. The Scottish girls are fed up, and Mike is working very hard at the moment on something called a "long firm fraud", when not reading Lord of the Rings.

I asked the Scottish girls if they'd had a good Christmas, and they all said they'd been back to their families. They asked what we'd done and I said we'd had a couple of friends round.

"I don't think I can stand this place much longer," said Kirstin at lunchtime, kicking her chair. It was another dull day and we looked out on the dreary scene.

"Can't wait till I get back to sunny Aberdeen!" said Flora.

"Don't be a silly billy, the sun NEVER shines in Aberdeen!" said Kirstin. "And all the houses are grey. It's worse than London."

"I thought London would be exciting," said Flora. "I thought people went to nightclubs every night. And we're stuck out in the hostel, going to the pictures in hen parties."

"They talk about the bright lights, but we never see them!" said Kirstin.

Somehow we dragged through the afternoon. Joanna asked me if I wouldn't mind staying on for half an hour to finish what I was working on, and I said OK. It was just her and me and the dark outside, again, and I jumped whenever anybody slammed a door or shouted "Goodnight!"

I finished the tape in the end and handed the pages over to Joanna and said goodnight to her and rushed off to wash my hands and fix my hair by pushing the hairpins back in. Someone came in behind me and came up to the mirror – it was Melusine. She had a scarlet lipstick in her hand and drew her mouth back on in a different shape to the real one. I wanted to tell her it looked old-fashioned.

She caught my eye in the mirror.

"Off home?" she grated, in quite a friendly manner, for her.

"What does it look like?"

"Could you pop up to my office for a moment — there's some stuff you could take down to the front desk for me. I'm not going for a bit."

"Oh, all right," I said, "Anything to oblige." So we got in the lift and went up to the top floor and into her office. I stood about while she fiddled about with some files on her desk. I wasn't going to mention that I knew she'd asked them not to book me any more. Perhaps she was trying to make amends.

"I just need to make a phone call."

She dialled a number and when somebody answered she said "Yes – right away," and put the phone down.

"The papers aren't that important. I really just wanted a chat," she said.

"Really? What about."

"I wanted to say you shouldn't worry about going on working here. I sorted it out with Mr Magister. I'm not going to ring your agency."

"I see. Well, that's OK then. Is there really something you wanted me to do for you?"

"Yes. Take these files —" She handed them to me. "And go down and leave them with the person on the front desk. As you're going that way anyway."

I took them, and said goodnight, and went back to the lift and down to the foyer. There was nobody there but the head guard, Mr Gremory, sitting behind the desk writing on a form in a big lever-arch file. I went up and handed over the folders.

"I'm supposed to give you these," I said.

He took them and looked into the first one.

"More bloody time-sheets!" he said. "The admin in this place gets more ridiculous by the day. It's like painting the Forth Bridge."

He put them in a drawer, then stood up. I said, "Well, goodnight," and walked towards the glass door turning my coat collar up because it was raining outside.

"The front door's locked," he said, coming round the desk. "And the gate. It's on a time switch and we can't over-ride it. We'll have to let you out through the carpark and the fire exit."

Just then Melusine came out of the lift. I wondered why she couldn't have taken the files down herself. She was wearing a smart coat and a scarf over her head, tied under her chin, and she came over to us and said: "Are you going to let us out the back way?"

"Follow me, ladies!" said Mr Gremory, and unlocked the concealed door in the wall. His eyes were still bloodshot, as if he smoked dope. Perhaps he does. We walked down a little corridor, with him on one side of me and Melusine on the other, and down some stairs, and through another door and came out in the carpark.

"Here we go — it's a bit of a walk, but you'll be able to get a bus from the other end," said Mr Gremory. The carpark entrance was shut with a grille. He took my elbow, and opened another door that led to a concrete tunnel with lights in the ceiling. "It's just the back entrance," he said.

Now he was holding my arm tightly, and Melusine came round to my other side.

"Couldn't you unlock the gate? How does Mr Magister get in and out?" I said.

"I told you I can't over-ride it!" he said crossly.

"Mr Magister can't help you now," rasped Melusine. "You didn't really think I'd just let you come back, did you? Come on, Kane."

And Mr Gremory grabbed both my arms from behind and pushed me further down the tunnel. It bent round so I couldn't see where it led. I tried pulling away from him, but he dug his fingers into my arm. We struggled a bit and my hair fell down. I threw my weight forward, and then back, and stamped on his instep. He staggered a bit, and I sagged at the knees and straightened up suddenly so that the top of my head hit his chin. I could hear his teeth click together and he let go a bit, so I lunged forwards and muttered "Hermes, help me!" and took off down the corridor, because they were between me and the door we'd come through and it had shut again.

I ran round the bend in the corridor and on. I seemed to be running so fast that the air whistled past my ears and my hair streamed out behind me. At the end was an opening with a concertina door which was half shut and I zoomed through the gap and out into a little alley full of dustbins and old cardboard boxes. It was raining harder and I could hear footsteps pounding along the passage behind me.

I ran out of the alley and took a chance and turned to the left, and found myself in a street that looked familiar — it was the one with the Stella Orrin agency in it, and there were lights in the windows. I looked back and saw the two of them scoot out after me, so I rushed to the door of Stella Orrin and pressed the doorbell. I shouted "It's Anna!" into the intercom and somebody buzzed me in and I got inside and shut the door behind me and whizzed up the stairs.

There was a different girl behind the desk, not Janice. She was wearing a big purple jersey and rather a lot of makeup.

"Hi!" she said. "I'll just call through. I thought we were all here now."

"I'm not booked," I said, panting a bit. "But I work here sometimes. Can I dry off a bit until the rain stops?"

"Of course you can. I thought I recognised you." She pointed to the wall, where they'd hung the picture of me in the field. "I'm Delphine. I'll tell Helmut you're here. And how about a cup of tea?"

"No need to bother him," I said, but she said he'd like to know and phoned through and he came out of the studio.

"Anna, my pet! You are soaking!"

"Delphine's just gone to make some tea."

"Oh, good, bring it into the studio, Delphine," he shouted into the kitchen. "Come and see what we're doing, Anna. You look quite grown up in your work clothes."

We went into the studio and there were a lot of girls sitting around in dressing gowns or nylon "negligees" with lace and ribbons, and a girl in jeans with the usual clothes rail with a sheet thrown over it.

"Delphine is bringing us some tea," said Helmut. "This is Anna, who sometimes works here."

I took off my wet coat and draped it over a chair. The girls were all rather tall and large, but they were very smiley and friendly and found a towel and dried my hair for me, and one of them insisted on brushing it.

"No rush, anybody," said Helmut. "Anna, you don't want to go back out into that downpour. Do you need to ring home?"

"No, Mike will be working late."

Delphine came in with a tea tray and we drank tea and ate biscuits — I was pretty hungry by now. One of the usual men with straggly hair and a moustache was arranging a curtain and some plinths.

"Anna models children's clothes, but she is not a child, as you can see," said Helmut. "I wonder if we've got any clothes to fit her?"

"How about the white stocking set?" asked the girl in jeans, who must be the stylist. Another bloke came in carrying an armchair and they put it on the plinth.

"See if you can find something. No need to feel left out, Anna! And this is better money, you know. I'm sure we can use you today."

"Still chucking it down," said one of the girls, pulling a blind to one side and looking out of the window. "Stay and watch. We always have a laugh."

"Now I'd like Merlina and Amethyst," said Helmut. Two of the girls stood up and slid off their negligees. Underneath they hadn't much on — one was wearing a corset with suspenders and stockings and high heels, and the other had on a bra and pants and the same. Helmut got them to pose around on the plinth and pretend that one of them was taking the other's measurements and stuff like that.

The other girls carried on drinking tea and knitting, and Helmut said Merlina and Amethyst could rest now and called two other girls up. They were wearing even less, in fact one of them had nothing on top. They stood about while the blokes brought in some different props and chairs.

The stylist held up a lacy camisole and waved it at Helmut. "This would fit her, don't you think? And we've got a small belt and some white stockings."

"How about it, Anna?" said Helmut. "We could fit you in after these two." He was staring down his lens and twiddling dials on the camera. "The money's better in glamour."

"I think I'll go home now," I said, putting down my cup of tea and putting my coat on, even though it was still sopping.

"Another time!" said Helmut. "It's time you graduated. You're beginning to look quite 14."

"I hope she isn't!" said the stylist, rather snappishly. I left Helmut to explain, thanked them for the tea and went out through reception again.

"It's still cats and dogs, dear!" said Delphine.

"I think I'll chance it," I said, putting my sopping coat back on.

"OK, then, take care!"

And I went out and down the stairs. Surely Melusine and Mr Gremory would have given up and gone home by now, if they had homes.

CHAPTER TWENTY-ONE

There was nobody about, just a van parked further up the street. I shut the door behind me and stood on the step for a bit under the doorway. The wind had got up and the rain was slanting sideways. I walked north, hunched forward and with my coat collar turned up. As I came up with the van, the door opened suddenly. I stepped back, but someone behind me pushed me inside. He got in beside me and shoved me along the seat and we drove off.

"Bad luck!" said Melusine, who was sitting on my left, while Mr Gremory drove. She laughed nastily. I wondered how she could put on a pleasant face and voice to persuade people to invest in their holiday villages. Her headscarf and coat were soaked.

"You're pretty wet," I said. "Where are we going?"

"For a little drive," said Mr Gremory.

"I saw you go into that place," said Melusine. "I stood in a shop doorway waiting for you to come out while Kane went for the van."

"You run pretty fast," said Mr Gremory. "But not fast enough."

I supposed it had been all rot about not being able to open the front gate. The windscreen wipers slooshed back and forth, and the streetlamps and shop fronts were reflected wavily in puddles. I couldn't tell where we were going, but we had the river on our left for a bit and I guessed we were somewhere near Victoria Station.

"Who were your friends in Soho?" asked Melusine.

"It's where I work sometimes," I said.

"Good. Well you can go back there and stay — if you ever get back to London."

She was huddled against the van's door, looking even sourer than usual. She didn't say any more and we drove down the Kings Road where all the boutiques are though people say it's over now, like Carnaby Street. We went right down to the end and turned left and came out at the river again and some pretty houses on the right and a big factory or something with a chimney up ahead, and Mr Gremory parked the van.

"Just the night for a party on a houseboat!" said Melusine, and Mr Gremory got out on his side and pulled me after him. This time he held my arms in a half-nelson behind me.

"No more of your tricks!" he said. "You made me bite my tongue. It's really painful."

"Good!" I said. "I hope you need stitches."

Melusine went ahead of us and we went through a gap in the parapet and onto a slippery wooden walkway. The water was licking up against the stone wall of the embankment. There were a lot of houseboats moored, rather far out in the river, rocking a bit on the waves. There were lights in some of the windows, but most of the boats were dark.

"Most of the houseboaters come ashore in the winter," said Mr Gremory. "Sensible of them."

We walked along the planks, out into the Thames, then turned left where the bridge carried on between the boats, with a rickety-looking railing. We went almost to the end, where it was all dark. There were trees between us and the street lights now, but I could just see the rain hitting the boats' roofs and the water.

Melusine stepped onto the deck of one of the boats, and Mr Gremory lifted me onto it, then leaped on himself and grabbed my arms again. Melusine opened a door at the front of the boat, and he shoved me inside, and I fell forwards into the dark, tumbling down a short set of wooden steps and landing in a heap on the floor.

"We're just going to leave you here for a bit," said Melusine, looking in through the door as I picked myself up. "I wonder where you'll get to? The tide's going out. How do you fancy Holland? Just remember not to come back!"

She shut the door and locked it again and their feet thumped on the deck as they leapt off. There were some clanking sounds, and then I heard them walking away along the bridge, and then silence.

I was in what might have been a cosy room inside the boat, with seats round the sides, and little curtains. I tried looking out of the windows, but I could only see the blurred lights from the road, swaying back and forth, and moving about. The boat seemed to slip round sideways, and the lights and the bank got further away.

The boat rocked frighteningly and then settled down, and continued downstream. My eyes got used to the dimness a bit, and at least the boat was floating. The rain made a row on the roof, and I felt around and found a gas stove with a kettle, and a table with a drawer in it. I opened the drawer and felt inside and found some matches, but they were too damp to light.

Well, what now? I still had my handbag slung over my head and shoulder, but I didn't have a lighter or anything useful. I tried pushing the door, and it gave a little way. It was cold inside, and everything felt clammy and gritty. There was a chair by the table and I picked it up and tried hitting the door with that. It gave way a bit more, and I could see it was shut by a staple. The door frame felt quite crumbly and rotten, so I hit it again with the chair, and this time the staple came out of the wood and the door opened. I put my head out and saw that we were rocking towards a bridge so I went inside again and held the door shut so as not to see anything. We hit the bridge with a loud bang, and went sideways for a bit, and it got very dark, but then we came out on the other side and went on going.

I felt around in the drawer some more, trying to find some dryer matches. There were several boxes at the back, and I got one to light. Then I saw a lighter and a candle in a holder on a shelf, so I put that on the table and lit it. There were some glasses on the shelf, too, so I put one upside down on the formica top of the table. I looked out of the window at the choppy, dark water and tried to remember where the Fleet flowed into the Thames. It was probably a bit further down, but I made a quick invocation to the Naiads of the Fleet.

Naiads, naiads of the Fleet
Hear me from your watery seat
Maidens of the chilly wave
Hear me, hear me, come and save.

I had a little notebook in my bag, and I wrote out the alphabet and cut out the letters with nail scissors and put them in a circle round the glass. I put one finger on the bottom of the glass, and said quietly, "Frank, Frank, please move if you're there! It's Anna. I'm in a jam. If I ever needed help it's now. Can you come?"

Nothing happened, then the glass quivered and slid towards the letters. It spelled out F-R-A-N-K H-E-R-E.

"Frank!" I said. "I'm on a houseboat adrift in the middle of the Thames."

He said: "W-H-E-R-E?"

"I think I'm somewhere near Vauxhall Bridge by now."

"OK."

Then the glass stopped moving. I wondered what he'd do. I looked out of the door again into the driving rain. We went under another bridge, not hitting it this time, and I thought I saw Lambeth Palace coming up on the right. I came back into the saloon and there was Frank sitting on the chair by the table in the candlelight.

"Am I glad to see you!" I said.

"You are in a pickle, aren't you?"

"They shut me in here and then set me adrift."

"The bad guys?"

"Some of them. It's not always easy to tell who they are. Melusine and Mr Gremory."

"They want to get rid of you, anyway."

I flopped down on a little banquette seat and looked at him. He seemed quite at home.

"We're just passing Lambeth Palace," he said.

"We're going awfully fast."

"I don't like to leave you," he said, "But I think I'd better let somebody know where you are, though I'm not sure how."

"You need to tell the police."

"A message on a blackboard? Write them a note?"

"Tell Mike, my husband. He's a policeman, and I know where he'll be."

I wrote down Mike's name and the address of the police station on another page of my notebook. He didn't pick it up, but looked at it.

"Ah, I know where that is," he said. "But how do I get through to him?"

"It's OK — Mike can see you! The others can't, but it means you can just stroll in and go and find him."

"Excellent!" he said, getting up. "What does he look like?"

"He's slim and pale, with short brown hair in a widow's peak."

"Were you dancing with him at Halloween?"

"Yes, I was. It's such bliss having somebody to dance with."

"They never should have shut the Locarno," he sighed. "Well, I'll be off. I'll let you know what's happening. If you spring a leak, bail with that saucepan. You don't want to join us yet!"

"Some time — but not quite yet!" I said.

"Why don't you put that candle in the window?"

"Good idea — I wonder if there are any more?"

And he walked up the steps, out into the rainstorm, and disappeared. I felt around in the drawer and found a few more candles, and some old nightlights, so I stuck them in the windows and lit them all. I sat down at the table while the boat rocked about, sometimes with the pointed end facing East, and sometimes broadside on. I looked out of the window, but couldn't see any more bridges coming up. Perhaps they'd open Tower Bridge for me. Will I end up haunting London and see the future and flying cars after all? I suppose Lyons will shut.

We twisted about again and the door flew open and banged against something. I looked round, and Frank was back again, sitting on the banquette.

"Don't worry!" he said. "Help is on its way. I just walked into the police station and looked around for Mike. He was in an office on his own and I told him where you were — said it had been an accident and you'd got cast adrift. Said we were having a bit of a party down there by the houseboats. I'm not sure if he believed me."

"Never mind."

"Anyway, he shouted for Fred and Stan and told them to get on to the River Police. I think I can hear them now."

I couldn't hear anything, but then came the buzz of an engine, and men shouting, and a bang as I suppose they reached out with a boathook or something.

"I'd better be going," said Frank.

"Oh, thank you so much! Goodbye!"

"Until next time!"

He walked quickly through the kitchen and into what must be the bedroom, and was gone. Heavy boots landed on the deck, and there was a lot of yelling, and a bright light flashed in through the windows.

CHAPTER TWENTY-TWO

The door opened and Mike leaped down the little flight of steps and I flew into his arms and we stood there while the boat rocked and the candle flames quivered and guttered. He let me go as Fred came in.

"Here she is!" said Mike.

"You don't half get into some scrapes, young lady," said Fred. "Come on, let's get you into the launch. Well done lighting the candles – you were easy to spot."

"Are you OK?" asked Mike. "You're awfully wet."

"I got wet in the rain," I said. "When I looked out to see where I was."

"I gather it was a wild party," said Fred. I was glad Frank had briefed me.

"They're a bohemian lot down those houseboats," said Mike. Fred went up the ladder again and held out a hand to me and pulled me up on deck. The police launch was shining a bright light onto the river, and Mike and Fred swung me onto the deck of the launch where I fell against a man in a waterproof coat. He hung onto me, and Mike and Fred jumped onto the deck, and I was shoved into the brightly lit inside where there were banquettes like in the houseboat. After a bit more bumping, we set off. I supposed they'd tied the houseboat on at the back.

"Do you want to get a cup of tea at the pier, or would you rather go straight home?" asked Fred.

"Straight home," said Mike. I'd begun to shiver.

"We can have a chat tomorrow," said Fred. "After all, you're in police custody! Can't get away! We'll send you both home in the car. Mike, you're off duty."

We got off at the police pier, which was a bit scary and I had to climb a ladder, but they kept holding onto me, and passing me to each other. We went through a floating wooden office with phones and things, and up a ramp to the Embankment. There was a little crowd of people with umbrellas who must have been watching. A man in a bowler hat said "Glad you're safe!" and a woman smiled and nodded. She was getting pretty wet and her long skirt was trailing in a puddle, so the bowler-hat man courteously held his umbrella over her.

We got into the back of the police car that was waiting by the pavement, and Mike gave the driver our address. We held hands until we got home. We said goodnight to the driver and went inside, and I took off my wet coat and went and got a towel for my hair. Mike put the kettle on and some bread in the toaster.

"What time is it?" I said. "it feels awfully late."

"It's only about ten." He sighed. "You won't do this sort of thing again, will you? I don't know how you get away with it."

"I promise I won't. I really want to lead a very, very quiet life."

"Are you hungry?"

"Do you know, I'm starving?"

He got down a can of beans and opened it and poured it into a saucepan. I turned on the electric fire and huddled over it.

"It's lovely to be back indoors," I said.

We ate the beans on toast with tomato ketchup and it was about the nicest meal I'd ever had.

"So did Frank tell you where I was?"

"That shabby friend of yours who hangs out with the shoplifter — yes, he did. Told me where to look, but didn't really explain what had happened. There was nothing we could keep him for, but he didn't hang about. Perhaps he doesn't like the police. What did happen?"

I sent a quick thought to Hermes, Prince of Tricksters, and plunged into the story I'd been making up in the car.

"I bumped into Frank and Elsie as I was coming out of work. They said they were due at a party in Chelsea and did I want to come? So we got into Frank's sports car..."

"I wonder where he got that from? Perhaps he nicked it! Still that must be how he got to the station so quickly — and away."

"So anyway, we drove to Chelsea Embankment and parked the car, and walked along a kind of plank bridge to the houseboat — it was near the end. It was pouring with rain and we ducked inside and there were lots of people and we had a glass of sherry and olives and anchovies on little bits of pastry."

"Surely you can't fit many people in those things?"

"They were sitting round the sides — and on the floor. After a bit I thought I'd go home. I like Frank and Elsie but the rest of them weren't exactly my age group."

"When did you meet them?"

"When I first came to London. I met Elsie in a Lyons. We were sitting at the same table and we just got chatting. I remember saying it was hard to make friends."

"I suppose you were keen to make any friends. I don't blame you."

"Anyway, Frank said he'd see me back to the Embankment. So we went outside again and it was pouring even harder. He said it would be safer if we jumped onto the next boat, and so on, instead of chancing the walkway, which was slippery. So I went first, but the rope must have come undone and the boat floated out into the river. It all happened so fast. He shouted to me that he'd call the police and I told him to get you and where you were, and then I floated off, and I went inside to get out of the rain."

"I see. I hope you weren't too frightened?"

"I was pretty terrified when the boat hit the bridge, but then it missed the next lot. And I knew you'd come and get me."

"You're such a tough nut! We'll go down tomorrow and get the story from the other boaters. Why didn't he just phone? No phones on a houseboat, of course — I suppose he didn't want to waste time looking for a phone box that hadn't been vandalised. Though why didn't he go to Kings Road?"

"I told him to get you!"

"People don't always think clearly in an emergency," he said kindly, and added that he'd clear up while I had a bath. I was exhausted from the whole thing, and from telling all those lies. I couldn't have told him about Melusine and Mr Gremory, not while Christine and the Scottish girls were still working for Gilles, not to mention all the rest of the nice ordinary people in the building. And Lawrence was still in prison. Nothing must go wrong. I just had to keep on keeping quiet about everything. But what about work tomorrow?

****

It carried on raining half the night, drumming on the roof while the wind whipped the branches of the trees outside our window. Our bedroom is a little extension at the back, with the bathroom off it. Mike got up and had breakfast with me but he said he'd probably kip a bit more before he had to go to work.

I said: "You know, I don't think I'll do any more modelling."

"OK. But I thought you liked it."

"I've got a feeling the agency is a bit dodgy after all."

"What gave you that idea?"

"Well, the last few pictures they took of me... I mean, I was very covered-up, but it was more like a costume. Lots of frilly white petticoats, and camisole tops. And I've seen some of the pictures they took — they sell them framed in art shops."

"All within in the meaning of the act but..." he said. "Appealing to a certain type of older gentleman?"

"Yes, that's it exactly. They warned us at school against people like that. I'd better go to work." I slurped down some coffee.

"A bit early, aren't you?"

"I've got some extra stuff to do."

On my way to work I went into a phone box and rang Gilles on his private flat number.

"How nice to hear from you! Even at this early hour. Are you on your way here?"

"Yes, I am. But look — Melusine still isn't happy with me being there."

"She's never happy, hadn't you noticed?"

"Yes, I suppose you're right. But she tried to get rid of me again. Well, it's a long story, but last night she set me adrift on the Thames in a houseboat."

"How very ingenious! And you're here to tell the tale? It was a dark and stormy night!"

"Yes, the river police caught up with me."

"Our wonderful policemen! Of course, you're married to one, aren't you?"

"I was worried about coming into the building again. You see, one of the security guards was helping her."

"Really?" he asked rather sharply.

"Yes – the head one, Mr Gremory."

"Oh, I see." He sounded thoughtful.

"But I suppose you can just give him the sack, can't you?"

"I would love to do your bidding, but it may not be that simple. Anyway — how are your researches going?"

"I've got all the incantations and the stuff ready."

"Good. Don't worry about Gremory and Melusine, I'll have a word with them. Come straight in the usual way."

"They'll be rather surprised to find I'm not in Holland by now."

"Or Tilbury."

We said goodbye and rang off, and I walked into the building a bit fearfully. Fortunately Mr Gremory wasn't there, only Alan and another security man.

"Mike read that thriller – the one about She Who Must Be Obeyed!" I said to Alan as I passed.

"You should read it too, there's some good stuff about a flame of immortality."

"I will." I skipped off into the lift and the safety of the typing pool. I took off my coat and Joanna called me to her desk. She handed me an ordinary size envelope and said in a discreet voice: "Note for you – from the top floor." I put it in my handbag, and nipped off to the ladies to read it. It was from Gilles, saying to come up at five on Thursday, our date, so at lunchtime I rang him from a phone box again to say that was OK. I didn't want Kirstin teasing me about one of the porters being in love with me or anything – but perhaps I should pretend, for camouflage.

That evening, Mike came home at about ten as I was watching telly. I made us some tea, as he said he'd had some food in the canteen. He put a paper down on the table.

"It's nice and homely in here," he said. "You made the Evening Standard — thrilling rescue by River Police."

I hadn't turned on the wall lights, just the lamp on the table, though nobody seems to watch telly in the dark any more, or go on about it ruining your eyesight.

"I wouldn't want to live in one of those houseboats, though," he went on.

"Nor me."

"Never again, eh?"

"No — and they'd be cold and damp."

He was sitting on the sofa and I was sitting on the floor. He put his hand on my shoulder.

"We went down there earlier — some of those boats are quite snug inside. There were people at home in one or two and we asked them about the party. And of course we had to take your boat back and tie it up securely. Nobody knew how it had got adrift or 'slipped its moorings' as they say, and our river colleagues said someone must have tampered with it. And nobody seems to claim it, either. We're trying to get a list of who owns all the boats, but it's difficult. They're a law unto themselves. Can you remember anyone you met?"

"Not really, I was just talking to Frank and Elsie. They were all a bit middle-aged."

"Yes, they struck me that way. And bohemian. You know, red curtains and ladies in big skirts. Any excuse for a gin and tonic. Pottery with flowers on it."

"Yes, that's what they were like."

"Anyway, they didn't seem to know anybody had been having a party, or having anybody over. It was such a wild night that a lot of them had gone ashore because of the storm, and the ones that stayed put said they'd 'battened down the hatches' and prepared to 'ride it out'. But you said it was down at the end — the end boats were empty, and the people nearby said they'd gone ashore and stayed with friends. We described Frank and Elsie to them but they couldn't be sure if they'd met them."

"I forgot to say I love you again," I said.

"As long as you do. And I do too. You know what I mean."

"I could have written it on something."

"Good thing you didn't have to. You're safe, that's all that matters. Nothing else matters, really."

We sat and held hands for a bit, and I thought about the ritual.

CHAPTER TWENTY-THREE

On the day of the banishing, I packed the ingredients in my satchel as before, and some sheets of paper with the invocations. Mike was still working shifts and getting back late. Gilles had told me to come up at about five and go to his office, so I asked Joanna if I could leave a bit early again and she said that was OK.

So just before five, I put on my coat and scarf as if I was going home, got my bag and satchel, said goodbye to everybody and went out to the lift. It was dark outside and I could see the lighted windows of other office blocks through the mist.

I got out at the top floor and turned right into Melusine's office. She wasn't there, but there was a girl standing with her back to me, brushing her shoulder-length brown hair at a mirror on the opposite wall, and putting it in a pony tail.

"Um, hello," I said. "I've got an appointment with Mr Magister."

She turned round.

"Christine!" I said. "I knew you worked for Magister's sometimes but I didn't know you'd be here. I'm sorry, is it a secret or something?"

She didn't smile as usual – in fact she was staring at me as if she loathed me.

"You weren't supposed to come back!" she gritted. "But Giles told me to leave you alone. I wonder how long this partnership will last. I don't like being told what to do."

"I don't understand," I said feebly, taking a step backwards.

"Stay where you are!" she barked. I got the desk between me and her, and said: "I'd go, but I was asked to come up."

Lying on the desk were a pair of glasses, a handbag and a black wig. She pinned up her ponytail, picked up the wig and pulled it on.

"Christine's a friend of yours, isn't she?" she said. She added the glasses and was Melusine again.

"Yes, she is, I met her at the model agency. And she works for you, doesn't she?"

"How do you know that?"

"I saw you talking to each other."

"You're such an idiot! Fortunately."

"Oh, thanks."

"Let me spell it out for you."

She opened her handbag and got out a compact and lipstick and reapplied her mouth and carried on.

"I met Giles when I'd just applied to Regent Street Polytechnic. He had the money, and he wanted to make lots more, quickly. I told him about an idea I'd had. I have lots of ideas. He bought this building and the business, and I told him how to operate the scheme. But I'm the one who runs it."

"How clever of you. What is it exactly?" I hoped she'd be flattered.

"I couldn't spend much time hanging around at college, but I wanted to get my degree. I've got an IQ of 190, I don't have to work too hard. But I couldn't do all that chatting to people and going to the pub and the disco and on holiday. I couldn't be bothered. And I've never gone in for friends. But employers and investors don't just want a degree, they want proof that you're a normal person. You need pictures of yourself with mates on a Greek Island to stick up in your office. So I got a copy of Spotlight — that's the actors' directory — and looked through it for someone who looked like me. And there was Christine — the spitting image. It was like looking in a mirror. Her name is almost the same as mine, too! Christina is my middle name. I'm really Melusine Haywood and she's Christine Hayward. I can always say they made out the degree certificate wrong, or alter it. It's just a couple of letters."

"So you wrote the essays and read the books and went to the lectures?"

"Yes, and the rest of the time I was here, working out ways of parting people from their cash."

"And she came to the canteen and the disco with us, and had lots of friends and boyfriends."

"That's another thing everybody expects you to do." She was still looking at me crossly. "And she was great at giving presentations — as me, as Melusine."

"And it was her in the film — oh, I see. I saw you together and thought it was odd. Did you swap clothes? And she'd have to — it must have been terribly complicated."

"We synchronise schedules. I'm good at that – look at my charts! And she told me about her friends just in case I bumped into any of them, but if anybody talked to me I always pretended I was in a terrible hurry and just rushed off. I saw you there a couple of times but of course I wasn't going to say anything. I didn't want Mr Magister to find you."

"People just thought she was a bit absent-minded. But they couldn't understand when she did the work because she's popular and goes out all the time."

"She's got the brains of a prawn. She wanted to be an actress!"

"Well, it seems she's pretty good at it."

"That was why I wanted to study history. Machiavelli and Plato, they tell you how people are sheep, and will believe anything, especially if you tell them you're going to make them rich."

"But you're just selling people houses and holiday homes, aren't you? What's clever about that?"

"We're selling them films and glossy brochures, and dreams of fairy gold! They don't want to buy the houses, they buy shares in the projects. But there are no projects! They're all just Potemkin Villages!" She began to laugh.

"Potemkin Villages - what are they?"

"They were made out of cardboard to fool Catherine the Great!"

"And I thought it was a film set."

"And then you came along and threatened to spoil everything! But I couldn't get rid of you. Giles refused to give you the sack. He likes you. He moons over your picture."

"Oh please, it's not like that at all!"

"You're popular! I've seen you, at college, and here, chatting with your friends. But they're all empty-headed, I don't need them. I don't need people. I'm happy without them!"

She was still laughing, but crying at the same time. She pulled some tissues from her bag and took off her glasses.

"Don't you realise?" she went on, scrubbing her eyes with a tissue. "Humans are such idiots! They'll believe anything We just take the money and pay 'dividends' with it and they think they're going to make their fortune, but we will just cash in and disappear, and start up again somewhere else!"

"So, now you know how the business is run, Anna," said a deep voice. It was Gilles — he had come quietly into the room from his office and was standing by the door.

He said: "Come in. And you'd better come too, Melusine, and pull yourself together. Perhaps the strain of it all has been too much for you — juggling money, keeping secrets. But it's really not a good idea to give way like this."

"It's her! I can't stand her wan little face," sobbed Melusine.

"All the same, you'd better stay with us until you calm down. We don't want people asking questions."

He gestured to the inner office and held the door for us — Melusine grabbed her bag and followed me in as if she was used to obeying his orders, and collapsed on one of the black leather settees and wiped her eyes some more.

"Anna and I have a little job to do," said Gilles.

He opened the door of a teak cupboard that turned out to be a fridge and got her out a bottle of Perrier water, and a glass from a shelf.

"I don't know if you know it, but the building is haunted," he said, pouring her out some water.

"What rot!" she said croakily, taking the glass. "It was just a silly rumour."

"Haven't you noticed black smoke, and a dark shape that disappears when you look at it? And when you investigate, there's never a fire?"

"That was just an electrical fault!" She sipped the water.

He shook his head. "Anna is here to banish the entity that haunts these offices."

"So she's some kind of medium as well? I suppose you have a crystal ball at home! Are you going to tell all our futures?"

"I don't think anybody can do that," I said.

Gilles smiled and said to me: "You know, Melusine is the most purely evil person I've ever met. And thoroughly disagreeable, as you can see. But clever. She keeps track of everything, and robs Peter to pay Paul."

"I always wanted to try one of those tulip-bulb schemes," muttered Melusine. "Or the South Sea bubble. It's all there in Dickens. Anyway, get on with it, and then we can all go home."

"And we called the projects after demons," explained Gilles. "So that every time someone said their names, they would be invoked."

"We shall have to summon this one before I can banish it," I said.

Gilles helped me move the furniture out of the way and clear a space on the floor. I took off my coat and put it with my bag on one of the sofas, and got the stuff out of my satchel. I drew a pentacle on the floor, and some symbols, and a circle around the lot, and set out sulphur, salt, iron, powdered wolfsbane and mercury in little dishes at the points of the pentacle. I put four stones with holes in them at the points of the compass. I sprinkled some holy water. I lit a candle in the centre of the diagram, with the bottle of holy water next to it, and the bell, and Gilles turned off the lights. I threw some grains of incense into the candle. Then I pulled out my hairpins and let my hair fall down.

"I suppose nobody minds if I smoke?" grated Melusine. We didn't say anything and she got a cigarette out of her bag and lit it. She was huddled at the end of the sofa.

"Just don't interrupt," said Gilles.

"Oh, I'll be quiet," she said grumpily. "I want to see what fools you make of yourselves."

"Perfect, isn't she?" said Gilles, smiling again. He stood back out of my way, in the shadows.

I took off my shoes and stood in the centre of the circle by the candle. I picked up the temple bell, which I'd attached to a bit of string, and rang it three times. Then I intoned:

Creature of fire and smoke that haunts this place
By Thoth I summon thee
By Bast I summon thee
By Nephthys I summon thee
Appear! Appear to me!

The room got darker, and the candle guttered. I looked at the panoramic view out of the window, but it blurred and faded as mist and smoke blotted it out. Soon it was almost gone and I could only see a few light patches. Melusine sat very still. Her cigarette had gone out. Gilles made no sound.

Then dark fog began to seep through the edges of the window frames and pour into the room, falling to the floor as if it was heavy. It pooled just outside the chalk circle.

I recited:

Fight Water by Water and Fire by Fire
Unto the Red Sea may you flee
As the cleansing flame leaps higher
May you no longer threaten me.

Now we had to wait for it to appear. Nobody moved. Then we heard footsteps coming towards us through the outer office. I stayed still by the candle with my eyes fixed on the door. It opened and someone stood in the doorway, a black shape. The smoke shrank into a knot and rushed towards him and disappeared. He stepped into the room.

"Hullo, boss!" he said. "What's up? You called me, so I came. Can I help? What's going on? These young ladies causing any trouble?"

It was Mr Gremory, with his red-rimmed eyes, and acne-scarred, pale greenish face. I turned over a page of my incantation. The next bit went:

Avaunt and flee
Away from me
I banish thee to the Red Sea,
Upon the strand to make ropes of sand
Upon the shore for ever more.

But just then there was a howl from outside — from the forecourt, and a chorus of barking, and many voices raised in eerie howls. Melusine slid off the sofa, ran to the window, slid it open and leaned out. Gilles and Mr Gremory followed her and I stepped out of the circle, clutching my spells.

The fog was still thick outside, and the forecourt was seething with grey shapes. They were howling and showing their teeth, forming waves and jumping up at the doors. In the midst of the wolves stood Dorinda, dressed in one of her kaftans, or anyway in long dark robes, and holding a staff, with her hellhounds one on either side of her. Behind them I could see through the mist some towering black shapes standing in the shrubbery.

Dorinda raised her arm and brandished the staff. There was a flash, a crack of thunder and a deafening bang as the windows shattered. We all leaped back, and the room filled with real smoke, black and smelling of burning rubber. The floor was covered in broken glass and I shoved my feet back into my shoes. The fire alarm shrilled, and flames appeared in one corner of the ceiling and began to spread.

Gilles came up behind me and took the pages with the incantations out of my hand, and picked up the candle from the floor. It lit his face from underneath and cast a lurid light on Mr Gremory, who was standing beside him.

"Anna! Melusine!" said Gilles. "Go as quickly as you can! Run! Remember to take the stairs! And thank you for all your help!"

I grabbed my bag from the sofa and took Mel's hand and pulled her after me.

"What about you?" I called out.

"We're right behind you! Go!"

We ran out of the room through the thick smoke. Behind us I could hear his deep voice intoning: *"Procul O procul este profani!"*

We clattered round and round and down and down the emergency stairs. We could hear people running ahead of us and we came out into the carpark. The entrance was shut and Alan was standing at the door of the fire escape tunnel, waving everybody in. The alarm kept screaming.

We hared after the crowd and Alan shouted: "Anyone else up there?"

"Yes, two!"

"You go on!" he said. "I'll wait!" Then all the lights went out and Alan began to cough.

"Come on, Alan!" I said. "You'll suffocate if you stay there!"

I was still clutching Melusine's hand and together we raced along the tunnel.

Alan pounded after us, panting: "I can hardly breathe! Keep going!"

We ran on through the dark.

CHAPTER TWENTY-FOUR

We spilled out into the alley, with smoke following us. There was a small crowd on the pavement, with people counting heads. One woman was sobbing. I looked around for my friends, but couldn't see them — just Joanna. She saw me and called out: "It's OK – the others all left before the alarm went off! And I thought you'd gone home!"

Melusine pulled her hand out of mine — I'd forgotten I was still holding it. We could hear fire engines clanging past, and some firemen and policemen charged towards us. She pushed her way through the knot of Magister staff and disappeared in the direction of Shaftesbury Avenue.

"I hope the other two got out!" said Alan.

"They were just behind us," I said, "But I can't see them."

"It's hard to see anybody in this crowd, and the smoke," said Alan, looking around. "Who were they?"

"You know Mr Magister."

"He's hard to miss. Who was the other guy?"

"Your boss, Mr Gremory. Perhaps we should tell somebody."

There was nobody in the alley now apart from police and firemen. I went up to one of the policemen and said: "There are still two people inside. They were just behind us. Unless they came out through the front of the building."

"Description?" asked the policeman.

"A tall man with white hair, and one in a uniform like his," I said, indicating Alan.

The policeman talked briefly to the firemen, and they put on masks and went into the tunnel.

"Don't you worry," said the copper, moving us out of the firemen's way. "Everyone else is accounted for. You two get along and get a cup of tea. I expect you need it."

"Nothing I'd like more," said Alan, coughing.

"I'd better just take your names."

We gave them and he wrote them in a notebook.

"No point staying and getting overcome yourself, mate," said the copper. "And besides, you had this young lady to look after."

"There was another one," said Alan, looking about.

"She's OK, she cleared off," I said.

"I'd better just take her name too, and the names of the missing men," said the policeman. We gave them. Most of the other Magister staff had dispersed. I thought about Gilles saying "Thank you for your help" as if I'd just typed some letters.

"Let's go and get that cup of tea," said Alan.

"Yes, let's," I said. "There's an Espresso Bar near here."

I led him to it, and I rang Mike at the police station from a phone on the wall.

"There you are!" he said. "They said everyone was out bar two males. I do worry, you know."

"I'm fine," I said. "And so is Alan. It just got quite smoky as we were getting out."

"The fire service are there now, they're saying it was a lightning strike. It's mainly hit the top two floors, and you're usually in the middle, aren't you?"

"Yes, we ran down the stairs and out of the fire escape."

"Would you believe our blokes are busy rounding up some animals that have escaped from the zoo? Bloody animal liberationists! Anyway, come home and I'll see you later."

"OK, Alan and I are just having a cup of tea."

"Put in lots of sugar – it's good for shock!"

"I'll see you later."

I sat down at the table where Alan had got us two cups of tea.

"The police say it was lightning," I said, as I spooned sugar into the cup.

"I wonder if we'll have a job tomorrow?"

"We'll just have to turn up and see what's happening."

"I suppose so," he said. "You know it's a bit weird — there was a thick fog, and thunder, and then I suppose we were hit by lightning, but here it's just drizzling as usual. It was so foggy outside I couldn't see the forecourt. It looked as if the fog was pawing the windows!"

"Weird! Perhaps it was an electrical fire like the ones that kept breaking out."

"Yes – they never found the fault. Perhaps it just decided to go off bang! So what if the firm shuts for a bit — what will you do?"

"I had another job modelling, but that's fizzled too."

"Why was that?"

"Basically they wanted me to take my clothes off."

"Say no more," he said.

"What about you?"

"I was getting bored anyway. The plan is, you see, you get a straight job and then your mind is free the rest of the time. But I'm sick of standing about. At least when I'm on the desk I can read."

"What is it today?" I asked.

"Extraordinary Popular Delusions and the Madness of Crowds," he said, pulling it out of his inside pocket.

"My friend at college was reading that. What were the delusions?"

"Alchemy, tulip bulbs."

"Tulip bulbs? Did they eat them?" I asked.

"No, they sold them to each other for thousands of guilders. They bred different varieties. Somebody wrote a story about a black tulip that was worth a bomb. And then fashions changed and everybody went 'Oh they're just flowers after all'."

"And everybody lost their money again."

"That's about the size of it," said Alan.

I wondered if there'd really been a black tulip, but he didn't think there had been.

We finished our tea. Alan said goodbye and "Stay in touch, whatever happens!", and went towards Leicester Square, and I walked north and got a bus home. I never finished my spells, and I'd done nothing to repel Dorinda's attack. But there'd be no point going back now – the place would be full of firemen and policemen and wolves.

Mike came home late and said they'd been out with the RSPCA and keepers from the zoo taking the escaped animals home and looking for footprints and trying to work out how the beasts had been let out.

"No sign of who did it — and they usually leave a note. Just a whacking great hole cut in the fence. Torn, more like."

I said I'd had to leave my coat and my satchel, and I'd go back and see if I could retrieve them. Next morning he went out early and got a paper and looked at it while we had breakfast.

"This must be an old picture," he said, showing me a photo of the Magister building looking new and modern.

I read the short article. "This award-winning architectural masterpiece... thought to have been struck in a freak storm... Witnesses claimed to have seen a bright flash and thick smoke. Windows and front door shattered. Most staff escaped through a fire exit. All accounted for apart from two: Giles Magister, managing director, and Kane Gremory, a security guard."

"It only says 'unaccounted for'," said Mike. "They could have just failed to report. But it doesn't look worth your while turning up for work. It'll all be taped off. The building will be unsafe, no electricity."

Just then the phone rang and I picked it up. It was someone from the temp agency.

"Awful about the Magister building!" she said. "We had several girls placed there. Someone phoned this morning and said everyone had got out OK. Anyway, they're saying, don't go in until you hear. So you've got the day off! Try calling us tomorrow."

I thanked her and put the phone down. I spent the morning pottering about, then at lunchtime I went out and bought an Evening Standard and got a bus to Tottenham Court Road. There was a bit about the fire, and another bit about animals escaping from the zoo, with a picture of the hole in the fence. It said the wolves were back home, and had brought a couple of Egyptian hunting dogs with them which the zoo was keeping until they could find their owner. There was a photo of them in a cage.

There was quite a crowd of people standing outside the Magister building, and policemen stopping them getting any closer. There were huge cracs across the front winow and big shattered holes. The top floor was blackened, and the windows up there were empty.

"The top floor was pretty much destroyed," said a man standing next to me. "But I gather nearly everybody got out."

"Well, that's good, anyway," I said.

"It's odd that the front windows shattered, though," he said. "There's no fire damage – it was all on the top stories."

I agreed it was odd. In the forecourt men in boiler suits were sweeping broken glass into heaps. The flower beds and shrubs were all trampled by firemen's boots, but I could see a few paw marks. There didn't seem to be anything more I could do. I had left my ritual half-done, and Dorinda had done her worst. I should have guessed she might choose Imbolc to attack.

***

The temp agency said Magister's would be shut for a while, and got me some work in a different office for next week. It was another clean, anonymous modern block. I wondered what Joanna, Kirstin, Clemency and the others would do. I didn't even know where their hostel was. That's temping, perhaps that's life, you move on, and someone was your friend last week, and now you'll never see them again. There wasn't a canteen at the new place, just a drinks machine, so I went out and got cream cheese and cress sandwiches.

A few days later Mike was reading the paper again as we ate our toast and marmalade.

"Here's some more about Magister Enterprises," he said. "They haven't found a trace of those blokes who were missing. They think they must have got out through the front door or windows — most of the glass was shattered. One of them actually lived there in a penthouse, and of course that's gone now. That was Giles Magister — did you ever meet him?"

"He had a deputy who ran things and liaised with the staff."

If Gilles was still alive, he could still make trouble for me, so I'd better keep on keeping quiet. Was I breaking the law? Aiding and abetting? Compounding a felony? Perhaps I'd end up in prison reading Dickens.

"He could be anywhere," said Mike. "Probably in a posh hotel. Or perhaps he's got several gaffs. Other flats and houses. And the other guy, the security guard, never returned to his bedsit."

"But if Mr Magister just moved into a posh hotel — wouldn't he phone in and say he was OK?"

Mike shook his head and smiled.

"There's more to the story! He's got good reasons for going AWOL. And there's somebody else absent — the deputy, a woman called Melusine Smith. Weird moniker. She was seen leaving the building, but she never went back to her flat. Or if she did, she just took a few things and left."

"What were the good reasons?"

"The firm was about to go bust. Of course, the remaining executives swear they knew nothing about it, but I expect we'll see them in court. It was supposed to be a construction outfit, wasn't it?"

"Yes, they said that's what it used to be. But you know, I just type stuff."

"They'd just been selling promises, and getting people to invest, and offering them huge returns, the pot of gold at the end of the rainbow. It's called a Ponzi scheme. You keep signing up more and more investors and taking their money, and then you use that to pay 'dividends' to everybody. How did they keep track? It was all going to implode one day. Anyway — some of the records were burned, but there are plenty left. The fraud squad have got them now. They went through the filing cabinets while they were looking for the missing men, and somebody thought it looked fishy. So then they interviewed the other officers."

"Is it all in the paper?" I wondered if Marian had worked it out, or suspected something.

"Not all of it. And perhaps this other guy was in cahoots with them."

"But of course you know what's going on — because it's a crime."

"It's no joke for those people who've been rooked. Thought they were going to make their fortune. The firm stopped putting up real buildings, you see. What they sold was a fantasy."

So the police knew all about it – that was one less guilty secret. What is the word for not reporting a crime? Thank goodness Christine had been disguised as Melusine when she made all those promotional films, I thought. Surely she didn't know what was going on, and if nobody said anything they'd never connect her to Magister's.

"We'll probably get round to questioning you, again," said Mike. "You must be used to it by now. Who was there when you were getting out?"

"I did see Miss Smith, I knew her by sight, but she made off after we'd been counted. I came out with Alan, and I saw Joanna and she said the other girls had got out OK, and Alan and I went and had a cup of tea. But what will happen to all those employees? The canteen ladies, the porters, the Scottish girls? I know they live in a hostel somewhere, but I don't know where. Can I see the paper?"

He handed it over. There was a picture of the burned building, saying it would be closed until further notice, pending investigations.

"It was a good thing most of the staff had gone home. I could find out where that hostel is, if you like," said Mike.

"I would like."

"It must have been frightening" he said, holding my hand.

"I was a bit scared. But we had so many fire drills I got used to them."

I was still wondering what had really happened. Where was Dorinda? Had Mr Gremory — the djinn — disappeared? It looked as if Gilles had vapourised with him.

CHAPTER TWENTY-FIVE

The Evening Standard said that no remains had been found, but the missing men were still absent. There was no sign of Melusine Smith, either, and she and Giles Magister were now wanted by the fraud squad. Some investors might get some money back eventually, but a lot of it had gone. "Miss Smith was seen to leave the building. It appears she returned to her flat, packed a bag and left." I suppose she's got a passport with a picture of herself without the wig and glasses, and in another name. She'd told me her real one – something like Heywood. Perhaps there was enough in various filing cabinets to give her away. They must have had an escape plan, and salted away the money somehow, but Gilles knew the djinn would follow him wherever he went. If he is still alive, and the djinn is still with him, I shall hear from him again.

The paper said some of the wolves had gone back to the Zoo on their own, after running around the West End frightening people and being mistaken for large dogs. A hole had been ripped in their fence and there were lots of paw marks going both ways, and the prints of outsize bare feet. There was a cartoon of policemen in helmets looking at the paw prints through a giant magnifying glass while the wolves and some barefoot hippy activists laughed at them.

They hadn't found Dorinda's remains either, so perhaps she'd run away with the wolves. Unless she'd been vapourised. I hoped not. It wasn't like her to run around barefoot, but perhaps it had been part of her ritual, like mine.

I settled down at the boring office block. It was an ad agency called Perkins Gilman Cady Stanton, and all the girls were very smart, so I made sure I looked "well-groomed". My coat had gone up in the fire, so I wore a bomber jacket, and window-shopped for trench coats. The stuff we had to type wasn't too boring, either. There were some very posh girls who talked to each other all the time and went to the country at weekends, but there were some normal ones as well.

It looks like I can stay for a bit. I sit next to Lesley and Marianne who calls people "seketries". She said I'd soon be "part of the furniture" and asked me where I'd worked before. I said I'd had to leave my last job when the building was struck by lightning.

"Wasn't there a lightning conductor?" asked Lesley.

"There must have been," said Marianne.

"It was in all the papers," said Lesley. "It was a freak storm. Were you scared?"

"I suppose I was a bit," I said, "But we all got out through the fire exit and we were mostly OK."

"They're still looking for the rogues who defrauded all those people, though," said Ray, one of the men in suits. "Perhaps they set the fire themselves! Would you come in, Marianne, and bring your book?"

Mike found me the phone number of the Scottish girls' hostel, and I rang it. A woman answered, but she said that the place was closing down, and the girls had all gone back to Scotland.

***

I came home one evening to find a letter waiting for me on the ledge in the hall. It was written on thick paper with a swirly pattern, and it was addressed in pink ink. I ran upstairs to open it. Mike was there, and he put on the kettle while I took my jacket off.

"It's from Lawrence!" I said. "He's out of prison!"

"Well, I wonder how he swung that! Still, he was hardly the mastermind. Perhaps he got time off for good behaviour."

"Yes, he said he worked in the library. Anyway, he's giving a 'coming out' party at a dress factory in Soho and has invited us."

"Me too?"

"You too. He says 'Live and let live, eh?'"

So we went along and it was above a fabric shop in a room full of clothes on dummies. There was loud music playing, and a disco ball dangling from the ceiling. I wore black velvet trousers and a denim waistcoat. I introduced Lawrence to Mike and they shook hands.

"No hard feelings!" said Lawrence, and Mike smiled.

"Darling!" said Lawrence, kissing me. "I can't wait to grow my hair. Shall I dye it purple, or keep the grey?"

"I think it looks fine as it is."

"Now have a glass of this perfectly harmless pink champers," he winked at me and poured us all out a glass. He was wearing a gangsterish suit with a waisted jacket and wide lapels.

"I like your suit," I said.

"The whistle? That's rhyming slang you know, sweetheart. I'd better learn it and drop all that 'far out, blow your mind' garbage."

"It seems such ages ago."

"Doesn't it?"

Mike was talking to some other men in stripy suits and girls in 40s style dresses.

"So what are you up to?" Lawrence asked me. "I see you've been doing some modelling. I could always pull a few strings if you want to do more of that. That picture of you holding a hat is popular. I think I'll get a copy for our gallery!"

"Thanks – it was fun at first and nice getting all that money for just a day's work, but it got rather sleazy quite quickly."

"Yes, I can imagine. Not your scene at all!"

"No. I wouldn't mind going on pretending to be 14, but I don't think..."

"Don't think you can swing it for much longer? How old are you really?"

"I'm 20."

"Yes, you don't look quite so juvenile as you used. But you're still a perfect size six. You could make a thing out of being tiny! I'm sure Penelope Tree's only about five foot six. Or was that..."

"Ha ha, I'm not even five foot! Anyway, I'm working at an ad agency now."

"Cool! Come and meet my new colleagues."

"I meant to ask – how did you get out early? I mean, I'm glad, of course."

"Your guess is as good as mine! It was like magic! I was just told one day that I was leaving and I was practically spirited out of the building. I hardly knew where to put myself. But I didn't like to ask questions."

"So who's Penelope Tree?"

"She's a model who makes a thing out of looking childlike. A bit creepy, like you say. We've got a picture of her – come and have a look."

And he dragged me off to look at the posters of famous models like Twiggy on the walls. Penelope did look waiflike.

"You see ten years ago, fashion models all looked 40. Check out Barbara Goalen."

He pointed at a picture of a thin woman in a two-piece suit and a hat with her head thrown back.

"Wonder what this year will bring? The trend seems to be tribal, and layers, and crimped hair. It's the look of 1971!"

"It's easier to type, anyway! 1971, I mean."

We went and joined Mike and the others and people brought round cocktail sausages and tiny sandwiches on trays. Lawrence introduced me to his colleagues, who called Lawrence "Lol" and were all called Del and Gaz. Mike said: "I've already met some old friends."

"But we're all friends here, aren't we?" said Lawrence. "The past is the past and an awful long way away. Have a sani!"

I talked to some of the girls and told them I'd been a model and felt quite trendy. We ate a few more nibbles and decided to leave. I kissed Lawrence goodbye and said: "Good luck in your new job", and he said: "We're opening several boutiques – we'll need staff! Keep in touch!"

I put my jersey and jacket and scarf back on, and as we left it began to snow slightly. "You wouldn't want to go back to retail, would you?" asked Mike.

"I've got used to sitting down all day," I said. "And anyway, shopgirls get a pittance."

"They're nice blokes – they just don't seem to know how to stay inside the law! Though they seemed to be running a straight operation."

"I'm sure Lawrence would do anything to stay out of prison."

"Did he say how he got out?"

"No – well, he did try to explain, but it was a bit confused."

"Oh well – let's get this bus."

We got on the bus, which was full of people with soggy boots and umbrellas.

"Do you fancy Spain again next summer?" asked Mike.

"I don't think this bus has got the heating on." I shivered and huddled close to him.

"How about Cornwall, then? We could stay in a B&B, or a caravan."

"Everybody got on OK, then?" I said.

"At the party? Cops and cons do get on, you know. We tend to be the same kind of people, just on different sides of the law."

"In the Stone Age, Early Man worshipped the prey animal. Or did they worship predators? Wolves and bears and stags."

"Let's get some holiday brochures."

"There are always ads in the back of the papers."

"The zoo never did get all their wolves back."

"You're joking!"

"No – there must be some still out there. Living on cats and rats – or Kentucky Fried Chicken."

But I wasn't sure he meant it.

***

I hadn't seen Naheed at college lately, and she was the only one I could ask for news of Dorinda. Next time I went, I looked about for her, but the only person in the hall I recognised was Amit, the Indian student, so I went over.

"Look, they have cancelled my favourite lecture!" he said, pointing to the noticeboard. There was a CANCELLED sticker over the poster for Dorinda's series.

"I am so disappointed," he said. "I felt I was really getting somewhere! At least to the first heaven of the Gnostics."

"Oh, never mind," I said. "You'll find something else. I wonder what happened to the lecturer?"

"Perhaps she bored herself! Maybe it's time to study the culture of the Indian subcontinent – it seems to be flavour of the month!"

"I'm just going to the canteen for tea," I said.

"Will you be with your usual crowd?"

"I hope so. Are you coming?"

But then I saw Naheed coming down the corridor, with her hands in the pockets of a long green cardy over her sari. I told Amit I'd be along in a minute, and he went off as Naheed came up to me.

"Hullo, my dear!" she said. "How are you?"

"Oh, much the same. I've moved jobs."

"How was that?"

"Well, the firm shut down. It was rather sudden. I lost touch with my work friends – they all went back to Scotland. Just as I make friends with people we all move on."

"Life is a checkerboard of nights and days, as somebody says," she said, shaking her head and sighing. "We just move about like chess pieces. You see Dorinda's lectures are cancelled?"

"Yes, Amit told me."

"Another old crowd breaking up. She has left London, I think. Or at least, she has left her flat and I don't know where she has moved to. I asked about her at the College of Psychic Studies but they hadn't heard from her either."

"Oh, that's a shame," I said.

"Well, it was nice to see you, at any rate! I must get to my class."

"Goodbye!"

I hoped Dorinda hadn't been vapourised as well. I ought to be glad they'd all passed out of my life again, but I'd like to know what happened to them. I went into the canteen, where Amit was sitting with Rowena, Ginevra and Benny. I got tea and a scone and went over and joined them. We sat and chatted for a bit, and then Christine put down a cup of tea and pulled up a tubular aluminium chair and said "Hi, guys!" I looked at her nervously, but she was smiling, and her voice sounded normal, warm and friendly.

We all said "Hi!" too and she said "I've just called in to say goodbye to you lot."

"Goodbye!" said Rowena.

"Yes, I'm dropping out. Is it still fashionable?"

"Aren't you going to finish your degree? But your marks were so good!"

"Surely it's just au revoir!" said Benny rather anxiously.

"My heart was never in it really," said Christine. "I had a kind of acting job on the side, but that's come to an end early. Though they gave me a nice bonus as a payoff."

"How did you manage to study so hard if you had a part-time job?" asked Ginevra.

"Oh, I just juggled everything."

"And you were chaperoning Paula some of the time," I said.

"That was in the holidays."

"Well, I do think you're clever," said Benny. And she must have been, to know where she was supposed to be – and who she was being that day.

"Are you going to pursue the acting?" I asked.

"Yes, definitely. I've got some auditions lined up."

"You can always come back to higher education later," said Rowena, seriously. "Look at Ginevra."

"Yes," said Ginevra. "Having the baby made me realise I wasn't really into interior design and wanted to do something more serious."

"Perhaps I'll bump into you, Anna, at a modelling shoot one day!" said Christine. "I'll miss you all."

"I don't think I'll be doing any more modelling," I said. "I'm getting a bit old for it."

"Perhaps you do look a bit sadder and wiser," said Christine.

"I hope so. Is Paula still going to work for Stella Orrin?"

"Yes – and she's on the books of some other agencies."

"Maybe stick to them – I don't like that Helmut."

"Did he pinch your bum, or chase you round the studio?"

"Something like that. That's why I don't want to go back, really."

"Modelling is exploitation!" said Rowena. "It turns women into sex objects."

"Paula's getting a bit old herself," said Christine. "Mum is sending her for elocution and tap dancing lessons."

Rowena got some stickers out of her bag and handed them out to us. They all said "This exploits women".

"You stick them on adverts," she explained. "You can do a lot on the escalators on the tube," she said. "And they can't catch up with you so easily."

We picked up our stuff and coats and went out into the hall. Christine said: "I'm glad I saw you. Let's stay in touch."

"Did I ever give you my phone number?" I asked, and scribbled it on a bit of file paper and gave it to her. She wrote hers on the same sheet, and tore it off and gave it to me, and went out through the double doors.

"How she can walk away from such a good degree I don't know," said Rowena, coming up behind me.

"Perhaps she got someone else to write her essays after all," said Ginevra.

"Perhaps she was about to get found out!" suggested Amit.

We parted and Ginevra said: "Come and play with Richard some time."

I went into the ladies to see if I looked sadder and wiser. Whenever I do some magic that works I start to look a bit weirder. I stared at my face. Perhaps my eyebrows were more arched, my skin paler, and my ears pointier, and my eyes more amber than green. Perhaps if I remember to smile vacantly nobody will notice. Somebody came in, and I quickly washed my hands in case they thought I was vain.

***

So Christine passed out of my life, and we went and saw Ginevra and David one weekend and Mike played football with Richard in their back garden. I was at the ad agency most weeks, though I had more fun in an antique shop where they wanted a lot of labels typed and wording for a brochure. I sat and typed in the shop – some of the labels were for pictures which was more interesting than endless addresses, though you can always get some fun out of people's names. If I was called Whybrow or Smellie I'd change it.

When I had nothing to do I just sat in the shop in case anybody came in, to smile and say "Good morning", and watch if they stole anything. That was easy, and I read a book about Tiepolo's engravings which were all of witches and wizards. There's a kitchen behind the shop, where the shop-owner, who's fat with curly hair and called Pauly, was cleaning a picture, and some old brick sheds out at the back, where some blokes were restoring furniture and stripping pine dressers.

"I hope you can come back some time!" said Pauly at the end of the week.

"I hope I do!" I said. "I like your books. I'm studying stuff like that at college."

"Stuff like what?"

"It's called Classical Civilisation, gods and religion and myths and so on. I've got another essay to write."

"Sounds interesting! Keep it up." And we parted on good terms.

So, nothing much else happened, which was just as I liked it. I wrote some more essays, and the days got longer and it was spring. I picked some flowers and left them for Hermes and the Naiads of the Fleet in the Gray's Inn Road. I hadn't seen the Naiads, but I'm sure they had been there, that night in the houseboat.

I didn't think the staff of the British Museum would like it if you left flowers around. Mike didn't mention children again. We were learning about fertility cults, but I knew I couldn't ask for anything just for myself — it would rebound, if not on me, on someone else. Though I couldn't help hoping. Perhaps we could adopt somebody. We went out with his friends now and again and they teased me about always getting into trouble. "If you go and work somewhere, the building burns down!" When will they drop that one? Probably never, knowing people.

I nipped into the British Museum anyway and said a silent thanks to Hermes and the cat-like statues of Bast/Diana. I looked at their feet – they are outsize human feet rather than lion's paws. While I was standing there one of the guards came up to me. I thought he was going to tell me to move on or something, but he said: "Hello, young lady! Remember me?"

It was Jim, who'd given me a sofa and some tea the night I did the longevity-reversing incantation.

"Oh, hi there!" I said.

"Bunking off from your posh school again?" he asked. "Don't worry, I won't tell."

"Actually I've got some essays to write and I'm doing some research," I said, which happened to be true for once. I can always work Bast/Diana into one of them.

"Mind how you linger around here after dark, though!" he said.

"I won't get caught again! And now I must be getting back." To work, but I didn't say so.

"It's my belief they sometimes go for a bit of a wander round," he said, nodding at the black basalt goddesses. "I could swear I've passed through here some nights and someone's been missing from a pedestal."

"How would they get in and out without you seeing?" I asked.

"Perhaps they go through the loading bay," he winked. "The lock keeps getting broken, you know!"

"Oh, of course!" I laughed. "Well, thank you for the tea and the sofa that time."

"Bye bye. And be good!"

I walked out quickly and went back to the office. If the goddesses had protected us from Dorinda, and rounded up the wolves, I was more than ever in their debt.

CHAPTER TWENTY-SIX

Marianne said there was a personal assistant's job going, and why didn't I apply, but I don't think I could face keeping someone's diary and booking them airline tickets. I'd be terrified I'd get it wrong. I got some calls from Stella Orrin but I said I wasn't free, and in fact wasn't interested any more. But I did get the occasional call from the antique shop and took a day or two off from the ad agency because the people are lovely and it's fun looking at the stuff – the lace and teaspoons and jewellery and china and pictures. One of the boys said he'd teach me French polishing and the others laughed because it apparently it means something rude.

Then I got a call from Lawrence one night and he offered me a gig modelling clothes for buyers.

"They don't want six-foot beanpoles, they want normal-looking girls. You can look normal if you try, can't you? The perfect dolly bird, like I always said."

I said that sounded fun.

"You just get in and out of a lot of clobber and swan up and down. It's like a little fashion show and we put on drinks and eats. There'll be dressers to help. I don't suppose you know a perfect size 12 with a pretty face? Average height?"

"Oh yes, I do. She did some child modelling too and she wants to be an actress. I've got her number. Hang on, I'll find it for you. She's called Christine Hayward or Haywood, I can't remember which."

So I got some time off from the ad agency – they weren't as relaxed as Magister's where I suppose I could have done whatever I liked once Gilles knew I was there, but they said OK if it was another job and a previous commitment.

So I turned up on the day and there was Christine. She said she had a lot of projects in view and might do some catalogue modelling or a fringe play written by a friend.

"What's a fringe play?"

"They get put on in rooms above pubs – it's fun, you must come!"

They'd set up the main room with a catwalk down the middle, and chairs down the side, and pushed all the racks of clothes into another room, where we went. There were two dressers and they showed us the clothes and the order we'd wear them in, and then we rehearsed sashaying down the catwalk.

"Step, step, step, and then drop the hip!" said the dresser. We had to put one foot in front of the other, turn around at the end of the catwalk and look at everybody and walk back again, do another turn, and retreat into the dressing room. Lawrence said he'd put some music on when the buyers arrived. We had some tea and sandwiches sent up on a tray from a nearby café, and did our hair and makeup.

211

"I practically never wear makeup," I said.

"Never mind," said one of the dressers, "I'll do yours." So she gave me some ivory pancake foundation and pale mauve eyeshadow and black mascara, and lipstick about the same colour as the eyeshadow. Christine did her own. She'd had her hair cut shorter at the front than at the back and kind of rolled under, and had plucked her eyebrows.

"Now what are we going to do with your hair?" the dresser asked me. It was just down, so that they could do what they liked with it. "It looks nice like that, but the buyers won't be able to see the back of the garment."

"I put it up most of the time," I said.

"That'll look a bit mature," said the dresser. "You'd look good with a pixy cut. Have you ever thought of having it all off? Or shall we crimp it?"

In the end she did it in Red Indian plaits. She fixed a choker round Christine's neck, and they got us into our first outfits. We could hear the buyers chatting next door. Then Lawrence put some music on, the kind you can dance to, and we trotted up and down the catwalk in the clobber, remembering to drop the hip and smile and look around vacantly.

I wore skinny-rib tops with button-through denim midi-skirts and clogs, cheesecloth smocks (yuk), and a strange knitted thing in red and blue layers which the dressers said was going to be big. When we'd finished our show the buyers gave us a round of applause, and we got back into our own clothes (and I undid the plaits), and came out with the dressers and we all had canapes and glass of wine or Coke.

Lawrence kissed us goodbye and said "Come again!" and gave us our wages in cash.

"How did you meet Lawrence?" asked Christine as we walked away down the street. "He's nice!"

"He ran a boutique where I worked for a bit," I explained.

"Which one was that?"

"Huzzah! – there were several branches."

"It got closed down, didn't it? Drugs or something!"

"Yes, it did shut suddenly."

"I'm sure you weren't involved in all the goings on?"

"No, I really wasn't! I had no idea." Which wasn't quite true, but I've turned into such a godawful liar. Still, what else can I do?

"I've got a date to meet Benny in one of these coffee bars," she said. "Do you want to come and say hello?"

"Nice of you to ask, but I'd better get home to my husband!"

"I always forget you're really grownup, but I suppose you get a bit tired of that one. Anyway, let's do this again some time?" And she went off to meet Benny.

***

I got a letter from the lawyer saying not to forget I was going to get some more money when I was 21 and asking me to visit them and talk to them about it. I showed it to Mike.

"Might mean that house. Or a bigger flat with a garden," he said.

"We'd need a garden."

"If we had children."

"Is it time to go back to the doctor?"

"Maybe we should both go. There must be a clinic they could send us to."

"It's worth a try," I said.

"Or perhaps there's somebody out there who needs us to adopt him," said Mike.

"That's an idea."

"You know your friends Frank and Elsie? The ones with the houseboat?"

"I don't think it was their houseboat."

"I'm sure I've seen their faces somewhere – I mean, their mugshots in a file. I've been flipping through our recent customers, but I couldn't find them."

"I'll ask them what they've been up to! I'm sure I'll bump into them again before too long."

"So why did your parents go on the run? Or don't you know?"

"I know, but I'm afraid I can't tell you. It's their secret."

"OK. Do you want me to come with you to the lawyers?"

"Do you mind if I go alone?"

"No, that's all right."

So I made an appointment, and went to see the lawyers and they gave me some Earl Grey tea and explained about the money.

"I know you can't tell me where my parents are, if you know," I said.

"Yes, it's unusual, but we comply with our clients' requests." The lawyer looked at me curiously.

"Anyway, I'd like to give you this to look after." I got out a big envelope from my shopping bag and handed it to him. "It's an old book, and it's probably quite valuable. I just thought my mother might want it back one day. Would you lock it up somewhere extremely safe?"

"We can put it in a bank vault for you in a deposit box, but you would have to be present."

"Let's do that. And there's a photo album too, that she might like back." It was the one with the picture of Mum and Dad with different names and old-fashioned clothes, and the same faces, and the same ages, dated 1920-something. I'd copied out the whole of the recipe book by now, and kept it with my college work.

So we made a date for the handing over, and I met the lawyer at the bank, and put the envelope into a metal box which they put into a slot in the wall and gave me the key. I gave the key to the lawyer to look after.

***

We got an appointment at the fertility clinic, and underwent some tests that I'll draw a veil over, and they said they couldn't see any problem except that I seemed a little underdeveloped for my age. They said to keep trying for another six months, and then they might think about hormones. I said, "What about adoption?" and they said to give it time, and we were too young to adopt anyway. One of the doctors said that often women got pregnant after they'd adopted somebody, as they relaxed and were less nervous. Can people like me have children? My mother had me, so they must.

It got to be the end of the summer term, when we were actually going to do an exam. I'm sure nobody told me about that when I signed up, but never mind. I would do rottenly, same as I always did, and it didn't matter. All the other students were doing exams of some kind or the other and the classrooms were turned into exam halls, with little tables and chairs and invigilators pacing about.

I turned up to do mine, with lots of pencils and biros in case my pen ran out. I'd even been revising as I seem to have worked out how to do it. The others wished me luck – they don't do finals till next year.

As I was walking towards my exam hall, and checking if I'd got the right one – they had handwritten labels on the door – I thought I saw Christine coming out of one of the halls wearing a summer dress. There were lots of people jostling each other and looking at exam schedules. The girl who looked like Christine rushed past me, getting some sunglasses out of her bag and putting them on. She still had her old shoulder-length hairstyle. I watched her back as she hurried down the corridor and out of the front door.

So Melusine couldn't resist turning up and doing her finals and getting her brilliant degree. I suppose I could tell the police I'd seen her – but then it would get really complicated. How on earth could I explain, without involving the real Christine? I'm sure Christine hadn't known that it was all a scam and loads of people had lost their life savings. It had just been a job to her, even if it had seemed a bit odd, and she'd have had to keep quiet about it. Perhaps if you wanted to be an actress you accepted all sorts of weird jobs. I went into the exam hall and sat down and looked at the pile of lined paper on the table, and the invigilator said: "You may turn over your paper now!". I read the questions several times, choosing which ones to answer. I even read over my answers when I'd written them.

So that was the end of that. I met Rowena and Ginevra and the boys in a Wimpy one night and we talked about what we were going to do over the summer. They all had books to read and research to do. Benny, Hervey and Amit were going to try and get odd jobs and make a bit of money. Ginevra said she'd spend most of the time playing with Richard and taking him to the park.

"We're going to try to earn enough to go on holiday somewhere," said Rowena, meaning Hervey and her.

"I'm not sure what we're doing," I said.

"Come and play with Richard again," said Ginevra, and we made a date.

***

A couple of weeks later I got an official-looking letter – it turned out to be from the head of department at college saying she wanted to see me. Blimey, what now? But I went along, and met her in a tiny office with frosted glass windows looking onto the corridor. It was full of books and papers and little filing arrangements.

The head of department had short grey hair and specs and was wearing an old-fashioned brown and white stripy cotton dress and sandals. I wondered if she wore the same summer clothes every year and put them away in a trunk the rest of the time.

"Do sit down!" she said, pointing to a chair with a ripped leatherette seat. She struggled to open the window, which gave onto a little light well and had a lot of dead flies on the windowsill.

"Well, Anna," she said, picking up some papers on her desk. "You know you got good marks for your essays."

"Yes, I was surprised. I didn't do too brilliantly at school."

"And which A Levels did you do?"

"I never did any. Actually the school gave me the push!"

"Perhaps you were rather rebellious." She smiled, showing rather sticky-out teeth.

"Yes, and I got awful marks in my O Levels."

"Were there other distractions? Friends, boys?"

"It was my friends' problems really."

"Perhaps you got in with the wrong crowd."

"You can say that!"

"But now you're married – you must have got married rather young."

"Yes, I think I was 18." I wondered where this conversation was going.

"What did your parents think?"

"They aren't with me any more."

"I'm very sorry to hear that. Well, the reason I called you in here was to see if you would like to do a degree here. Your exam papers are quite impressive. You have such a genuine passion for your subject that it would be a shame to waste such enthusiasm. And you have a brain!"

"So they say. It's odd that school didn't think so!"

She made a little contemptuous noise. "Schools! Well, let's forget about them for a moment! This course counts as one A Level, and then you could do a couple more next year. How about History of Art? That's a one-year course..." She took some brochures from a shelf behind her. "What else could you do in one year? It's actually much easier outside the school context, there's none of that time-wasting stuff, you know, sport and choirs and country dancing..."

"Character-building?"

"You've had to grow up fast, I can see. I gather you work in an office?"

"Yes, I'm working as a temp."

"That can't be exactly fulfilling. And you can always have children later!"

She seemed to have my whole life mapped out. I almost told her I was thinking of adopting one when I was 25.

"Now, what about another subject?" She riffled through the brochure. "How about Botany? Philosophy? History of Medicine? I'm thinking you'd like to read Archaeology eventually. Or Archaeology and Anthropology."

"Wow, yes! If it means more about the ancient world."

"It certainly does, though in a more hands-on way!"

"Digging up stuff?"

"Yes, there are field trips and a lot of immediate experience."

"Can I have a look?" She handed over the brochure and I flipped through it. "I'd love to do History of Art, and how about Botany? I know a bit about it. Though what's it got to do with Archaeology?"

"You can date buildings by looking at tree rings, and anyway, it's a science and would train you in the scientific attitude."

"Right! Where do I sign up?"

"Many of our students work part-time, you know."

I thanked her profusely and took the brochure home to show Mike. He looked through it and said, "You really want to do this, don't you?"

I said, yes, I did.

"And there's the money from your parents."

"She said I'd probably get a grant since I'd worked."

"Perhaps we'd better not tell them about the money, then! It'll just slip our minds."

"And if I get pregnant..."

"We'll think of something."

"If we put it into a house, then we won't have it, will we?"

He shook his head sadly and said I shouldn't mix so much with the criminal classes.

I was back at the antique shop for a bit, and I told them all about it and they were pleased for me. Then Pauly came into the kitchen where I was making tea on a filthy gas ring, and said: "How do you fancy a part-time job here when your term starts? We can teach you a bit of restoring, and you can sit in the window mending china and luring in the punters."

I said I would love to do that.

CHAPTER TWENTY-SEVEN

I got another letter from Elspeth, this time inviting us to her and Murray's wedding, at St Stephen's Church, Haslemere! In September – I accepted, and put the date in my diary. I hadn't heard from Alan, so I called him one Saturday when Mike was working, and he sounded glad I'd rung.

"What are you doing this afternoon?" he asked. "Do you want to meet in that Soho coffee bar?"

An hour later we were drinking frothy coffee (cappuccino) at a formica-topped table.

"So they never found our former employer?" he mused. "Looks like he did a runner. Did you know they'd been operating some complicated scam, and a lot of people lost money?"

"Yes, Mike told me a few things that didn't get into the papers. Did Mr Gremory ever turn up?"

"Not that I know of! Perhaps he was involved too, like Miss Smith. But I got a month's salary in the post! I suppose as a temp you wouldn't have been eligible, but all the staff did, I hear. And I thought the whole place had shut down. Still – I put it straight in the bank!"

"Did you know all the time that Mr Magister was Gilles?"

"Yes, I bumped into him one day when I was rather on my uppers — I was a bit surprised, since I thought he was in prison. He looked different with white hair, of course. He asked me what I was up to and I said I was down on my luck and not doing much, so he offered me the job. And of course he asked me to keep my mouth shut. When did you find out?"

"I saw him a couple of times when I had to run messages to the top floor."

"And he could always persuade the police we'd been more involved in the drugs thing, so we'd be sure to keep shtumm. Isn't it difficult, being married to one, though?"

I shook my head. "I suppose I was sorry for him being in prison and didn't want to be the one to send him back there. And he was in there for a bit."

"Paid his debt to society, as they say. I got the impression he had several addresses — he's probably hiding out in one of them. Still, I don't feel any inclination to chat to the fuzz! So did you find another job?"

"I'm at an ad agency, and sometimes in an antique shop. How about you?"

"I've been doing some more security work – temping, like you. Boring most of the time, and then the building catches fire! No, really, that hasn't happened again. Perhaps I'll drop back into college. I was at Keele."

"What was that like?"

"It was a bit dead and alive. Full of engineers. And there's nowhere to go but Newcastle."

"I did a part-time course at Regent Street Poly. Classical civilisation and religion. They seem to take anybody. My friend Ginevra's doing history there and she dropped out before to have a baby."

"Far out!"

"He's a little boy now."

"How was your course?"

"I wrote an essay about Apuleius! And next year I'm doing some A Levels, and after that I might do a degree."

"Unreal! Perhaps I could come round and have a look at it – the college, I mean."

"Yes, why don't you? Everybody's friendly. And there are lots of Indian and Chinese students."

"Perhaps there's a course on Buddhism."

"Bound to be! They did one on astrology. And as you've worked, you might get a grant."

"I'd better."

We said goodbye, and I went to Oxford Street, which was packed as usual. I was glad everybody had got some money. But surely the staff records would have been locked in the building? Or had the police just taken everything away as evidence?

I went to John Lewis and looked at sewing machines bought a tapestry kit of a spaniel's head. I hoped Frank and Elsie might tie up the loose ends – and besides, I wanted to thank them. I hadn't called them in the usual way, but I thought about them as I trudged along the pavement. Then I went into "our" Lyons and sat down facing the door, and put the John Lewis bag on the opposite seat and spread out a bit. There were a lot of dirty cups and plates on the table too, which might put other people off. I ordered a cup of tea, and read a paperback. I deliberately didn't look up, to give Frank or Elsie a chance to shimmer in if they felt like it. After a while I heard a quiet voice say "Hello, dear!"

I looked up and there they were. I smiled at them.

"I've been wanting to thank you, Frank, for saving my life that time!"

"Think nothing of it," he said.

"You know, Mike thought he saw your photo in a file at the police station."

"He must have been looking through some very old records! Elsie and I met outside Court Three."

"I used to shoplift to order!" said Elsie. "Poacher's pockets inside my coat."

"And I had some wonderful schemes," said Frank. "Begging letters, chain letters — of course they only work if you start them yourself."

"You were a con man!"

"A con artist, please!"

"Like our old friend, Gilles Lemaitre. I ended up working for his firm — I think he'd summoned me by a spell."

"Magister and Smith!" said Frank. "We read about it in the papers. They thought big! You can't help admiring them. And we heard you'd been there."

I must have looked a bit puzzled and he added, "Through the grapevine."

"So I don't have to go into long explanations."

"You're one of us, in a way."

"I don't understand everything, though."

"The building was struck by lightning and caught fire," said Frank. "And the villains are still missing, and a lot of the records got burned. That's what the papers said."

"So..." I said carefully, "They didn't die?"

They just looked at me.

I said: "I thought not. Because nothing happened to Christine, and she got paid off with a bonus, and so did all the other staff, and Lawrence was sprung from prison. Gilles must have been behind it, so he's not dead. And they never found any 'remains' as the papers said."

"Looks like it," said Frank. "And of course one of the missing men was never truly alive in the ordinary sense of the word."

"The djinn! I never completed my incantation. Gilles took the notes from me and told us to run down the fire escape. Did he finish the incantation, I wonder? And how did he get out?"

"He must have had all the keys," said Elsie. "He was the boss."

"Yes," I said. I was thinking of his beautiful flat with the sculptures and leather furniture, all being burned. "He could have got out by the front door, or through the windows, they were all smashed. But the forecourt was full of wolves from the zoo. I didn't have time to do anything to help. And what happened to Dorinda?"

"She's gone back to being a medium," said Frank. "She's moved to the South Coast and is breeding dogs in her back garden."

"So why didn't the djinn destroy Gilles?" I mused. "Perhaps it attacked Dorinda and the wolves."

"Something got rid of them," said Frank.

"And Gilles told Mel and me to save ourselves," I said.

"You'll understand it all one day," said Elsie.

I didn't want to think about that too much.

"Anyway, I'm going to do two A Levels next year, and if I do well enough in them I'm going to study archaeology!"

"Good for you!" said Frank.

"It would be cheating to use magic, though, wouldn't it?"

"But you might find another Roman villa and become rich and famous!" said Frank. "Write books, charge people admission!"

"I don't think it would be safe – something always goes wrong. I mean it would be as risky as looking for buried hoards of gold."

"They're usually guarded by a dragon of some kind," agreed Frank.

We chatted a bit more, and they said they'd always be around. So perhaps they don't want to move to a higher plane – or maybe they can't.

"I hope they never close Lyons," I said. "Even 200 years from now."

"The dear old place never changes very much," said Elsie. "London, I mean." And they got up and passed through the crowds shoving in, and disappeared, and a waitress came to clear the table and I moved my John Lewis bag out of people's way, and paid and left too.

There was so much they wouldn't, or couldn't tell me. Perhaps I'd never know. When I got home, Mike wasn't back yet, so I got out the crystal ball and set it on the table by the window, on its piece of black velvet. I had seen the past in it at least once. I gazed into it and saw the miniature reflection of the trees outside the window, but I was thinking of Dorinda outside the Magister building, surrounded by ravening beasts. I may see things people want to keep hidden, but sometimes I see people who need help. Though Gilles and Dorinda were too skilled at magic to let any ordinary clairvoyant know what they were up to. I didn't expect much.

I gazed at the green branches, not thinking of anything in particular, and then I saw the Magister building, from outside, shrouded in mist and with shattered gaps in the front glass wall. I saw two figures emerge from the gloom. One came closer – it was Mr Gremory. His eyes were like burning embers, and then there was a bright flash, and only one man was left inside what remained of the glass doors. He stepped through the jagged opening, and the picture fragmented and crumbled, and the green branches were back.

Just then Mike came in. I couldn't hide the crystal ball so I just sat there.

"What can you see?" he asked. He was holding a big thick envelope.

"Just the reflection of the trees."

"Let me have a look. Yes, just the trees and the window. Perhaps you have to stare in it for longer. Oh, look, it's getting smoky! Just joking. Where did you get it?"

"In an antique shop." Which was true – except the antique shop was in Haslemere, and I bought it ages ago when I was still at school.

"Well, don't put it in the window. They can start fires."

"Yes, that's what they told me in the shop." I picked it up and wrapped it in its black velvet and went to put it back in the cupboard.

He was still clutching the envelope and now he emptied over the table. Out fell a lot of estate agents' details.

"Why not put it on the shelf?" he said. "It's pretty. Let's have a look at these. What have you been up to?"

"I met Alan in Soho," I said, arranging the black velvet on the shelf and putting the crystal ball it. "He's thinking of going back to university, too."

"It's mostly three-bed houses round here. We might have to go for Battersea."

I started leafing through the literature. "Alan said he'd got a month's salary from Magister's. But I thought all the money was gone?"

"Yes – Magister and Smith had salted most of it away. But there was still some in a pension fund, and enough to give people a month in lieu of notice. Anyway, what do you think of this one? Louvred windows to front, woodchip wallpaper throughout, Victorian conversation — I think they mean 'conversion'."

We laughed at the spelling on the details and imagined ourselves living in the different places. Did we want a garden flat? Or somewhere with a balcony? In the end we picked out several, and on Monday we went to look at a few nearby flats, which weren't much different from the one we were living in.

There was just one small house, two-up, two-down, in a cul-de-sac between Parliament Hill and Highgate cemetery. It had a white fence in front, half broken off, and an old sofa in the front garden. It was one of a little row – the others looked more cared-for.

"It's still full of the previous owner's furniture, I'm afraid," said the estate agent.

It was pretty dirty inside, with old wallpaper, and ancient gas fires, and the kind of tables and chairs you find in bedsits. There was a slight smell of gas leaks and boiled cabbage.

"It would be quite easy to clear all this out," said the agent. I was looking at some rather nice views of the Bay of Naples which you could just see under the cobwebs and dust.

225

"I think there's some stuff we could keep," I said. "Don't touch it for the moment."

"The kitchen is through here," said the agent, ushering us into a back room. "You could easily put fitted units."

We opened the door into the back garden, which was full of brambles. We said we were interested and said we'd go home and do the sums. The agent looked relieved and babbled about mortgage brokers and surveys.

"Let's go out and celebrate," said Mike. "It just needs cleaning up. And you're right – that furniture's OK. It's homely."

"I could hang onto that kitchen cupboard – or get a cheap dresser from the antique shop."

"I asked about the Hammersmith Palais — it's still open. It's quite a long way on the tube, but shall we go?"

We dressed up and went, and there was a DJ playing Olde-Tyme records, and elderly people dancing. There were little tables to sit out at and we did all the dances we could remember.

"Look – there are your dodgy mates!" said Mike. "Funny how we keep bumping into them."

Frank and Elsie were waltzing under the glitter ball, their clothes spangled in little squares of light. The floor was crowded, and they danced into the shadows at the side of the floor and I couldn't see them any more. There were some other people at our table, a bit younger than the rest.

"Did you spot a friend?" asked a girl in a yellow dress with a big skirt. "I never see anyone I know here. It caters to the older crowd! The London Casino is the place to go."

We asked here where it was and she said Old Compton Street and she said she hoped she'd see us there, so we said we'd definitely go one day.

"We could go once a week," said Mike, leading me onto the dance floor. "Hand in hand, they danced on the strand. Everything's wonderful." And we waltzed away under the glitter ball.

THE END

Printed in Great Britain
by Amazon